'You just want my library, that's what it is,' he stated calmly. 'I saw you leafing through it with lust in your eyes. You wish for undisputed title.'

Admiral Slovo admitted the possibility with a shift of the shoulders. 'Well, that may have something to do with it, but I'd thank you to keep your voice down. Bibliomania does not accord with my professional image. The crew might nurture false notions, requiring bloody suppression.'

'That library has been generations in the acquiring,' said the Venetian firmly. 'I'm not giving it up.'

Admiral Slovo stood up and stretched. 'I'm rather afraid you are,' he said. 'To prepare yourself for Paradise, your books and heart must surely part. Now off you go, there's a good chap.'

The Venetian glowered at the half circle of buccaneers below him but realized that his position was futile. 'I do not consider this conversation to be at an end,' he said equably. Then, with as much dignity as could be mustered, he turned and walked off the plank into the Mediterranean sea.

Also by John Whitbourn in VGSF

A DANGEROUS ENERGY

JOHN WHITBOURN
POPES
and PHANTOMS

VGSF

First published in Great Britain 1993
by Victor Gollancz

First VGSF edition published 1994
by Victor Gollancz
A Division of the Cassell group
Villiers House, 41/47 Strand, London WC2N 5JE

A catalogue record for this book is
available from the British Library.

ISBN 0 575 05763 7

Printed and bound in Great Britain
by Cox & Wyman Ltd, Reading; Berks

✣ Contents

Being Chapter Headings and Topic-titles, sole remnants from the otherwise lost: 'THE NEW MEDITATIONS: MEMOIRS OF A STOIC PIRATE, PHILOSOPHER AND PAPAL GHOST-HUNTER', BY ADMIRAL SLOVO OF CAPRI, ROME AND ELSEWHERE.

VATICAN MISC. INCOMPLETE PAPERS – 16th century. Library 2.
Stack 23. Shelf 15.
Attrib: Slovo (floreat 1460?–1525?).
Collection of: Bishop Fredo Dionisotti of Palermo (1685–1780).

PAGE 9.   The Year 1525. *'How did I get to here from there and was it really worth all the trouble? The consolations of flesh and philosophy.'*

PAGE 28.   The Year 1486. *'SWIMMING LESSONS: After a sad and lonely childhood, cast as an orphan into the wicked world, I discover my vocation and philosophy of life. Piracy suits me very well.'*

PAGE 46   The Year 1487. *'I find service with a Master of my chosen trade and meet new and frightening people with my best interests at heart.'*

PAGE 53.   The Year 1488. *'By possession of a beautiful bottom (but not my own) I secure a new position in life and acquire respectability and a wife!'*

PAGE 75.   The Year 1492. '*INSTALMENTS: In which I become impatient and incite some nostalgics to ambitions of destroying the human race. Little by little, I learn something.*'

PAGE 90.   The Year 1493. '*I die in Germany. Afterwards, I am enrolled in a conspiracy.*'

PAGE 105.   The Year 1497. '*A STAB IN THE DARK: I apply liberality to the dispensing of Justice and assist a soul in torment.*'

PAGE 124.   The Year 1498. '*I offer hospitality, but for which* Notre Dame *would become a Mosque.*'

PAGE 134. The Year 1499. '*GREAT EXPECTATIONS: I save a dynasty, dabble in racial politics and have my portrait painted.*'

PAGE 159.   The Year 1500. '*In which some stony-hearts confide that I am important.*'

PAGE 166.   The Year 1506. '*BE ASSURED, HE IS NOT THERE: I commission a masterpiece of Western art and learn the key mystery of Mother Church. A friend is glad to hear he has not wasted his life.*'

PAGE 190.   The Year 1508. '*PUTTING OFF THE EVIL DAY: In which I render a god homeless, mingle with Royalty, learning their dark and disgraceful secrets, and do the world a great favour for which it is not particularly grateful.*'

PAGE 207.   The Year 1509. '*In bed with the Borgias. Cannons and cuckoldry in Northern Italy. An ordeal not entirely in accord with my tastes.*'

PAGE 213.   The Year 1510. '*THE FLOWERING OF THE REFORMATION & FATHER DROZ'S LITTLE OUTING: A symposium on faith, carnal lust and sausage. I guiltily sow weeds in the fields of Mother Church.*'

PAGE 248.   The Year 1520. '*A LIGHT TO (AND FROM) THE GENTILES: In which I decide the fate of the Universe and become Lord of the Isle of Capri.*'

PAGE 276.   The Year ?. '*ENVOI: The Devil's gift-box contains only unsweet sorrow. A comfortable life, another wife and additions to the tribe of Slovo. A bath seems increasingly attractive however.*'

❧ The Year 1525

'How did I get to here from there and was it really worth all the trouble? The consolations of flesh and philosophy.'

In the year 1525 yet another European nation – Denmark – discovered the joys of Lutheranism and the ex-friar Luther discovered the joys of matrimony (with a former nun). At the same time, Admiral Slovo, Lord of Capri, Papal Knight, sometime *Gonfaloniere* (banner-bearer) of His Holiness's armed forces and subject of 'death-on-sight' notices in Venice, Geneva and sundry other places, decided it was time for his bath.

True, the sunrise was beautiful, the sound of his little children playing most diverting, but they were no longer sufficient to delay him. That bath, so long put off, now seemed overwhelmingly attractive. Gathering his heavy black gown about him he hobbled down from his seat on the hill and into the grounds of his villa. The gardens were quite superlative, not a bloom or blade of grass out of place. It was, in fact, that one day of the year that comes to all well-kept gardens when there is not a thing left to be done and perfection hangs in precarious balance. *An auspicious time for my ablutions*, the Admiral thought.

Inside, he smiled at the antique statue of the Roman

Emperor, he smiled at the handsome grooms and pretty maids who comprised his household staff. Had she chosen to show herself, Admiral Slovo would even have smiled at his young wife but, as ever, she was keeping out of his way.

The bath was sunken and made of the whitest marble. His love of antiquity had made him lavish vast sums on it to recreate the old Roman bath-house style, but even all that gold had captured only the shape, not the spirit, of the thing. The whole concept had turned out to be a disappointment, like so much else.

Whilst painted lads and lasses hurried with steaming water at his command, Admiral Slovo limped about to check that he had all that he would need. There within easy reach was the sponge, the strigil, the tub of cleansing grease, a towel. Beside these was his writing tray with vellum, quill and inkpot (in case inspiration should strike) and the special wax-treated, steam-and-water proofed, bath-time copy of the immortal *Meditations* that he'd had made.

'No, not today, thank you all the same,' said the Admiral to the implicit query of the Tuscan brother and sister who'd poured the last great terra-cotta amphora of water into the brimming pool. This was one occasion when company, for whatever purpose, would be inappropriate.

When these two had left the chamber, Slovo stooped down and placed the one remaining necessary item beside all the others. It was vital that there be a razor to open his wrists.

Before immersing himself, Admiral Slovo recalled the bottle of Falernian he had spent a prince's ransom on some years before and which had been recovered from a shipwreck of the Imperial Age by sponge divers off Carthage. A Castilian middleman had known enough of the Admiral's tastes to seek him out and earn the means to retire. The seal was good, the contents unblemished (so far as could be told) and Slovo was unable to resist the temptation to partake of a vintage such as Horace or even the divine Marcus might have known. To enjoy it now seemed happily in accord with the moment.

In the event it was disgusting. The bouquet that escaped the bottle's fifteen hundred years of meditation could have stripped the villa's walls of their painted murals; the contents seemed capable of dissolving the bricks behind them. The appropriate response to the Judas concoction would have been to dash it to the floor but, now more than ever proof against the storms of emotion, Admiral Slovo merely placed it down and wandered off, naked, to fetch a flagon of rough Capri red.

At the bathroom door he came face to face with a stranger and knew straightaway that all his plans, his bath, his dignified exit from the world, were now postponed.

Because of all he had done and the causes he had served, Admiral Slovo's home was surrounded and penetrated by subtle security. Cold-eyed soldiery supervised every movement in and out of *Villa di Slovo*. There was even an outer band of vigilance based in Naples Harbour, monitoring access to Capri itself. However, this man in black had walked through them all and thus whatever he might have to say demanded respectful attention.

Admiral Slovo did not fear for his life since he had been about to take that himself. Anyway, the visitor did not appear in the least malign but merely curious. Peering past Slovo's head at the scene behind, his gaze was caught by the utensils laid out by the bathside.

'It seems I've arrived just in time,' he said, his voice betraying only indifference at this turn of fate. 'Our calculations suggested events would not be so far advanced . . .'

Admiral Slovo, knowing full well who this man was

11

although they had never met before, felt relieved that here at the close of play, one short step from boarding Charon's ferry, he was not so much a puppet as to be *entirely* predictable. 'As you can see,' he said politely, 'I am about to embark on a journey. If you have further work for me you've left it too late.'

The man held up his hands to express exaggerated horror at such a misunderstanding. The sleeves of his cowl fell back to display, to the Admiral's surprise, the cold pale flesh of the northern barbarians. 'Goodness no!' The man spoke as before in impeccable Italian. 'I should not wish to disturb you by suggesting that you can be of any further use to us.'

'Just as well,' said Slovo, turning back to the bath. 'My days of doing are done.'

'And so they should be. You have achieved so much for us, our Masters could hardly ask for more.'

'*Your* Masters,' corrected the Admiral. 'I was never more than a jobbing-contractor, a mercenary in their service – nor wished to be.'

The visitor plainly disagreed, but hid the spirit of discord from his unkind blue eyes. 'Let us not quarrel today of all days,' he said. 'It would not be seemly to part on bad terms. My superiors would not lightly forgive me for that.'

'Forgiveness hardly being one of their principal traits,' said Slovo, matter of factly.

'No,' the man concurred. 'Or yours, come to that – from what I've read.'

Slovo shrugged, accepting the charge lightly.

'Your present nakedness doesn't inhibit you, I note. Does that also stem from your admiration for Romano-Hellenic culture – along with the Stoicism[1] and all that?'

'Yes,' answered the Admiral, with the mildest of grimaces. 'Along with the Stoicism "and all that". Besides,' he added in acid tones, 'in all the cultures I've ever encountered, it is

12

customary to disrobe before bathing. Is that not the case in your . . . England?'

'Wales, actually.'

'Same thing.'

'I beg to differ. Look, Admiral, I appreciate that I have interrupted a matter of surpassing importance to you but my purpose is not an idle one. Realizing that you were likely to soon depart, our Masters sent me to convey the gratitude that I have hinted at. I am entrusted with a final message as to the warmth of their sentiments for you.'

'I dislike sentiment,' said Admiral Slovo. 'I despise it with a passion in paradoxical opposition to my Stoical beliefs. Your journey from your land of rain and emotional dysentery has been wasted, I fear. I could happily have had my bath not knowing this burning news you've brought me.'

'It was suspected as much,' the man said, 'and so mere farewells are not all I have brought. I have *The Book* with me – or at least a copy of it.'

'Ah . . .' said the Admiral rapidly re-evaluating, 'that may be different. The complete work?'

'Alpha to Omega, first to last page, unsullied by excision.'

'I see . . .' mused Slovo. 'That alters things.'

'I hoped it might.'

'You are more senior than you seem – to be so entrusted.' The Admiral eyed the stocky young Welshman with more respect.

'One sees more of true human nature as someone of no apparent import.' The man shrugged, 'And no, your unpredictability is well known of old; you couldn't ply that famous stiletto blade of yours and just take *The Book*. In such an event it would simply self-combust. If preparation is of any value at all then I am proof against anything you can muster.'

'Fine,' said Slovo, still engaged with the output pouring from the computer-forerunner that he had made of his mind.

'Very well. I will talk with you. I won't fill the bath with my blood just yet.'

The Welshman nodded agreement. 'Excellent. I think we will both learn thereby.'

The Admiral smiled sadly. 'I fear the only things I could tell you would shrivel up your soul and make you a thing of stone,' he said.

'Like you? Well, yes, I have hopes of that.'

'Whereas I,' said Slovo, 'am curious merely to hold *The Book*, to learn from it to what precise end I have devoted my life.'

'Then the bargain is struck,' grinned the Welshman.

'It was struck long ago,' disagreed the Admiral, 'and I suspect it was not fair-dealing. One side or the other was rooked.'

'There's commerce for you,' came the answering quip. 'Now, shall I call some of your ganymedes to help you robe or is there anything I can do for you?'

'They are more used to assisting with the opposite process,' responded Slovo magisterially. 'As to yourself – yes, go and fetch a bottle of good wine. We'll sit in the garden and drink it while we discuss the end of things.'

They issued out into the sunlight arm in arm. In passing, Slovo ordered a servant girl, who was almost dressed in a white silk chiton, to usher his children indoors. His distant affection for them dictated that there were some things they should not see or hear.

Both men were conditioned to admire the excessively formal gardens of Italian Renaissance high culture. In other circumstances they might have wandered *Villa di Slovo*'s symmetrical paths with relish. Indeed, the entire estate was designed for the promotion of calm and stately thoughts in both beholder and those who dwelt within. The close proximity of the ruins of the *Villa Jovis*, Emperor Tiberius's notorious pleasure-palace, merely emphasized the point; their sad state evidencing the reassurance that all things will pass and the folly of unrestrained passion.

The sun was climbing fast in the cloudless blue sky and there was every indication that the day would become sultry. The Welshman, left to himself, would have hurried to the hill-top summerhouse. The Admiral, however, was more used to the direct and relentless kiss of Sol. It had baked the galley decks he had trod long ago and now it was a friend that warmed the aging limbs which his sluggish Slovo blood betrayed. Therefore he took his time and made inventory as he went, admiring his gardener's savage corseting of nature. Everything he wanted to see was present and correct: the box-hedges and laurels, the potted palms, the orange and lemon trees. Indeed the deliberate gaiety of it all might have seduced him into delusions of normality, as if today was just another day and tomorrow would be likewise. He tried hard to recall that this was not the case and quickened his pace accordingly. There was just a last item of business to be dealt with, best seen to speedily, and then he could be off.

With his companion, he headed for the replica of a classical temple that had slender fluted columns and gleaming cupola, all made of marble. At the centre, round the pedestalled bust of Jupiter the Unconquered Sun, the interior was marvellously cool and airy. Admiral Slovo fetched another chair so that they could sit either side of a tiny table bearing dishes of drying fruit. The Welshman opened the flask of wine he had procured and filled them each a glass.

'It's good!' he said eventually, licking his thin, pale lips.

'What is?' asked the Admiral. 'The wine? The view? Your mission?'

'Them all,' came the answer. 'Your wine is robust and

15

spicy. The view over the gulf to Naples is all one could wish. And I enjoy my work.'

The perspective over the *Villa di Slovo*, taking in the Palace of Tiberius, the blue of the sea and a distance-blessed image of the seething hell of Naples, *was* exquisite. Admiral Slovo had always intended that he would finally take stock of the world from such a place. Whole summer days had passed, remote from family and ordinary things, without him leaving its precincts. Now he sipped his wine expecting consolation but, like rebelling outposts of a failing empire, his taste buds were joining in the swift erosion of his faculties. Everything tasted sour nowadays – even this specially sweetened vintage. Still, to be positive right to the end, it was better than the Falernian.

'I'm glad you are made happy by my hospitality. Is there anything else I can get you?'

The visitor leaned back in the wicker seat and downed another cup. 'I am content,' he said briskly. 'Are you?'

Admiral Slovo had had ample years in which to tire of the verbal games of young men. Only his philosophical beliefs kept a note of tetchiness from entering his reply. 'Of course not,' he said. 'You must know my history and why that should be so.'

'Intimately,' came the agreement. 'I have read both your case-file and your memoirs.'

'How so?' Slovo interrupted, referring to the latter. 'I possess the only copy.'

The man turned to look at the Admiral with a pitying smile. 'Come, come, Admiral,' he said gently, 'you, more than anyone, know our ways.'

Slovo nodded. 'You are everywhere you want to be,' he said heavily.

'And see everything we want to see,' the visitor added.

'Don't be bashful, Admiral, these memoirs of yours are excellent stuff. They deserve to be printed for a wider public.'

'Although they never will be,' Slovo said before the Welshman could.

'No,' the man agreed. 'We can't permit that.'

'So may I see this "case-file" – since you have read my version of the same events?'

'Sorry, no, Admiral. I have come to give you a fuller story, admittedly – but not the *full* story. I'm sure you'll understand.'

'But you do have *The Book*.'

'Yes indeed.'

'I'm honoured.'

'I should say so!' The answer was an exclamation. 'There's been a mere handful similarly favoured the last few centuries.'

'May I see it then?'

The man considered. 'It is your first sight, is that not so?' he asked.

'That's correct,' replied the Admiral, looking away. 'It was discussed on the occasion of my initiation, but otherwise . . .'

'So you are, in fact, a virgin in such matters and I would accordingly counsel patience. You may have *The Book* in all good time but you doubtless appreciate the associated perils . . .'

'Of course,' said Slovo. 'Knowing the guards, magical and otherwise, that surround *The Book*, I'm surprised that you can even carry it and live.'

'Likewise. I have been provided with powerful wards but, even so, the stewardship is a trifle unnerving. If it's all the same to you, Admiral, I'd be happier if we minimized its exposure to the world, for that's when its guardians are most vigilant.'

'And hungry,' said Slovo helpfully.

17

'Just so.'

'I'm happy to wait then,' confirmed Admiral Slovo, to the Welshman's evident relief.

'Thank you,' he said, clearly desirous of a conversational diversion. 'Incidentally, is that the height from which Tiberius's victims were thrown?'

Slovo knew the general direction of the gesture was correct but, with a stubborn residual concern for truth, he turned to make sure.

'Yes – or so it's said. "Tiberius's Drop", the local peasants call it. He's a legendary monster hereabouts.'

'But you disagree?'

Admiral Slovo shrugged. 'I have no strong opinions one way or the other. Perhaps he did have his partners, willing or otherwise, of the previous night flung to their death from a cliff, that is his business. We have all felt that way at one time or another.'

The visitor seemed slightly shocked, but said nothing. Instead, he looked out over the Gulf of Naples and considered how to regain his lost advantage. 'It has been a long and weary old road for you, Admiral, has it not?'

'I can hardly deny that,' answered Admiral Slovo equably.

'And do you blame us?'

Slovo's smile was like a shine on a razor. 'That would hardly be fair. My particular die was cast long before my recruitment to your "Ancient and Holy Vehme".'

'That's very reasonable of you. However, would you maintain that famous Stoic poise were I to tell you that we enlisted you even before that? What if I were to say that your service to the Vehme was of far longer duration?'

The Admiral considered, 'I'm not sure,' he said in due course. 'Is it the sort of thing you're likely to say, Master Vehmist?'

'I'm afraid so.'

'Well,' said Slovo, in thoughtful tone, 'I should hope that I would not so abandon my Stoicism as to be unduly perturbed. It rather depends on the precise nature of the revelation.'

The black-gowned man poured himself another, quite generous, glass of wine. 'And there you have hit the nail squarely on the head, Admiral! My business here is revelation. I have come, with the blessing of the Vehme, to shed light on the dark places of your history. It is our earnest wish that you should understand all – or nearly all. Whether you will *like* all that I shed light on is another matter.'

'Valuing my life as lightly as I do,' said Admiral Slovo, 'I have successfully banished fear and recrimination from it. You term yourselves *Illuminati*, do you not?'

'That is another name for the *Vehmgericht*,' agreed the Welshman cautiously, his middle-German as faultless as his Court Italian.

'Then pray illumine,' said Slovo. 'You cannot hurt me now.'

The Welshman raised his eyebrows at such presumption. 'Well,' he said, 'let us start at your beginning . . .'

About the time that Turkish Imperialism seized another bit of Europe and rolled into Herzegovina, in the year that Charles the Bold became Duke of Burgundy, a small child, the blank slate that was to be Admiral Slovo, thought of something disastrously clever.

It started when another youth in the classroom that fateful day gave voice to the question that would give Slovo away.

'Honoured sir,' piped the stocky ten-year-old, bursting with the desire to display new found knowledge. 'May I ask something?'

The schoolmaster looked up from the Latin text in which he was following the class's painful recitation. An astoundingly liberal pedagogue for his time – indeed notoriously so – he was known to welcome signs of intellectual curiosity among the sons of the upper mercantile classes. Sensible queries were never deterred and could, on happy occasion, postpone the tedious work in hand. He lifted his pointer from the book and signalled for the conjugating chant to cease.

'I've been thinking about Aristotle and Plato, sir.'

'I am so relieved to hear that, Constantius,' came the unpromising reply. 'Why, to think I was under the impression that you laboured unwillingly in the vineyard of their works!'

It was a cheap bit of schoolmaster sarcasm and he instantly regretted it as the class dutifully laughed at the boy's expense.

'I am sorry, Constantius,' he said loudly, bringing the merriment to an instant end. 'I did not mean to crush the tender shoot of budding enquiry.'

Rehabilitated, Constantius looked warningly around at his classmates. 'Well, honoured sir, I just wondered ... where did they go?'

'Why, to the grave of course, like we all do.'

'No, I mean *after* that, sir. Where then?'

The schoolmaster stroked his beard and gave the boy a very cool look.

'I now see the direction of your question, child,' he said. 'It is an interesting one.'

The boy swelled with pleasure at the unaccustomed approval.

'Is anyone else similarly intrigued?' asked the master.

Until the lie of the land was absolutely clear, no one ventured to risk such a confession and, noting this, the proto-Slovo was reluctantly obliged to raise his own hand.

'Slovo ...' said the schoolmaster, feigning surprise.

'Another dark horse of classical curiosity rears up in our very midst. Let's see if you can develop the question. Proceed!'

Under the conducting baton of the master's pointer, the seven-year-old was left with little option but to reveal more of his thoughts than was natural to him. 'The paradox that struck me, honoured sir,' he said slowly and gauging the reaction, 'is whether ancient men of virtue such as Aristotle could enter Paradise when they did not – and could not – possess the true faith. But, if they are damned, for all their goodness, for not professing what they could not have known, then is that just? And if it is not just, then how can that be, since God is, by definition, just?'

'What he means, honoured sir,' said Constantius, butting in, 'is that Plato and his fellows couldn't have been Christians, could they? They died before Christ was born ...'

'I understood what Slovo meant well enough,' said the schoolmaster with awesome finality. 'And I can settle the debate quite simply by stating something you all should already know: *Extra Ecclesia nulla salus*: There is no salvation outside the Church. Your question, Constantius, is impious and inappropriate for an immature mind. However, since it was also a *good* question, I shall take the matter no further. Now return, if you please, to the verb *habere*, to have, and,' he waved the pointer like a wizard's wand, 'con-ju-gate ...'

'The point is,' said the schoolmaster, now very differently attired and accorded even greater respect than before, 'that the question was Slovo's. Every schoolroom has its spies and I knew it was he who'd primed the purely average Constantius, who longs to shine, with the query hatched in his own mind.'

'So,' said the black-cowled leader of the Tribunal facing the schoolmaster, 'he makes arrows for others to fire.'

'Precisely,' agreed the schoolmaster. 'For all his fortunate birth, he is the most distrusting boy I've yet to meet. He operates behind screens of deception and reticence, never saying all of what he means, even when it is of no import. Everything is buried beneath layers of artifice.'

'That might just be cowardice,' suggested another of his interrogators.

'I, too, thought so,' said the schoolmaster eagerly, 'and so observed and tested him. He stands his ground in all the tiny wars of the play-yard. He is no coward, merely preternaturally controlled and nerveless.'

'Do the other infants abhor him then?' The question came from within the dark-clad ranks of those standing round the walls of the cavern.

The schoolmaster politely sought to reply to the correct face but it was lost in the shadows between the torch embrasures. 'No,' he said. 'That is the confirming point – his detachment is a seamless garment. To the other children he pretends to be a light-hearted and natural boy and they are deceived.'

He turned his head slowly to take in the assembly and lifted his hand to solicit support from the hundreds gathered there. 'I ask you to trust me,' he said, addressing the whole gathering. 'He is intelligent and calculating, cold-hearted and yet ethically aware. He is a seven-year-old that entertains theological speculations. While his peers play ball he wonders about Aristotle. I really think that he might serve.'

Thus saying, the schoolmaster bowed his head and stepped back two paces in the prescribed Vehmic way, showing he was before the mercy of their judgement. The noose hanging round his neck made the point even plainer. The recommender of a rejected prospect was hung forthwith. This balanced the glory attaching to a successful proposal, for the Vehme wished their ranks to exclude all but the most promising recruits.

The Tribunal conferred, their heavy cowls lending privacy to the deliberations. The schoolmaster and all his brothers (and some sisters) waited patiently and in silence.

At last, the head of the Tribunal stood, a strategically placed torch bestowing a halo of fire around his head to those viewing from below. 'We are minded to say yes,' he announced. 'Are there any who would disagree?'

In a belief-cum-organization-cum-conspiracy that aspired to democratic ideals, it was always left open for dissatisfaction to have its voice – or even its way, if feelings were strong enough. On this occasion no one spoke.

'So it shall be,' concluded the Tribunalist. 'The Captain of Nemesis will arrange what is necessary.'

Therefore it was because of young Slovo's precocious thoughts that an arrow took his father in the throat whilst he was out hunting. No one saw the archer, though a search was made; no one was ever charged with the crime. The flint-tipped and black-fletched little arrow still protruded through his neck when they bore him home, but the light had long since left his eyes. The whole household was inconsolable and even the boy Slovo, for all his famed control, could not hold back childish tears.

Madame Slovo simply vanished one day soon after, and that was even worse in its way. She was last seen busy in the dairy and then, no more. No note, no token, not even a spray of blood was left to account for her passing.

A brother died of the 'sweating sickness', an uncle hung himself for no good reason – one by one the Slovo clan went down. Neighbours began to get the message and avoided them.

The final barrier between the boy Slovo and the outside world was his aunt. She – because the Vehme, whilst never merciful, could sometimes be whimsical – ended up as the erotic plaything of a Syrian princeling. Even more strangely, lust and hatred slowly mutated over the years into affection and what started as abduction ended in honoured matrimony. This would have been small comfort for the child Slovo, even if he could have known or understood it.

Next, the *Vehmgericht* subtly incited the lawyer holding the Slovo estate in trust to pillage and defraud it (though he was going to do that anyway), so that at the age of eight, the boy Slovo found himself rapidly sans family, home and livelihood and the tender mercies of a far-away Church orphanage were extended to him.

The Ancient and Holy Vehme began one of their long and infinitely patient watching briefs.

'Oh . . .' said Admiral Slovo numbly, meanwhile engaged in the most heroic struggle of his life in order to control his features. There was a lengthy pause as, in some frigid inner sanctum, he strove to accept the long-suppressed suspicion. 'So that was you, was it?'

The Vehmist beside him had taken the precaution of donning fine-mesh body armour beneath his gown before arriving. Not knowing that the Admiral's favoured stiletto blow was a strike to the eye, he felt reasonably confident of survival. In the event, his trouble and present itchy discomfort in the heat were all wasted. Admiral Slovo prevailed in his supreme test, denying and overcoming the inner howl for revenge.

'Sorry, yes,' answered the Welshman. 'You had potential, you see, but we had to find out what the world could make of you. For what we had in mind, a secure upbringing in the warm bosom of the family probably wouldn't have been suitable.'

'No,' agreed Slovo, looking into a private middle-distance and speaking his words as though translating. 'I can see that.'

'It's just a shame it was so hard on you personally,' said the Vehmist, reasonable to the point of mockery.

'Only to start with,' Slovo reassured him.

'Yes. That was noted at the time,' agreed the Welshman, nibbling at a dried apricot. 'You rapidly became endlessly adaptable – and that suited us very well.'

'I'm pleased to hear my savage education gratified someone; tell me, who was reporting for you?'

'Oh,' mused the Vehmist, 'a variety of people. Our first move was to replace the Orphanage Superintendent with one of our own folk.'

'And *what* a sow she was!'

'Only by necessity and only in your case, Admiral. Actually, she was quite a kindly person in normal life – I knew her well in her old age.'

'I trust her death was attended with drawn-out pain and degradation,' said Slovo.

'No,' replied the Vehmist. 'It came very swift and merciful.'

Admiral Slovo looked away. 'I'm heartbroken,' he said.

'Naturally, there were others. We would never rely on merely one opinion. Of course, your spectacular escape didn't exactly make our task any easier. We lost you for a number of months.'

'Oh, I'm sorry to hear that!' said Slovo. 'At the time, I had no idea I was inconveniencing anyone.'

The Vehmist smiled wryly, studying a flight of small birds winging overhead. 'I dare say those whose throats you cut on the way were a trifle put out . . .' he observed.

'Mere youthful high spirits,' explained Admiral Slovo, 'added to a residual desire for justice.'

The Vehmist shrugged to signify his indifference. 'Anyhow,' he said, 'there was no real harm done as far as we were concerned. We picked up your trail in Bohemia by dint of the local mayhem.'

'Bohemian political life was ever thus,' countered Slovo.

'Quite so – but you added a delectable degree of style and art to the process. The refreshing change caught our local agent's attention.'

In travelling memory lane, Admiral Slovo seemed to have found some consolation. His eyes looked on the sparkling sea with renewed favour. 'I rather enjoyed life in that river-flotilla,' he said. 'Rising so fast entailed a lot of responsibility on my young shoulders, it's true, but I found the work very ... healing. Of course, between the Turk on one bank and the quasi-human frontier tribes on "our" side, we had quite a torrid time of it.'

'All of which we fully approved of,' said the Vehmist. 'Likewise the Town Governorship that followed and the condottiere service in Thessaly. Banking in Ravenna was something of a departure, but a welcome one, a valuable broadening of experience. You see, Admiral Slovo, all our judgements were made after the event – we were hard pressed to keep up with each new incarnation and your name was rarely off our trace list. You certainly got to see Christendom, didn't you?'

'Something kept me moving,' agreed Slovo. 'Forever in search.'

'Of what?'

'I can't recall, actually,' answered the Admiral. 'That Slovo is lost and gone. It's like speaking of a different person.'

The Vehmist appeared to accept this. 'The leap from banking to piracy took us by surprise, I must confess. That radical departure – and its suddenness – meant we lost you once more.'

'In fact,' said Slovo, 'there are closer affinities between the two professions than cursory thought suggests. Piracy seemed a logical extension to what I had been doing – and a more honest way of life.'

The Welshman again deferred to the older man's judgement. 'By the merest stroke of fortune,' he said, 'it was that choice that caused our paths to cross again, never to part. Only then could we closely study what we had created – and scarce forbear to cheer!'

'Oh,' said Admiral Slovo, 'you mean when I had my swimming lessons . . .'

❧ The Year 1486

'SWIMMING LESSONS: After a sad and lonely childhood, cast as an orphan into the wicked world, I discover my vocation and philosophy of life. Piracy suits me very well.'

'No, I'm sorry. I'm afraid you'll have to walk home.'

The Venetian nobleman looked down at Admiral Slovo and raised an enquiring eyebrow.

'Well, yes, I know,' explained Slovo to the man poised on the deck rail. 'Call me faithless if you like ...'

'You are faithless,' obliged the Venetian. 'You promised me my life.'

'Agreed,' conceded the Admiral, folding his arms and leaning convivially against the rail, beside the Venetian's feet. 'But that was then and this is ...'

'Now. Yes, I quite see,' interrupted the nobleman. 'And I must say I take your decision personally, you know.'

'Oh dear, I do wish you wouldn't,' replied Slovo, reasonably. 'Put yourself in my shoes ...'

Some of the crew, who had nothing better to do than watch the show, found grounds for bestial amusement at this aside but the Admiral silenced them with a glance.

'What I *mean*,' he continued, 'is that despite doubtless genuine grounds for grievance, you are refusing to see the problem in the round. His Holiness and your Serene Repub-

28

lic are nominally at peace at this juncture. It would not do, therefore, for me to return to Ostia bearing the sole survivor of a forbidden piratical venture, would it now?'

They both turned to look at the nearby once-grand galley, now afire and sinking; its crew (bar one) dead in battle or by subsequent murder, still aboard.

'Come to think of it,' the Admiral mused, 'my commission from His Holiness even precludes attacks on fellow Christians. Venetian though you may be, I assume that you come within that category . . .?' And when the nobleman shrugged, Slovo added, 'Well, there you are then, you see the quandary my greed-inspired oath puts me in.'

The Venetian looked underwhelmed by the Admiral's dilemma. 'You just want my library, that's what it is,' he stated calmly. 'I saw you leafing through it with lust in your eyes. You wish for undisputed title.'

Admiral Slovo admitted the possibility with a shift of the shoulders. 'Well, that may have something to do with it, but I'd thank you to keep your voice down. Bibliomania does not accord with my professional image. The crew might nurture false notions, requiring bloody suppression.'

'That library has been generations in the acquiring,' said the Venetian firmly. 'I'm not giving it up.'

Admiral Slovo stood up and stretched. 'I'm rather afraid you are,' he said. 'To prepare yourself for Paradise, your books and heart must surely part. Now off you go, there's a good chap.'

The Venetian glowered at the half circle of buccaneers below him but realized that his position was futile. 'I do not consider this conversation to be at an end,' he said equably. The pirates smiled. Then, with as much dignity as could be mustered, he turned and walked off the plank into the Mediterranean sea.

*

'Stop oars!'

The strokemaster's roar echoed off into silence. All the crew were shifting in their appointed stations and straining to see.

'Keep to your places, if you please,' said Admiral Slovo to his Bosun. As intended, he relayed the command to the crew in louder and coarser terms. There was a just acceptable lowering of the level of frenzy.

'Look, there he is!' shouted the look-out in the stern. 'Out there!'

Slovo strode to join him and peered into the distant blue. 'It's possible,' he conceded eventually. 'How interesting.'

The Bosun, who had no other name known to man, had for career's sake emphasized the animal within but in fact he retained a worthwhile intellect and was invited to join them.

'Can't be sure at that distance,' he barked. 'It's blurred – might be jetsam.'

'I think not,' said the Admiral authoritatively. 'I have never heard of swimming jetsam. Look, one can see the rise of an arm.'

'There's any number of overboards in the sea,' replied Bosun indefatigably. 'It don't mean it's our man.'

Slovo nodded his tentative agreement. 'I don't see how it can be the Venetian either. He could hardly have lasted two days in the water. On the other hand, it does look awfully like him. If only he'd come a little closer so that his face was less . . . indistinct.'

Bosun looked shocked at the expression of such a wish. 'Let me go and get my crossbow, Admiral,' he asked. 'That'll sort him!'

'I think not,' answered Slovo slowly. 'If it's a mere lost sailor, the sea will soon deal with the matter. Should, however, it be the Venetian, I cannot but feel that our weaponry will be of little avail. If we must be pursued by a revenant, I'd prefer it not to have a crossbow bolt in its brow.'

Bosun was thinking this one through when, with a voice of joy, he noted that the figure had gone. In an explosion of relief, the crew threw discipline to the winds and scrambled to line the sides. No one had the heart to reprimand them. In a silence broken only by the call of gulls, everyone searched the waves for their obscure and elusive companion of the last day and night.

'Down to Hell and fare ye well,' said Bosun at last, when all agreed that sea and sky were all there was to see.

The celebration was spoilt by the sound, starting low but rising to a thunderous roar, distorted by its passage through water and hull, of knocking from beneath the ship.

After a further day of being shadowed at the very edge of sight, quite regardless of whatever turn of speed that wind and oar could produce, Admiral Slovo decided to head for land. For all he cared, the dead Venetian could follow him and hammer on his ship for eternity. Alas, however, the crew were not so philosophical. Even Bosun, who feared neither God nor State (not fully understanding the power of either) was getting edgy. Slovo, who maintained control by a record of success and the occasional exemplary death, knew when not to push his luck too far.

As they rowed home with unusual will, Slovo dallied at the stern and considered what problems this change of heart would bring. His words to the Venetian about inter-Christian piracy had not been idle ones and should their companion remain, a leech-like embarrassment, when they came to dock, then . . . difficult questions would be asked.

Still, never mind, thought the Admiral at length, never one to worry long. *Better the chance of a Papal scaffold than the certainty of mutiny*. He even waved to the Venetian with his newly acquired reading book, *The Meditations of Marcus Aurelius*.

'This is good stuff,' he shouted. 'I'm much obliged to you.'

Slovo was awoken by the sound of a ragged rattle of oars and a lack of progress. He had only to raise himself up from the deck to discover the reason for both.

Half a league off and silhouetted against the dawn was the Venetian, standing on the water and blocking their path.

Order took a bit of time to restore, even with the flat of a sword, and in the end it was easiest just to tell them to put about. That at least, the crew were glad to do.

One bank of oarsmen fidgeted on their benches whilst the other furiously tore at the sea and, bit by bit, gradually turned the galley's back on the sodden, silent, watcher. Then, using their joint efforts, they sped away from home into deep water, for once not needing the strokemaster's hypnotic call.

Admiral Slovo, seated at the stern, studied the swiftly receding Venetian and the compliment was returned in kind. Then, mission apparently fulfilled, the corpse slowly slipped back, inch by inch, beneath the waves, its guessed-at gaze never deviating until the water closed over its green, floating locks.

Bosun shuddered, not caring who saw him do so.

'I've not seen the ship move so fast since that encounter with the Ottoman harem-ship,' said the Admiral, jocularly. Bosun appeared not to hear him and Slovo felt entitled to allow his disgruntlement a further outing. 'I spent what was it?' he mused, 'on the Satan's-head ram which adorns the prow of this ship. Why then, Master Bosun, did we not employ it to sunder apart this persistent little man who dogs our steps?'

Before Bosun could reply, the look-out called out. 'Ahoy! He's back!'

They saw that this was so. The swimmer had returned.

'Might is right – but not always applicable,' said Bosun in reply to Slovo – inadvertently revealing, in his agitation, hidden depths and a secret taste for metaphysics.

'You could just be right, you know,' said the Admiral, making a note to keep an even closer eye on this dark horse. 'Perhaps philosophy is the answer. Tell them to up oars.'

Very reluctantly, the rowers were persuaded to desist whilst their Captain came to stand before them. He delayed a moment to achieve the required mental downgrading to permit communication.

'It's like this,' he said when finally prepared for the contamination. 'We're being chased – us, chased! Us wot as faced the ships of Sultan Bayezid and put holes in the galleons of the Mamelukes! Now, tell me, is this right? Is it proper?'

He paused for dramatic effect. No one answered. Only from beneath the ship came the sound of urgent knocking.

The following day, Admiral Slovo woke to the more than usually sullen stares of the crew and knew straightaway that something had happened. He enquired as to the state of play from Bosun.

'As soon as we get too far for his fancy, he blocks our way and the crew put about, orders or no. We're going nowhere fast.'

'Ultimately, life is like that,' said Slovo sharply. 'As a philosopher, you should appreciate that.'

'And the look-out is gone.'

'*Gone?*'

'Sometime during the night and silent as you like. Only I should say, he's not *entirely* gone.'

'How so?'

'The Venetian left half the rib-cage behind.'

Slovo refused to be out-cooled. 'That was considerate of him,' he said. 'At least we're left in no doubt.' Then, quoting from *The Meditations*, he said, 'It is not the thing that disturbs thee, but thine own judgement about it?'

Bosun looked ruefully towards the rising sun. 'This is quite some "thing" we're facing here, Admiral,' he said. 'Do you reckon Look-out made his judgement of it before it got him?'

Eventually Slovo was called on by name and he was glad of it. It was undignified being harried back and forth, subject to the impertinences of a restive crew, and far better matters should end this way rather than in death by thirst or mutiny.

The Venetian, afar off and a mere matchstick figure, clung to an ancient buoy and added his voice to its doleful bell.

'SLO-VO!' he called, over and over, in time with the bell-note. 'SLO-VO!' Despite the distance his voice was loud and clear.

Without being bidden the crew had upped oars and thus declared themselves spectators while the galley drifted, becalmed.

The prisoner of his professional image, Admiral Slovo remained impassive. Lolling in his Captain's chair, he called across to the Venetian, confident that in nature's present suspension his unraised voice would carry. 'Well then, hello again,' he said. 'And what can I do for you?'

There was a long pause before the Venetian replied. 'MY BOOOOOOOOKS!' he howled at last.

Slovo had anticipated this. He signalled to Bosun that the

prepared cask of book-booty be cast overboard like its former owner.

Before the noise of the splash had died away the Venetian called again, 'AND THE *MEDITATIONS* OF AURELIUS . . .'

The Admiral grimaced. That particular book had spoken to him on levels he did not know he owned. He'd very much wished to keep and finish it.

'So be it,' he answered eventually and, fetching the text from its hiding place, flung it over the rail.

The quiet returned. Slovo fancied the Venetian was savouring his post-mortem triumph. In order to spoil this gloat, he resumed the conversation. 'And what now?' he asked.

Another long pause and then: 'NOW I'D LIKE YOU TO SWIM WITH ME.'

Most of the crew turned their attention to the Admiral. How he dealt with this would determine his position in the Mediterranean pirates' hall of fame.

'I can't swim,' he answered simply.

There was no shame in this. Most mariners of the time preferred not to learn how to prolong the agony should Mother Sea claim them. *Not a bad point*, judged the crew and looked back at the Venetian.

'YOU'LL MANAGE,' he shot straight back. 'YOU'LL FIND, AS A CORPSE, YOU HAVE A CERTAIN FACILITY IN THE WATER.'

His shipmates were still reeling this one in as Slovo countered, 'You are not being a reasonable man.'

'THANKS TO YOU,' came the reply, 'I AM NO LONGER A MAN AT ALL.'

There was no real answer to this and Slovo subsided into his seat.

From below the galley there erupted the hammering of many hands. Unlike hitherto, the Venetian remained visible. It seemed he could now call on helpers.

35

'IT IS TIME,' came the call. 'COME TO ME.'

The pounding on the hull rose and threatened to turn it into matchwood. Slovo realized that between the vengeful ghost and the fearful crew there was little to choose: his life was over and all that remained was to leave it with style. When he rose and snapped his finger at the Venetian, by nods and mumbles the crew signalled their approval of this defiance in the face of despair.

The sea erupted and bubbled. All around the galley and for some distance outwards, the water was alive – no other word for it – with floating corpses.

'THEY WILL BEAR YOUR WEIGHT, ADMIRAL,' wailed the Venetian. 'COME TO ME.'

Slovo ignored a final spasm of weakness which made him wish he could turn and look to his crew for support. He knew that he had lost them; their reservoirs of primal dread outweighing any such latecomer concepts as loyalty or courage. Nothing else for it: Admiral Slovo was alone again. He vaulted over the ship's rail.

The dead men dipped and rocked but, as promised, they formed a path of sorts. Ignoring their undead stares – eyeless or otherwise – Slovo made his way to the Venetian. Close up, he saw that three days in the company of King Neptune and his little fishes had not been kind to the body.

'Hello, Slovo.' The greeting was uttered through nibbled lips.

'We meet once more, Master Venetian.' So saying, Slovo raised his lace kerchief to his nose. The once exquisite nobleman was now less than social in company.

'You wouldn't believe the number of us down here,' said the Venetian by way of small talk and indicating his carpet of comrades. 'Many of them put there by the likes of you. That fact may account for the assistance vouchsafed me in my quest. Even the sea has moral standards, it transpires.'

'Who'd have thought it?' quipped the Admiral.

The man and the revenant regarded each other with mutual distaste. Then the Venetian left the rusted buoy, causing its bell to toll, and reached out to grasp Slovo's throat. He did not meet any resistance and the saturated flesh of his plump and swollen fingers easily covered the Admiral's neck from ruff to chin.

Eye to eye with his nemesis (save that *its* eyes were in some fish somewhere), Slovo patiently awaited the application of pressure – and whatever lay beyond. After a while he realized that pain and death were a long time coming. The Venetian, poised upon fulfilment of his last wish, appeared undecided.

At last, the green mouth opened and, on a gale of salt-breath, it spoke into Slovo's face. '*Never allow yourself to be swept off your feet,*' he quoted. '*When an impulse stirs, see first that it will meet the claims of justice . . . to refrain from imitation is the best revenge.*'

'*Meditations?*' croaked Slovo.

The Venetian rocked his wobbly head. 'Of the divine Marcus Aurelius,' he confirmed. 'The guiding light of my life – both of which you took. One has been returned but the other . . .'

Admiral Slovo said nothing – mainly because it would have hurt too much.

'His Stoic principles attended my every thought and action: to the very point where I quietly trod a plank at your request.'

It seemed to Slovo that the vice-grip on his windpipe had eased somewhat, although he did not yet dare to hope.

'You did not deprive me of my faith during life,' mused the Venetian, 'why should you have that victory in death?'

'Why indeed?' Slovo hissed.

The Venetian nodded again. 'I will not kill you,' he said.

Less happy than he should be, the Admiral waited in vain for the hand to release him.

'I will take from you less than what is owed me,' the Venetian went on. 'I will have from you the energy to sustain my half-life – and thus condemn you to the same fate. There is justice in that, a moderation of vengeance. Such restraint is truly Stoical.'

With this, he applied his lips to Slovo's and they grappled in an obscene French kiss. Nauseated beyond endurance, Slovo felt himself losing . . . something, and then was calm.

The Venetian dropped him and stood back. He seemed reinvigorated and exultant. 'Your life-force is good,' he said. 'It will last me till my flesh and sinews at length decay. I *shall* have time to read my books!'

Admiral Slovo regained his footing and wondered why he felt so uninvolved.

'And you,' the dead man said, answering the unspoken question, 'I have left you with enough to live out your life. Life, of a sort, at least. I have been merciful.'

'Then thank you,' said Slovo politely.

The Venetian smiled – which was the worst sight of all. 'You are changed already,' he said. 'Such aridity! I afflict you with a curse and you thank me!' So saying, he sank beneath the waves.

Admiral Slovo turned rapidly back for his ship, not knowing how long the ex-human footway would last. In a gentle kind of way he was looking forward to the reunion with his crew and, still a way off, favoured them with a tigerish smile. Their disloyalty no longer worried him. He felt happy about the changes that would be made – by knife and rope and shot. And he was less troubled, less disturbed by flibbertigibbet thoughts and his own emotions than before. It might well be the peace of the desert, but at least he had found peace of mind.

Vengeance? he thought as he clambered over the side and the sea-dead fled to their proper place. *A curse? I'd have paid good money for this!*

After a wide-ranging and enjoyable discussion on Plato and the efficacy of the spells prescribed by the god Hermes Trismegistus in his masterwork, *Corpus Hermeticum*, the senior of the two Vehmists indicated that they should proceed to more mundane business.

The lesser brother, a member of the Rhodian Military Order of St John and appropriately armed and dressed, was weary after coming direct to this interview from his long journey. Even so, he sat up straight in his ornate carved chair and awaited some sign that he might deliver his report.

The other man, older than the first but clothed in equal splendour in the High academic gown of the Gemistan[2] Platonic School, levered himself up and crossed the room. There he checked for potential eavesdroppers and then closed and locked the door. Only after that, with a wave of his ancient and be-ringed hand, did he urge his guest on. Even in their Grecian citadel at Mistra, the Vehme had varying degrees of trust.

'Honourable Master,' said the Knight of St John, his Greek, though probably not his first language, faultless and courtly, 'I can convey both a measure of success and failure . . .'

'I know you, Captain Jean,' smiled the old scholar, 'your failures are ordinary men's glorious triumphs. Your past service to the cause would excuse a thousand disasters to come. So, tell me all without fear of reprimand.'

The Knight savoured the high compliment before proceeding. 'I have discovered the fate of our man,' he said, 'but failed to retrieve his murdered body.'

'How so?' asked the scholar.

'The sea has him, and her returning of borrowed objects is most capricious. We have scanned the likely rocks and beaches unsmiled on by fortune.'

'At this remove of time,' the scholar mused, looking idly out of the diamond-paned window down the spur of Mount Taygetus and at the landscape of the Morea (or Sparta, as he would archaically have termed it) below, 'I doubt there would be anything whole or wholesome for us to revere with burial.'

The Knight nodded his agreement. 'You are undoubtedly correct, but I fastidiously forbore to mention the point. Some of the cadavers we *did* discover were quite ... impermissible!'

'Just so, Captain. Very well then, let our brother roll in the embrace of the waves. He shall have his oratory hymn all the same. Its composition is near complete – as doubtless is his decomposition – a most moving conceit in which the styles of Pindar and Sappho meet and conjoin.'

The Knight smiled warily. 'A most unlikely mating,' he said, 'given the predilections of either poet.'

The scholar chose to miss the allusion. 'In the Academy we have talents capable of such ... problematic graftings,' he said. 'The art of the ancients may be incomparable but we have come to be passably good mimics. I think the death of our Consul of the Venetian Vehme merits some little exertion on our part – even if it's only artistic, don't you? Incidentally, did you ascertain who killed him?'

The Knight's face suddenly became hardened, the speed and ease of transformation suggesting that this was its normal state. 'It was a pirate,' he said lightly. 'We know that much, but not his name. He must be a new arrival in the Middle Sea or else we would have him already.'

'An alternative explanation might be that he is subtle

and full of craft beyond the norm,' ventured the scholar gently.

'There is that possibility,' said the Knight, forcing himself to consider the proposition. 'But it does not affect the ultimate issue – merely its timing. He will be found, in due course, and made to render full restitution for his crime.'

'It will be so,' agreed the scholar. 'We are enacting a morality play for the benefit of the gods and those generations who are yet to come. Let it be done then to our script and according to virtue.'

'Amen!' chorused the Knight. 'He's as good as dead.'

'Goodness, no!' said Enver Rashi, Pasha of the Ottoman-conquered *sanjak* of Morea. 'Quite the contrary!'

He had just informed the Gemistan Platonic scholar that the name of their Venetian brother's killer was already known to him. The scholar had promptly vowed the murderer's speedy extinction.

'Esteemed little brother,' he said to the puzzled older man, 'I fear your donkey trek from the Mistra Citadel to my court was partly wasted. Our late companion has already found means of conveying your news to me.'

The scholar, being complete master of his chosen academic field, was little used to radical surprise.

'This dead ... colleague ... has told you?' he stumbled, eyeing the Pasha for signs of mockery or, almost as bad, a trap. The shameless hussy laid out on the couch beside her master in turn lazily surveyed the Greek as if he were some unappetizing carcass.

'Effectively,' confirmed the Turk. 'At least, he permitted me to know.' As he signalled to the towering Janissary guard by a side door, a bedraggled captive was shoved into the dazzling white reception chamber. 'This man was the actual conveyance the message took,' he explained.

This unfortunate, a European of obvious base birth, was well rehearsed. Under the baleful gaze of the Janissary, he recited his tale to the stranger present. 'I was fishing,' he said, in what was clearly – and painfully – rote-learnt pigeon Turkish, 'off Malta where I live.'

'Lived,' corrected Enver Pasha. 'Past tense.'

'*Lived*. Then the man – or what was left of a man – rose out of the sea before me and stood there like he was on solid land, or he were Christ upon Galilee.'

The scholar, whose love of Greece and Rome led him to fear and resent Christianity and its founder, daintily curled his lips at such a reference. The Circassian girl, bored beyond measure, yawned and prepared to doze.

'Then he told me where I was to go, what I was to say and to whom. He promised me great riches if I did as I was bade and damnation if I did not. And so here I am.'

'And there you go!' quipped Enver Pasha, capping the fisherman's speech and indicating with one fat hand that he should be bundled from their presence. 'The Venetian,' Enver then gravely advised the scholar, 'did not forget his duty either side of the grave. He was one of our finest.'

'Perhaps still is . . .' hazarded the scholar.

'No,' replied Enver Pasha airily, 'the sea and its inhabitants do the most horrible things to lifeless flesh. His magic could not counter those sundering influences for ever.'

'So that is it!' crowed the old scholar, who knew all too much about the rapid dissolution of the body.

'Of course,' answered the Pasha, beaming a smile of white and gold. 'How else? You must know that the *Hermeticum* instructs how to instil divine essence into a statue . . .'

'I do,' the scholar confidently affirmed. 'And thereby we preserve the Pagan pantheon for future days.'

'Just so. Well, the Venetian had access to a deeper teaching by which the fleeing soul may be chained just a little longer to its prison of meat.'

'I had no idea!' gaped the scholar, forgetting considerations of image for a brief moment, such was his amazement.

'Being so menial in our counsels,' said the Pasha brutally, 'we chose not to enlighten you – until it was necessary. The fisherman was instructed to tell me one thing only – the name: Captain Slovo.'

'But you do not wish me to remove this ... grit in our sandal?' asked the scholar, his private world now all turned topsy-turvy.

'No,' said the Pasha, gently stroking the gauze-clad rump of the *houri* prone beside him. 'I want you to find him.'

'May I ask why?'

The Pasha nodded, his hand now moving to an even more intimate role. 'At your new – as of this moment – level, yes, you may. It transpires, by the strangest of coincidences – in which, as you know, we do not believe – that this Slo-vo is one of ours. Of all those available for the job, the Venetian found the one pirate in our ranks to be killed by. How odd, how strange, that this man should simultaneously return to our attention *and* create his own vacancy. He is clearly as favoured as the Venetian was not. In fact, I learn that he is a major investment, a piece of steel of our own forging. That is why, when he is found, I want you also to activate the Papal Chapter, excluding only the deepest buried treasures. It appears Slo-vo figures in many divergent plans and so, far from killing him, you will bring him home and pave his way.'

'It shall be so,' said the scholar and bowed as deeply as his traitorous joints would permit him.

'It must be so!' answered the Pasha. 'Now please leave – amorous instincts are storming the walls of my rational faculties.'

Being a mischievous as well as a learned old man, the scholar turned back after reaching the door to the outer audience chamber. As he'd hoped, proceedings were already well advanced and the *houri*'s lustrous head was buried deep in the Pasha's crotch. 'And the fisherman?' he asked innocently.

Enver Pasha regained control of his eyeballs and disengaged his intimate accomplice. 'Service in the galleys of the Sultan seems best,' he said as evenly as he could. 'The man is used to a martime career.'

'But no riches?'

'It is possible,' replied the Pasha, leaning back in anticipation of a professionally choreographed hour or two to come. 'Once every decade or so, a ship gets in such a desperate position that it frees and arms its galley-slaves. Of those unfortunate ships a few might even go on to win the fight. A rare sea-captain, one whom life has not yet hardened beyond human gratitude, might reward a slave who'd fought, performed mighty deeds of valour, and yet survived. It could just happen ... and certainly he had no greater chance of fortune as a Maltese fish-grabber.' Enver Pasha managed to sound the most reasonable of men. 'Therefore of what have we deprived him?'

The scholar conceded the point by withdrawing and closing the double doors. He then made haste to leave the Pasha's Athenian palace since sight of its present state, captured, altered and debauched to Islamic tastes and usage, upset him. Other more worthy feet should be treading the same ground. Perhaps even ... *his* step could have graced that ravished spot. It didn't bear thinking about he decided as the silk-glorified Janissaries grimly monitored his exit from the premises. Outside, he was careful to avert his gaze from the dishonoured Acropolis above.

How monstrous, mused the scholar, as he threaded his

44

donkey through the decayed streets of once-Imperial Athens, that anything should presume to exist without reverence for the gods, Plato and antiquity. High time that civilization was rearranged so as to compel it!

✆ The Year 1487

'I find service with a Master of my chosen trade and meet new and frightening people with my best interests at heart.'

'I came to Tripoli because I was so *tired* of Europe,' said Admiral Slovo. 'And with what they are trying to do there.'

'Are they trying to do something?' asked his elderly companion. 'I could never discern any cohesive project – and I am old, whereas you—'

'I have an old mind,' answered Slovo. 'And, for all your years you have never experienced at first hand the frenetic chit-chat going on over there now. I perceived a burgeoning wish to render life ... rational – understandable, even. Impossible, of course, but the attempt makes for a lot of misery, physical and spiritual. That doesn't deter the merchants and philosophers, naturally.'

The old man looked up from his beautifully drafted star-charts and studied Slovo by the shifting light of the giant candle. 'If what you say is true,' he said eventually, having characteristically thought the matter through thoroughly, regardless of socially awkward silences, 'then I would agree. To attempt to understand, let alone explain, the mind of Allah is the life-project of the fool. Yet all I see of you Christian infidel races suggests little such ... dryness. My prevailing impression is one of quite appalling vitality – combined with a propensity for violence far beyond the needs of the situation. That, I suggest, Slo-el-Vo, is a recipe for boisterous expansion, not boredom.'

'Perhaps, esteemed Khair Khaleel-el-Din,' suggested Slovo with polite hesitation, 'you have merely met the wrong people.'

The old man nodded, his great green turban adding enormous gravitas to the simple gesture. 'Possibly. As a pirate, or latterly a chief of pirates, I have encountered perhaps an unrepresentative selection of your kin. It may be that I simply recall, across a gap of sixty years, what my tutor in the trade impressed upon me. *Respect the ships of the Christians*, he told me, *even as you sink them. Be prepared to wade in blood, and not necessarily someone else's. On the surface they may seem soft – with all their talk of love and charity – but underneath . . . well!'*

'He may have had a point,' Slovo conceded. 'I detect a lazy tendency in myself of late, of preferring to attack ships from the Moslem world. I don't say, of course, that we discriminate or run, but given the choice . . .'

'Your meaning is taken, Captain,' said the old man warmly. 'I could cap it with an anecdote from my own experience about a mad Austrian who preferred oblivion embracing a barrel of gunpowder to capture and ransom.'

They paused as Khair Khaleel-el-Din's tiring heart was gladdened by the arrival of a meteor shower he had earlier predicted. Neither man knew what it was they were looking at or had any inkling of the cause of the celestial fireworks. Ignorant of whether the Heavens were infinite or mere miles away, they both watched the inter-planetary pebbles flare in final glory within the atmosphere of earth.

Slovo did not know what to think. He had not yet resolved

whether Stoicism permitted moderate enjoyment at the party-tricks of nature.

By contrast, the older pirate allowed himself to succumb to joy and felt that, however briefly, he had been honoured to dabble his fingertips in the stream of Allah's thoughts. His life-long reading and all his painstaking calculations had been rewarded and when the storm had quite finished he bowed his head in silent, thankful prayer.

'They came as you said they would,' Slovo congratulated him. 'I am very impressed.'

'They came,' smiled the old man, 'and, *inshallah*, they will come again. Neither of us will be here to see them – fortunately it is not given to humans to live for centuries. Allah guides these lights in the sky and directs them to the beautiful world He has made for us. Ah, but perhaps my talk seems over-pious to you?'

'I can see that in accepting meaning and perfection as belonging to God alone, you spare yourself a lot of anguish,' Slovo rejoined.

'It's not as good as you make out,' commented the old pirate. 'Many a noseless whore looks good at fifty paces. Still, there must be *something* in your religion – fully half of the ships I command are now captained by Christians. Perhaps one day, when I am safely dead and gone, every so-called Barbary pirate will be an infidel.'

'The difference is,' said Slovo carefully, 'that these men you speak of are not Christian at all. They are the foul air which has bubbled up from the fens of Christendom and floated your way. Which is not to decry their seamanship,' he added swiftly, not wishing to disparage his master's judgement. 'However, I would stake my ship not one in a hundred has ever entertained a thought emanating from above the belly-line.'

The corsair smiled gently, 'Whereas you . . .' he said.

'I did not come to Tripoli just for gold,' answered Slovo firmly. 'I came to find my soul and perhaps to save it.'

'I beg of you, Slovo, memorize what you have just said, burn the words into your heart. If you come to be as old as I, you will find that funny things are in short supply. On that day, if you can recall your last words, oh how you will laugh!'

Slovo could have been offended but simply said, 'I will do as you ask.'

'I know you will,' replied Khair Khaleel-el-Din, 'and that is because you are clever. I like you, Slovo, in so far as I like anything beyond my star-charts. You live here because your Stoa-whatever . . .'

'Stoicism,' said Slovo helpfully.

'. . .Stoicism accords with what you perceive as our fatalism. You'll see through that misconception soon enough and move on. Meanwhile, you're a one-off I can make a great deal of money from. Do you know your ship is one of my most profitable?'

'I surmised as much,' said Slovo, 'principally because I do not cheat you.'

'You hand over all that you take,' agreed Khair Khaleel-el-Din. 'That is true – and rare. However, you are also more daring and less squeamish than most. I would not want any child of mine to do what you have done, but nevertheless you do have virtue welded to your wickedness and that is a most unusual and useful combination. I shall re-employ you, Christian; your licence is renewed for a further six months.'

'I'm grateful,' said Slovo impassively.

'That might even be true,' answered the corsair. 'We'll agree and sign off the previous period's accounts tomorrow, when it is light. You will be pleased with the bonus I have in mind for you.'

Books, a new knife and a fair-skinned slave to experiment

with, thought Slovo – and was instantly ashamed of his weakness.

'Oh, and one other thing.' Khair Khaleel-el-Din made the question sound so casual that Slovo's defence mechanisms were immediately alerted. 'Have you been writing to anyone?'

'No,' said Slovo very firmly. 'I agreed not to enter into any communications.'

'Just so,' replied the pirate-lord. 'Well then, have you been making enquiries into the higher realms of the Islamic faith?'

'Would that I could,' said Slovo. 'My Arabic is still such that I can only dimly hear the apparently sublime cadences of your Qur'an.'

'Persevere,' said the corsair as an aside. 'It is well worth it. Meanwhile, I have received a letter concerning you. There is someone keen to meet you, my Captain Slovo, and I do not think I dare to deny them. It will be next month – are you agreeable?'

Slovo shrugged. 'What have I to lose?' he quipped.

Khair Khaleel-el-Din gave the comment far more consideration than it merited.

'That,' he said, running an index finger pensively along his withered lips, 'is a very good question.'

At the time appointed for the meeting, Khair Khaleel-el-Din was more forthcoming. 'This enlightened being who deigns to look upon you is the Principal of the ancient Cairene University of the Mosque Al-Azher. He is known as the *Shaduf*, after the original water-lifting implement of his nation, since he likewise brings life to the parched fields of the mind from the refreshing waters of truth. As a fellow respecter of wisdom, Slovo, you should abase yourself before him, as I do.'

In fact, neither of them made a move to do any such thing. Slovo took the minute movements of the little Arab visitor's implausibly neat beard and moustache to be outward signs of facial expression, and presumed it was a greeting. He made a semblance of a bow in return.

'I thank you, master privateer,' said the Shaduf. 'You may now leave us.'

Slovo wondered just what was in store. And it transpired he had the opportunity to ponder for some while. The Shaduf simply sat and studied him at first. Considering a trial of stares unwise, Slovo pretended to examine the galleys in Tripoli Harbour far below.

'Yes,' the Shaduf eventually drawled, clearly expectant that Slovo would give way to ecstasy at first hearing of that word. 'Yes, you will do.'

Slovo cleared some imaginary dust from the knee of his breeches. 'Well, that's a great weight from my mind,' he said. '*Do* for what exactly?'

'For what we have in mind,' replied the Shaduf concisely, not obviously disappointed by the infidel's reaction. 'But that needn't concern you unduly at this stage in your career.'

'I was unaware of owning such a structured concept,' said Slovo. 'And, incidentally, who is this "we"?'

For the Shaduf the interview was patently over but he remained willing to humour this impudent Christian. 'Firstly,' he ticked off one elegant finger, 'you may be presently unaware of a pattern to your life but that is not to disprove its existence. Secondly,' another digit was coaxed to bend over, 'the "we" to whom I referred is a collective called the Vehme.'

Slovo's data-retrieval faculties travelled gingerly down the hall of memories, careful to avoid some of the more monstrous items slumbering lightly there. 'I recall hearing that word,' he said, frowning to recollect, 'in Germania, amongst the City States. I have heard things . . .'

'But not the truth,' interrupted the Shaduf dismissively, with confidence that convinced. 'That is something that can only be learned gradually. It is this that we propose to you.'

Captain Slovo already had the experience to scent overwhelming power. Physically, the Shaduf might be no match for the youngest trainee pirate aboard Slovo's ship but it was clear to the Captain that he himself was very much a slingless David to the Arab's Goliath in this encounter.

'Just out of curiosity,' he asked, 'is it open for me to refuse?'

'It is open to all men to die,' answered the Shaduf.

❦ The Year 1488

'By possession of a beautiful bottom (but not my own) I secure a new position in life and acquire respectability and a wife!'

'Details, mere details,' said Captain Slovo.

'They may be mere details to you, Captain,' replied Bosun, 'but to us it's life and death. Come on – slit your throat and spill the news.'

Ever since the blowing of his cover, revealing him as an amateur philosopher, Bosun had been manifesting dangerously democratic tendencies. Slovo would never have tolerated it but for the fact that he had only one more voyage to make and that replacing Bosun would be inconvenient. Otherwise, the upstart tiller-tugger would have been over the side in short order, to join the Venetian.

'A reliable source,' Slovo explained with a patience that should have stirred Bosun's neck hairs, 'informed me of a particularly succulent "fruit of the waves", that is all. We sally forth to pluck and devour it. What could be more natural?'

Bosun made his protest with a discreet lowering of voice. 'But a Caliph's ship! That's not been our way. We're just a *galiot* and she'll be *laterna* size – we'll never hack it. They'll be all over us!'

'That prospect might be more attractive than you think,'

53

answered Slovo. 'A Princess's ship will carry a hefty contingent of maidens and eunuchs-in-waiting, in lieu of fighting men. The odds will be more even than you suppose. Besides, I am assured that we will be assisted by an agent aboard.'

In between his reflex ten-second checks on the crew's devotion to duty, Bosun found time to construct the message 'unconvinced' on his features. 'You've got a lot of faith in this *source*,' he said cautiously. 'That's not like you.'

Nor indeed was it but, in the face of the arguments arrayed in battle order by the Shaduf, Slovo had seen little option but the leap of faith. If the Principal of the world's oldest university said that a dowry-laden daughter of the Egyptian Sultan was en route to matrimony with a Turkish rival, Slovo found himself with no alternative but action. The additional consideration, that Slovo was soon to be declared an 'Enemy of God' throughout the Islamic world, made imminent departure very attractive. Bit by bit, the Vehmic conspiracy had narrowed and straightened the path before him, and then firmly pushed him on his way.

'What more can I say?' asked the Captain of his Bosun, preparing to deploy his 'doomsday instruction'. 'Trust me.'

There was no safe answer to that and Bosun swung away, launching into compensatory abuse of the crew. Those seamen not wedded to the oars teemed about like ants trying to appease him.

The galley fairly ripped through the water as the rowers settled easily into the mindless rhythm of the strokemaster's ancient song. Bosun had been permitted to tantalize them with hints of a bounteous prize ahead and they pulled away with a will. Only Bosun himself remained discontent, pacing the rowing deck and scanning the sea ahead, but there was nothing so unusual about that.

Slovo, by contrast, was looking forward to what was to come. For once in his life he did not need to worry about preparing for every eventuality. The Shaduf – and through him, the Vehme – had instructed him down to the last detail. Such tender care recalled dim memories of family, and might have cheered the Captain but for what the Venetian and Stoicism had jointly worked on him.

While the Shaduf had said next to nothing about the apparently all-embracing Vehme, he had been generous to a fault with other thought-provoking 'facts'. The Deity, however one conceived him or it, he had said, was possessed of seventy-three proper names and those infinite few who knew any of them were termed the *Baal Shem*.

Slovo had confessed himself intrigued by such theological information, but he was a working pirate with a living to steal. Exactly how did such revelations assist him?

The Shaduf's patient explanation that the hearing of such names was destruction to an unprepared mortal and that the Vehme would secrete one of their own Baal Shem aboard the Sultan's ship, went a long way to convince Slovo. Now he understood why the Vehme would pit a mere hundred fighting men against the floating fortress he knew they would meet. A deep and secret leviathan was being awakened on his behalf and the opposition would be vouchsafed a glimpse of God – at the price of their lives.

There were inconsistencies and unanswered questions Slovo would have liked to pursue but he'd felt it indelicate to do so. He had purchased waxen earblocks for all the crew and put his trust in his new employers. It was this unprecedented sentiment that had so alarmed Bosun. Slovo couldn't find it in his heart to blame him.

Then, just as he was pondering the degree to which the Islamic fatalism of Tripoli was influencing his present decisions, the look-out bellowed, 'Ship-ahoy!'

*

Even the Captain had second thoughts when they drew close to the monster containing the Sultan's daughter. The great galleon sat heavy in the sea, indicating the manpower packed within, although she moved along nippily enough when heaved by myriad banks of oars. The ominously huge bow and stern cannons discouraged proximity and the side facing Slovo was packed with a crowd of armoured welcomers.

It was to Bosun's credit that he moved swiftly to silence the murmurs of dismay. To encourage the others he split the head of one too plainly frightened sailor. Thus exhorted, the crew embraced the wisdom of their Captain's wishes and closed for battle, urged on by the strokemaster's *allegro* song – and an impulse to get the thing over and done with, one way or the other. Slovo noted the skilful positioning of the Egyptian ship to permit her stern gun to fire, but allowed Bosun to judge when to make the vital 'flick' to port or starboard that would avoid the crushing ball. True, the ship was bigger than any they had faced before but the basic play had been run through a hundred times. And, supposedly they had a friend aboard.

When the Bosun had done his job and they were all soaked by the vast impact in the sea a score of paces to port, Slovo wound his ship up to attack speed. Then, reverentially on one knee (but weapons to hand), Slovo commended himself to Mary and her Son, not forgetting a word of praise to Jehovah (since Judaism seemed occasionally persuasive).

The galley *Slovo* was liberally hosed down with Egyptian bow and shot and men started to slump at the oars. The crew would normally have returned suppressing fire and plainly wished with all their hearts to do so. However, above the noise of the dying, Captain Slovo forbade it. At the same time he ordered his men to insert their earplugs.

Obeying the stupid Barbary pirate custom of the ship's Captain standing fearless and prominent to face the worst the enemy could throw, Slovo at last had the opportunity to study his target at leisure – even whilst it tried to end his observations for ever.

It *was* a behemoth! A forest's worth afloat, made to look even more unnatural atop the waves by the rich, primary-colour decorations the Mohammedan Royals seemed to like so much. After painful translation and with mounting amusement, Slovo noted that the mighty white sail was emblazoned with a profession of faith: *There is no God but God and Mohammed is His prophet.* He smiled even as a whistling arrow's passage disturbed the fall of his hair. One God there might well be, he mused, but there was the hope that they might soon learn that He went under a number of names.

Abandoning attempts to escape by slave or sail from their more nimble pursuer, the lumbering Egyptian craft shipped oars and more or less awaited what might be. Happy to show them, a mere two lengths off and still weathering a storm of missiles, the galley *Slovo* banked for the cannon-free side and the final approach. The iron grapples and boarding platform were made ready and, since no ram was intended, the oarsmen were ordered to abandon their charges and tool up, allowing momentum to finish the job.

Slovo traversed his ship to join the elite group of particularly bestial sailors who always led the first charge. In lieu of commands they could no longer hear, he smiled encouragement.

The Royal Egyptian ship was high-sided but, burdened by her load, she sat low and permitted a clear view of her deck from the galley *Slovo*. Ordinarily, at this point it would have been time to hurl the fiery naphtha-pots and baskets of vipers to shed confusion and worse amidst the massed enemy, but Slovo ignored the pleading looks of the toughs around him.

This time, just this once, he would have faith right up to the last possible moment.

The Baal Shem very nearly did leave it too late and exhaust Slovo's feeble trust. The grapples had dropped, the platform had crashed down, its spikes biting into the Egyptian deck, before he showed his hand. The front ranks of pirates and marines were already in intimate and deadly embrace before his voice was heard. It was as well he acted, for they were hopelessly outnumbered.

Standing beside the gorgeous divan within the Royal pavilion, was a negro among a frightened huddle of courtiers. Unhurriedly laying down his ostrich feather fan, he stepped forward and began to speak.

What he had to say carried above the clamour and what he said caused all clamour to cease.

One by one the Egyptians stopped what they were doing, their attention now clearly held by something far more important than a mere life-and-death struggle. Some of the pirates unchivalrously took the opportunity to dispatch their distracted opponents. And now that the identity of their helper was known, Slovo seized his own chance and took out the ship's Captain with a crossbow-bolt to the throat.

In the event, he need not have bothered. At the call of the Baal Shem all those who could hear began to cry – with joy or horror Slovo could not discern – and then they started to die. A few pirates who had seen fit to discard the earplugs rapidly joined them.

Soon the Egyptian deck was choked with dead and dying, either neatly in rows as with the captured Christian oarsmen, or in twitching heaps of armoured marines and silk-garbed courtiers. Slovo had hoped to be able to watch and read the Baal Shem's lips but it had all happened too fast, and perhaps that was just as well.

The surviving pirates howled with pleasure at such wild

success and, casting their earplugs aside, poured on to the Egyptian prize. Their Captain followed suit. Then the coal-black Baal Shem stepped forward to meet them and thereby reversed the tide, leaving Slovo irritably wondering why he was being buffeted by routing men just as the battle was apparently won. But the crush before him cleared and all his doubts were resolved. As the Baal Shem casually advanced upon him, Captain Slovo found it supremely easy to forget courage and purpose and dignity. He discovered himself strangely willing to leap athletically back to his own ship and trample anyone between him and its familiar deck.

Fortunately it was all just by way of an effect, and the Baal Shem turned off his aura of approaching death-plus-something-worse as abruptly as he'd inflicted it. He leaned on the grappled rail of his galley-hecatomb and studied the shivering pirates with a neutral expression. 'How much do they know?' he asked in a touching falsetto, speaking directly to Slovo, and gesturing towards the crew.

'Just enough,' Slovo said, his speech emerging as a croak, 'and no more.'

'Then let them come and play,' replied the Baal Shem, 'while we talk.'

He stood aside and bowed everyone back aboard, the action as smooth and practised as that of any Sultan's flunkey. The prospect of good plunder overcame the pirates' fear and, like mice bypassing a watchful cat, they cautiously edged on to the ship of the dead, where they regained their normal instincts and fell whooping upon the fallen.

The Baal Shem in turn clambered stiffly on to the galley *Slovo*, making heavier weather of it than was customarily seen in pirate circles. He was obviously older than appearances suggested.

'There are survivors in the pavilion,' the Baal Shem said, almost as an aside, 'together with an object which will be of inestimable use to you. Instruct your creatures to respect its boundaries. All else they may have – even my trusty old ostrich fan.'

Captain Slovo so instructed Bosun and he so implemented. Even in the present madness, their management-record was such that they were confident of being obeyed.

The Baal Shem allowed himself to be directed to the Captain's deck at the stern and was settled upon a canvas stool. Slovo procured a goblet of wine each, the Baal Shem partook and then smacked his lips.

'Delectable!' he said with open pleasure. 'This is the first fruit of the vine I've imbibed since my Islamic servitude began. Thank you, Captain!'

'Every man needs access to intoxication,' said Slovo, 'in order that he may escape being himself.'

The Baal Shem nodded wholeheartedly. 'I agree, Captain. However, to business straightaway: how and why, I suppose?'

'If you don't mind,' replied Slovo, eyeing him cautiously whilst trying to conceal the impoliteness of doing so. 'What was that magic word you cried? It won us the game, sure enough.'

Wiping his lips with a broad hand, the Baal Shem explained, 'One of the names of the infinite, whereupon any mortal within earshot withers and dies. It is as simple as that.'

Slovo frowned slightly. 'But you mentioned survivors?'

'Ah, yes.' The Baal Shem looked meaningfully at the dead wine flagon but Slovo didn't take the heavy hint. 'It was always intended there should be one – aside from myself, of course – you'll need the Princess where you're going. It did come as a surprise though there being two who lived. Have you the time for me to explain?'

Slovo looked over his deserted ship to the wild scenes

unfolding across the way. 'They will be like badly brought-up children if they do not have their full measure of fun and profit,' he answered.

'Well, it will be enough for you to know that my life's vocation – up to mere moments ago – was to fan the brow, and other parts, of the Princess Khadine. Now, it so happens that she is famous in the Islamic world for the divine beauty and perfection of her curvaceous behind . . .'

'Oh yes, I have heard of her,' said Slovo helpfully. 'I once saw an indecent woodcut highlighting her attributes.'

'I'm not surprised,' said the Baal Shem. 'Our "lustrous jewel of the Delta" is quite a celebrity. Anyway, coincidentally, it also happens that the Caliph-Sultan Bayezid of Istanbul is famous for his interest in such matters. Accordingly, in order to avert the scandal of a war between Moslems and the deaths of untold thousands, the girl's backside is to be pressed into service and she is being rushed into matrimony with him. I am called upon to keep her cool while she is ferried thither, post-haste.'

'I still don't understand why she is alive,' Slovo said. 'Surely a body-slave such as yourself must have ample grievances you wish to repay in full? There is also the question of how you ensured her immunity.'

'She survives,' answered the Baal Shem, now casting reticence aside and rattling the empty flagon in Slovo's direction, 'because you need her – in the most honourable sense. She, and her ransom, will be your guarantee of welcome at your destination – not to mention the riches aboard her ship and the mighty craft itself: a welcome addition to any navy. There is also, as part of her intended dowry, a relic prised from the bony hands of Coptic monks: part of the pelvis of St Peter or some such: long revered and smothered in gold and baubles. Your next employer will love you dearly for the handing over of that.'

Slovo declined to rise to the dangled bait about his future and held to the question in hand. 'You neglected to touch upon the subject of *how*,' he said politely.

'Ah yes,' said the Baal Shem, clearly impressed by the Captain's restraint. 'Well, it is possible with some effort, and some magic, for me to circumscribe the name of God so that it fails to harm certain categories of person. It appealed to my sense of humour to exclude those possessed of a beautiful bottom . . .'

'Oh, I *see*!' said Slovo.

'Although that fails to account for why an accompanying Rabbi of the Hebrew faith should hear the blessed name and live.'

Surely he doesn't . . .?' asked the Captain.

'Goodness no!' replied the Baal Shem. 'He is exceedingly plain, prematurely middle-aged and dumpy – a shape gained through excessive study and prayer. No, it transpires that he already knew the name – presumably by dint of those last two activities – and so did not share the general fate.'

'I should like to meet this man,' said Slovo, as though asking a favour.

'And so you shall, Captain. His fortunes are entirely in your hands. You may allow him to proceed on his embassy from the Cairene Hebrews to their Ottoman fellows, you can converse with him or simply ditch him in the sea. It is up to you.'

Slovo at long last had mercy on the Baal Shem and fetched another flask of wine from his personal store. 'I should have thought,' he said, averting his eyes from the ensuing noisy imbibing, 'that with such a man anything but the sweetest good treatment would be most unwise.'

'Ah . . .' answered the Baal Shem, reluctantly disengaging his lips from the purple flow, 'that is the difference between he and I, between his . . . philosophy and that of the Vehme.

He might *know* an ineffable name, but he would never use it!'

Just then a peculiar cry went up from the captured Egyptian ship, different from the sounds of insensate joy that Slovo and the Baal Shem had got used to. They looked round to see two pirates hoisting a golden-skinned youth on to the ship's rail for all to see.

'We've found a live-un,' explained Bosun to the Captain. 'He was hiding under a pile of deaders.'

'Well, gracious me!' exclaimed the Baal Shem. 'This *is* a day of wonders!'

Slovo said nothing but for once allowed a butterfly feeling of pleasure in his stomach to live out its brief, fluttering life. Assuming this adolescent wasn't a precocious theologian, the current voyage might be even more interesting than anticipated.

Once they'd all made themselves at home in the Egyptian behemoth and sunk the galley *Slovo*, the Baal Shem announced that he wanted to be taken to Sicily. All things considered it was generally felt best to humour him in every respect and Slovo set the course.

The Captain was mildly sorry to lose his maritime home, his means of livelihood for the last few years, but there were simply not the numbers to move the Egyptian prize even under full sail, *and* tow the *Slovo*. For old times' sake, they waited long enough to see the forsaken galley point its stern skywards and then rapidly make its way, arrow-like, beneath the waves. Slovo even sought inspiration for a poem in the poignant sight but nothing suitable occurred to him.

Thereafter, the Baal Shem would not speak but retired to the Royal pavilion to think private thoughts that no one dared to interrupt. Captain Slovo thereby met the evicted

Princess Khadine and the fortunate-in-his-studies Rabbi of Cairo.

The Princess was disappointingly clad in voluminous black and in a state of permanent rage. After a full day of having his ears incomprehensibly assaulted, Slovo toyed with the idea of handing her over to the crew so that, just for once in their stunted lives, they might get to see how the other 0.0000001 per cent lived. Common sense prevailed, however, and peace was finally restored by the completion of her chadoor-clad modesty with an equally thick, black sack to muffle her head. Whatever future complaints the Sultan of Egypt might levy against the Captain, lack of concern for Islamic dress restrictions would not be among them.

The Rabbi was called Megillah and Slovo's first thoughts were to put him to much-needed work on the oars. It was unlikely his soft frame would last the trip, but he would at least perish in the good cause of putting distance between Slovo and the revenge of Islam in general, and Egypt in particular.

As it turned out, Rabbi Megillah saved himself (all unknowingly) with a masterful exposition over dinner that first evening of the five Noachian Commandments. Since Slovo continuously sought to balance his activities between the flesh and the spirit, he decided to retain the company of both the golden youth *and* the Rabbi – which Megillah mistook for an act of kindness. Between the two of them the journey became quite a pleasure cruise, and to compensate, Slovo experimented with praying before the pelvic bone of St Peter.

However, all good things must come to an end. The coast of Sicily was sighted, one dull and rainy dusk. Without being told, the Baal Shem awoke from his trance, and with the crew shrinking from him like puppies from a bath, he made his way to the ship's rail and beckoned Slovo to join him.

'I'm off now,' he said as pleasantly as his tin-whistle voice could allow.

Slovo looked uneasily at the dark and choppy sea. 'Right now?' he queried. 'Can't I get you nearer?'

The Baal Shem shook his head. 'No, that's kind, but not necessary, thank you. I'll walk from here.'

'I see . . .' answered Slovo, not going so far as actually to doubt him, 'but . . .'

'Another of my little skills,' explained the Baal Shem. 'It comes with knowing what I do.'

'Which is?' said Slovo swiftly. There seemed no harm in asking.

The Baal Shem merely smiled, proof against temptations. 'Which is that you must now go to Rome,' he said.

'Rome?'

The Baal Shem was looking longingly to shore, eager to be away. 'Yes, that is where your real life is to begin, the life you're going to share with us. You should be pleased, you know, we have great plans for you!'

Slovo found it easy to take the news equably. 'Are you prepared to tell me what they are?'

'Not yet, Captain. Besides, they're still somewhat fluid. Don't worry, all you have to do is be yourself.'

'That should be easy,' observed Slovo dryly.

The Baal Shem turned back, suddenly troubled. 'No,' he said, his voice as grave as high C would allow. 'I can reveal this much – it won't ever be easy.' So saying, he clambered laboriously over the rail and jumped. The sigh of relief from the superstitious (and highly racist) crew was almost audible.

Slovo looked over the side and found himself still almost eyeball to eyeball with the negro who was standing on the water as if it were an undulating platform.

'You'll be met at Rome,' he was told. 'Pay off your crew;

give the Princess, the ship and the relic to the Pope. Do not hold anything back – we are trusting you.'

'Don't do that!' advised Slovo.

'Make a clean break with your past life. I wish you well. As does the Venetian.'

'*Who?*' said the Captain.

'The Venetian,' replied the Baal Shem, indicating a patch of sea beside his feet. 'He tells me to wish you well with the job – despite everything. Oh, didn't you know? He's accompanied all of your voyages – particularly since he learnt you're one of ours. Here, look!'

Slovo did as he was asked and, even in the gloom, now saw that a man-sized area of sea was coated in a film of green-blue slime and grease. It suddenly began to bubble and boil and Slovo hurriedly recoiled. 'Is he still human?' he asked, looking more closely. The slime blistered again.

'Nominally so,' explained the Baal Shem. 'Higher minds can still communicate with him, although he says long association has brought increasing empathy with marine-life. It's just as well because he'll be joining them fully before too long, as the process of dissolution continues.' The Baal Shem looked at the darkening horizon and saw that day was almost over. 'Anyway,' he said, 'I can't stay here chatting; I've got a dynasty to destabilize.'

And with those words, he walked off over the sea and into the fast falling gloom.

Whilst very careful not to look properly, Slovo waved cheerfully at a certain bit of sea below him and gave the order to row.

The great Egyptian ship slowly began to move and, shining brightly in the light of the moon, a patch of oily water – and something extra – dutifully followed.

*

'Here's to the Captain! May his stiletto never rust!'

The pirates cheered Bosun's drunken toast and recommenced drinking themselves insensible and to an early grave.

Captain Slovo smiled thinly and soberly raised his modest mug of wine in response. He would be glad when this meaningless charade was over. The chilliest portion of his mind had suggested turning the crew in as 'apostates' and 'barbaries' to be hung at the nearest beach-strand at low tide. That would have made the very cleanest of cuts with his former life style. Certainly, the obliging potentate of the Roman Colonna clan (and Vehmist) who had greeted their arrival at Ostia Port would happily have arranged it.

In the end though, it just seemed simpler to pay them off with profligate lavishness, and a warning that they should now forget all. Asia, Africa, even Scandinavia, were all calling out for men of their calibre, he'd said – everywhere except Italy. The Italian climate would be bad for their health. Knowing the Captain as they did, they got the message and, as newly rich men, they could afford to be reasonable and oblige him.

After an initial frosty moment, caused by the appearance of their Islamic warship hoving into port, they had received a warm welcome at Ostia. The reception turned positively ecstatic when the full extent of their haul became apparent. The Colonna-Vehmist handled everything beautifully and the very next day a Cardinal, no less, with all the trimmings in terms of personnel, arrived to escort St Peter's pelvis to a place of respect and reverence. Commanders of the Papal naval forces descended to drool over the captured Egyptian galley and a flurry of nuns took the cursing Princess Khadine out of Slovo's life and to goodness knows what fate.

Rabbi Megillah blessed the Captain's head and went off to contact the Roman Jews and seek solace – perhaps even a permanent home – in their midst. It seemed wise, he said, to quit the Moslem world for a while and, anyway, he'd tired of his barren Cairene wife. He was still blissfully unaware of just how narrow his escape had been.

So everyone was happy from the Pope downwards, and Captain Slovo decided to take his crew out for a final (with the emphasis on *final*) drink. The Colonna baron, wisely espying what sort of an evening it was going to be, graciously declined to join them. The Captain's new position in the Vatican apparatus was all arranged, he'd said. Any . . . unfortunate aspects of his personal history had been expunged from the relevant records. Slovo should report for duty tomorrow and never look back – or contact the Baron again.

After three of four hours' bulk consumption of alcohol, proceedings reached what Slovo always called 'the knife-edge' – that moment when the collective mood pivots wildly from jollity to jumpiness, and a pirate's thoughts lightly turn to the blade at his side. Confined on board ship, such a moment can be relatively harmless, a stab, a scar or two, one killing at the most. Onshore, and in a big city however, Slovo was less sanguine. He did not wish to be held responsible for whatever might transpire – it was time for him to leave.

With a farewell wave that few noticed, he rose to go – and directly bumped into a body. The reaction to arm and strike was overridden, just in time, by the recognition that it was merely a little old woman, one of many working the taverns.

'Read your palm, my love, my sweet?' she said, not appreciating the greatness of her own recent good fortune.

The delay allowed the pirates to notice their Captain's act of departure and the message passed down the line of tables. 'Go on!' they shouted, sentimental all of a sudden and anxious to forestall their beloved leader's exit. 'Go on – give the old cow some money. See what's in store for you!'

Christian orthodoxy frowned on such practices and ordinarily Slovo would not have indulged. However, on this occasion he saw no way out that would not be a noisy and embarrassing anticlimax. Besides, he was embarking on a new life, why not bless it with a kindness? He gave the old girl a whole ducat and, smiling, held out his hand.

Also smiling, she took both and studied the upturned palm. She studied it – and studied it – and gradually the pirates became silent.

Then she dropped Slovo's hand as if it were hot and gave him back his money. Never taking her eyes off him, she retreated stiff-legged backwards to the door.

❧

'We were astounded,' said the Welsh Vehmist back at the other end of Admiral Slovo's existence, where the fever of life and activity now seemed very remote. 'Such a change in life and yet you took to it like the proverbial duck to water.'

'A poor metaphor, I think,' said Slovo. 'It was the chaos of Neptune's realm that you had me leave.'

'Good point,' nodded the Vehmist. 'Yes, we required your career to take on the soundness and stability of land. However, we were fully expecting a transitional period, a space where we would need to apologize for you and nudge you along the path of propriety.'

'For me,' Slovo mused, 'it was a novelty to behave like a normal man. Obedience and work, advancement and sub-mission, they were a heady brew – for a while.'

'But how you supped at it,' smiled the Vehmist. 'Dutiful hours in the Vatican, a home, making love to women, a Christian wife even! We didn't know what to expect next!'

The Admiral turned to look at his guest, an ill-natured light in his eyes. 'That's the very point,' he said. 'You knew all too well . . .'

*

It was around the time that Mikhail Gorbachev died.

The Archaeologist allowed his Italian assistant to sound the call for 'major find' – 'Aaaaaaa! Hereeeeeee!' she sang sweetly.

That meant the rank-and-file diggers could 'take five' and quit their trenches to see what was turning up. The Archaeologist thought such concessions good for site morale.

As the sun-browned mob arrived, the Archaeologist scraped away with mounting enthusiasm. He didn't even notice that some personnel had lit up strictly forbidden on-site cigarettes. 'This is going to be good,' he announced to all. 'It's a grave slab – not classical, late medieval, I should think. Joy, pass us the brush, will you?'

A finely constructed, sloe-eyed English girl handed down the required tool. The Archaeologist used it, with the ease born of practice, to flick away the remaining soil.

'Oh bugger! It's broken. Wayne, have your crew been using pickaxes down here?'

'No way,' answered a tall Anglo-Saxon in John Lennon glasses. 'I watched 'em – trowels only.'

'Well someone's given it a crack. There's a central strike with radial fault lines.'

'Looks ancient to me,' said Wayne authoritatively, leaning forward and peering into the trench.

The Archaeologist stood up. 'You're probably right,' he muttered. 'What a shame. Well, folks, I didn't expect to find anything like this. As far as we know there was never a church here, so either this slab is displaced from somewhere else – and has deliberately been broken – or else whoever's it is, is still underneath, buried outside consecrated ground. All in all, a nice little bonus before we hit classical levels.'

'Can you read any of the markings?' asked Joy.

The Archaeologist leaned closer and worried at the stone with his brush. 'There's a lot of stuff but in very bad condition, and the fault lines go straight through it. Latin, I think. Also there's some larger script up one end. Let's see, SL–O–V–O: Slovo. Well, well, well!'

'There was a villa here called that,' explained Wayne for the benefit of the native Caprisi diggers. 'Fifteenth to sixteenth century – where the Villa Fersen subsequently was. We've already uncovered some other stuff from it, fragments of statuary, that nice ornate key we showed you yesterday: bits and bobs, that sort of thing.'

'Maybe this was the guy himself,' mused the Archaeologist, smiling. 'How neat! Right, no more work just here for a space. We'll make arrangements to lift this beast and conserve it.'

'One thing,' said Joy hesitantly. 'I mean, maybe it's my eyes playing up or just the grain of the stone but ... well, look – I don't think that's a natural break.'

She stepped lithely into the trench and knelt beside the slab. The consequent coffee-and-cream cleavage display awoke slumbering engines in the Archaeologist's mind and he failed to hear her next remark.

'Pardon?'

'I said it's a V,' she repeated, stretching forward to trace the relevant line, thereby worsening the Archaeologist's concentration problems. 'A great big V!'

When the 'break' did indeed prove to have intricate radial ends and exquisite lightning bolts carved about the lower portion, the Archaeologist felt impelled to do some research in his free time.

A raid on the Anglo-Italian Institute's library in Capri Town produced Dr Grimes's famous *Dictionary of Sign & Symbol*, a comparable V and the entry: 'Vehme (supposed)' beside it. This in turn led him to the two-volume *Oxford English Dictionary* and greater enlightenment in the form of: 'Vehme-Vehmgericht: a form of secret tribunal which exercised great influence in Westphalia and elsewhere from the 12th to 16th centuries.'

Intrigued by now, the Archaeologist continued his pursuit of the silent dead. A week or so later he struck oil when the post delivered *Secret Societies* by Professor Royston Lyness Ph.D. (Oxon) (OUP 1990). Sitting in his tent, reading by the inadequate light of a camping solar lamp, he discovered the following – and as he read he became more and more oblivious of the mosquitoes' loving attentions.

The Vehme, in legend at least, combined the function of a secret police, an alternative judiciary and a subversive enforcer of justice against prevailing powers. In these and other respects, they seemed akin to the earliest manifestations of the MAFIA/COSA NOSTRA (q.v.), although they allegedly predate their Sicilian counterparts and seem to have greater, albeit dimly glimpsed, ambitions.

In the contemporary popular imagination they appear as avenging angels, in the guise of masked men from nowhere or black-clad knights, the equal in arms of anything Church or State could set against them. Much is made in surviving stories of the mystery of their origin, the grimness of their judgements and the implacable inevitability of execution. A typical tale would involve a summons nailed to a castle or palace door and the named person, terrified and alone, presenting him or herself at an appointed wilderness or crossroads, there to be led blindfolded by a black-gowned usher to the Tribunal of the Vehme.

This invariably took place in some vast underground cavern or vault, often a great distance from the victim's home. After the questioning, sentence would be pronounced, always at midnight. Then the blindfold would

72

be removed and the justified or condemned man would see his first and last sight of the 'Masked Free Judges in Black' – for a second summons could only bring death, as did non-appearance. Numerous stories recount the fate of the recidivist or coward, found slain under the very noses of their guards, with the Vehme's terrible cruciform dagger buried in their chest and the proclamation of sentence attached. It is also said that they relentlessly pursued a faithless or refractory member, even to the throne of King or Bishop, with steel and cord.

The actuality of the Vehme is attested to by the 'Code of the Vehmic Court', found in the archives of the Westphalian Kings and published in the *Reichstheater* of Müller, under the grandiose and fulsome title of *Codes and Statutes of the Holy and Secret Tribunal of Free Court and Free Judges of Westphalia, established in the year 772 by the Emperor Charlemagne and revived in 1404 by King Robert who made these alterations and additions requisite for the administration of justice in the Tribunals of the Illuminated, after investing them with his authority.*

Quite what is to be made of this is by no means clear. Whilst it is the one single mention of the Emperor Charlemagne in connection with Vehmic origins, other, equally compelling – or dubious – authorities attribute their founding to the Roman Emperors Hadrian or Julian the Apostate. What is significant about the Müller codex is the reference to the 'illuminated' who alone, it was explicitly stated, could look upon the writings or face of the Vehme. Quite what 'illumination' was shed, on what subjects, and for whom, is nowhere elucidated and looks likely now to remain forever unknown.

The post-war Nazi 'Werewolf' organization claimed to carry on the Vehmic tradition but in reality it seems likely that the group, conspiracy, belief or whatever it was, did not survive the social tornado of the Reformation and Thirty-Years War.

The Archaeologist looked ecstatically into the middle distance (circa twelve inches away in the context of his tent). *So*, maybe the dry old bones they'd uncovered under the slab today and neatly bagged in plastic, had once been clothed in 'illuminated' flesh. Or perhaps they belonged to a Vehme victim and so were unworthy of the Archaeologist's doggedly Marxist-leaning sympathies. Either way, for good or bad, the Vehme, whoever they were, seemed to have chosen to mark the old boy's grave with their sign. What a brilliant footnote to his report it would make!

Turning off the bug-encrusted solar lamp, he laid his bearded head to rest, well pleased.

The report was never written. Slovo's grave remained obscure, though his bones got to fly to London, for cursory study – and then covert disposal in a Holborn dustbin. Some of the nicer finds were gifted to London museums that were prepared to take them.

Meanwhile, the Archaeologist, still troubled by the howl of the libido and the unavailability of Joy, slowly succumbed to the siren call of Capri. A mere week into his ensuing pleasures with the island's abundantly available wallet-related love, the poor man contracted the HIV virus that would more than fully occupy the remainder of his short life.

✣ The Year 1492

'INSTALMENTS: In which I become impatient and incite some nostalgics to ambitions of destroying the human race. Little by little, I learn something.'

'Almighty Lord, on the reasonable assumption that you exist and that your wishes for Mankind are actually as related by the various revelations honoured by my time and culture, please forgive me for the things I have done, do, and will do. Generally speaking I mean well – except when I mean ill; which is probably too often (although my employers are usually responsible for that). Please keep my melancholia within acceptable bounds. Overlook my ambivalent attitude to Judaism: conversion is not, you'll surely agree, a practical course of action at present. Look kindly on my adherence to Pagan Stoicism: I mean no disrespect. Bless my wife, I suppose, wherever she is. I'm mostly sorry about the people I've killed this year . . .'

A confident tap on his shoulder interrupted Admiral Slovo's prayers. He turned swiftly, his thumb poised over the spring release on his blade-loaded opal signet ring, to see that a long-haired young man was standing behind him.

'No thank you,' whispered the Admiral, remaining on his knees.

'To what?' replied the elegant youth, puzzled.

'To whatever you are selling: yourself (currently fashionable in Rome so I'm told), your sister, choice sweetmeats or indulgences. Whatsoever it may be, I'm not interested.'

'You are being offensive,' said the youth; more hazarding a guess than making an accusation.

'And you are interrupting my prayers,' said Slovo. 'I will have to go back to the beginning now.'

'So?' the young man replied. 'Each moment spent in proximity to a Christian place of worship costs me dear. Even this brief conversation will have shortened my lifespan by perhaps one hundred of your years. Another five minutes so close to consecrated ground and I will die.'

'And?' asked Slovo, unconcerned.

'My message will require more than that time to relate. I am not asking for sentiment, Admiral, it is merely a matter of practicalities.'

'I am a reasonable man,' said Admiral Slovo, slowly rising to his feet. 'We will adjourn elsewhere.' Speaking to God he said, 'Please overlook the interrupted prayers, but this Elf wants to talk business.'

The young man did not actually mean to swagger, but his natural grace, compared to the other citizens of Rome, made it appear so. Once out of the Church of *San Tommaso degli Inglesi*, he replaced his broad-brimmed hat, arranged his red locks upon his shoulders and then set off briskly down the Via di Monserrato. Admiral Slovo kept pace, well aware that despite his childhood deportment training he appeared like a shambling ape beside his companion.

It was early evening, the between-time before commerce ceased and revelry began. The crowds were thin and incurious, the humanity-generated humidity bearable.

'Issues have developed,' said the youth, not deigning to turn his head. 'Elements mature beyond expectation. Your commission is accelerated by one of your months; extra funding will be provided. At your lodgings,' he continued, maintaining the same seamless conversation, 'you will find delivered an oaken cask. Within is a jewelled tiara, formerly the possession of Queen Zenobia of Palmyra; together with a solid gold sword used by the Roman Emperor Caligula for purposes that you would doubtless consider disgraceful. We are not expert at determining human pecuniary values but it is judged that these items, once realized into currency, will be more than adequate for your purposes.'

Admiral Slovo could hardly contradict that assertion but remained less than content. 'Always these curios,' he said. 'Solomon's breastplate, Attila's gold spittoon, Cleopatra's intimate utensils: do you realize how famous I am becoming for selling such things? Questions are being asked by anti-quarian professionals. And my wife, who is Genoese and highly acquisitive, shrieks to retain such valuables. Why can't you fund me with gems? Those I could hide from her.'

'They have no value to us, Admiral,' said the youth in all innocence. 'We give them to our offspring to play with, if we pick them up at all. Be satisfied with what you have – oh, I beg your pardon, that is another thing that humans are unable to do, is it not?'

'Most of us,' Slovo politely agreed. 'If you don't mind me saying so, you seem a trifle inadequately briefed.'

The youth nodded casually. 'Possibly so. The tuition I received was sufficient but my attention to it less so. By and large, we find discussion of your kind rather disgusting.'

'I see,' said the Admiral.

'For instance, I think I must now turn the conversation to your personal reward for these endeavours; failing which you will become disaffected.'

'Yes; what's in it for me?' said Slovo, going along with the racial stereotyping for weariness's sake.

The beautiful youth appeared pleased to find his prejudices

confirmed. 'The King sent you this,' he said, drawing from his purse a tiny cylinder of green-discoloured bronze. 'One month advanced, remember. Do not fail us or there will be no more.' So saying, he handed the cylinder to Slovo and was off.

He need not have hurried for the Admiral's mind was now elsewhere. Most rare of events, Slovo was obliged to struggle to control his actions. With nigh-on trembling fingers and an expression threatening to break on his face, he unscrewed the cylinder into its component parts. He didn't pay attention to the masterly craftsmanship or the intricate scenes carved on its side. All of the Admiral's thoughts were concentrated on the scrap of vellum within. It was the merest corner of a most ancient page, roughly torn across.

Admiral Slovo stood oblivious in the middle of the street and studied the Classical-Latin text: ... *like the castle of a Parthian ... do not accumulate distress but instead, contemplate the meaning of man's existence which is that* ...

Slovo fought and won a titanic inner battle and, in victory, was accordingly proud of his adherence to Stoic principles. 'How frustrating,' he said calmly.

'One month from now,' said Admiral Slovo.

'*Difficult*, perhaps ...'

'Quite recently,' said Slovo matter of factly, 'I had the good fortune to find the Emperor Caligula's golden sword, and sold same to Cardinal Grimani for an indecent sum. Accordingly, I have here a bearer-payable draft of deposit upon the Megillah Goldsmith's house in Rome which should put any such *difficulties* in proper perspective.'

After the armourer had fetched his wife to read the bond, he wholeheartedly agreed that all difficulties had evaporated like Florentine Citizen militia before Swiss pikemen.

'I will employ every skilled worker in Capri,' he said with a proud flourish. 'If need be, I will subcontract across to Naples. Your arquebuses will be ready in time, honoured Admiral: trust me.' With this, the armourer, doubtless envisaging villas, farms and a secure old age, grew expansive; almost familiar. 'Capri has never known an order like it,' he rejoiced, breaking out a wickered jug of (it transpired) quite impermissible wine. 'So many hundreds of guns! Before this, I made one or two a year but now, with your patronage, with the apprentices I've indentured, the blue sky itself cannot contain me or my good fortune!'

Oh, yes it will, thought Slovo, frowning at his wine, *and, sadly, sooner than you think*. He looked at the happy armourer and if he had not trained himself otherwise he would have been filled with compassion. Naturally, the fellow could not survive the contract's completion: that was yet another thing that would have to be arranged. He could not, alas, offer any reprieve or sympathy, so instead he praised the wine.

'We grow or diminish,' said the King, 'in direct proportion to our power – in the tales of humankind, that is. Once we were giants and titans, now we are merely tall. I do not doubt that before long people will disbelieve in us altogether. Your literature will have us as mere pixy figures suitable for the ends of your gardens.'

Admiral Slovo smiled pleasantly and thought to himself that the King was considerably behind the times. As the serried ranks of Elf soldiery in the valley below fired off another practice volley, it occurred to him that a lot of people were in for a shock.

'And that's another thing,' continued the King angrily, 'this garden business! Everywhere your species goes: gardens.

Why must you try and improve on what Nature has provided?'

Nature made it our nature, thought Slovo but said: 'It is not my place or inclination to defend mankind, Your Majesty. I am merely your gun-runner.'

The King turned to look at him, his yellow cat-eyes burning out from within his bronze helm. 'And quite a good one – for a renegade; I think we might run to a full page for you this time.'

Admiral Slovo controlled his excitement and looked impassively around the training site. From their high vantage point he could see the tops of the forest trees running on to what seemed like infinity. Rome was a long way away. Slovo had never been so far from sympathetic civilization before. He was therefore comforted to find he did not particularly mind the lack.

Down in the clearing, the Elf warriors fired again, tearing into the facing fringe of trees. Slovo had seen better displays of marksmanship, but recognized that it was early days yet. Noting the clumsiness as they proceeded to reload, he hastened to forestall the King's next demand.

'The iron content is at absolute minimum,' he said. 'A greater proportion of bronze would have caused performance problems too tedious to elaborate. Your people's aversion to iron is known to me but in this respect, if no other, you must defer. It was for my weaponry skills that I was hired.'

'That and your humanity,' agreed the King. 'Man's knowledge of us is not so faded that I could send my own golden-eyed folk to commission myriad guns of bronze for long-limbed sinistrists. Besides, you understand the money thing and the ways of tradesmen. Your high Vatican position is excellent cover and your lack of racial loyalty so . . . stimulating. You were the obvious choice.'

'Your Majesty is too kind,' said Slovo, bowing slightly.

The King gazed away into the middle distance. 'We will learn to tolerate the burning touch of iron,' he mused. 'We were dispossessed by iron and with iron (well, a proportion of it) we will regain the land. No more flint and copper against blades of steel: this time we will be as deadly as you . . .'

Having lately been in charge of the Roman state-armoury inventories, Admiral Slovo took leave to doubt this – but said nothing. He was toying with the alarming discovery that he found some of the lithe Elf youths sexually attractive.

'I know what you are thinking,' said the King.

I hope you don't, thought the Admiral.

'You are thinking that we are few for such an enterprise; that our martial skills and arquebuses notwithstanding, your Swiss, French, English and German soldiers . . .'

'Italians also fight on occasion,' protested Slovo.

'. . . will overrun us by the weight of numbers. You are thinking that your kind swarm and breed quickly whereas we reproduce only with effort and good fortune: is that not so?'

'No,' replied the Admiral truthfully, 'my mind was not resting on that.'

'Well, even so,' said the King, refusing to be deprived of his speech, 'should you be planning to think of it, you would be wrong.'

'Doubtless,' said Slovo obligingly.

'We are a vanguard, Admiral. This is an unprecedented array. Here I have the very best of all the scattered feuding tribes. All those who dare clutch the iron and dream of restitution are coming to me; the old chieftains are powerless to stop them. No more skulking in the wild places and fleeing your expansion. We are learning from you. Unheard of amongst the Old Races, an Over-King has been crowned and I am he. Our old ways and institutions are being remoulded by my dream. We will arm and learn to use your guns. Our day is returning and when we are ready we will take a human town and kill all within it so that not one usurper is left. And when that is heard abroad, all the hidden Elf Nations will unite and rise!'

'Very commendable,' said Admiral Slovo, the soul of gentlemanly toleration towards the pet projects of others. 'I suggest Pisa. Its walls are in a lamentable state and I once spent a most unhappy season there.'

The King, like any common Elf or person, resentful of being humoured, lowered his voice an octave or two. 'And then it will be your turn to eke out life in the forests and foothills,' he concluded grimly. 'Meanwhile,' the King continued, recalling the present necessity, 'commission another thousand handguns, and twelve demi-cannon. I presume the previous gunsmith is now dead?'

'Regrettably so,' confirmed the Admiral.

'Then have them made elsewhere; somewhere far away.'

'Venice?' suggested Slovo.

'An excellent choice; we have that place well infiltrated. My emissary will contact you there.'

'The same youth as before, Your Majesty?'

'No: his visit to your ... church, impaired his health; therefore he was killed.'

'I see.'

'He fully agreed with my judgement, Admiral. There are no bystanders here; merely martyrs and would-be martyrs. Come and see.' The King rose from the fallen tree on which they had rested and gestured that Slovo should accompany him into the valley clearing. 'Do not fear,' he said, 'you will be safe – the only human of whom that can be said.'

Even so, a low but musical growl of disapproval greeted Admiral Slovo as he approached the Elfish army. Powerless to alter matters, he found it easy to ignore and soon was in the midst of the be-plumed and feathered soldiery.

According to their tribe or inclination, some were in plain black, or green, or gold. Others were as gaudy as a Cardinal in all his glory. Over long evolution, far longer than humans had had to develop, their swords and halberds of bronze had mutated into wild and complex multi-edged forms, contrasting with the earnest practicality of the man-made guns.

Who knows? thought Slovo, *Perhaps I am wrong, maybe they do stand a chance*. The smallest, most ill-favoured Elf towered six inches over his own head, he noted.

'You are impressed,' said the King, 'and rightly so. The old chieftains counselled patience – arm if you must, they said, but do not gather; lie low. Wait for the usurpers to slip; for a plague, a famine, world-wide war, for anything to shorten impossible odds. But we have waited too long; like rats, your kind survives every misfortune and grows even stronger. The younger and better of us grow impatient and slip away from their people. They join and merge with the human victors and become great artists, soldiers and suchlike – not for their own people, no – but for you!' The King shook his helmeted head. 'That must all end,' he said. Suddenly he drew out his two-handed sword and hacked down a nearby warrior. 'Which it will not do,' he continued, wiping his blade on the Elf's sundered body, 'whilst Elf-kind display such personal laxity as that individual. His hair was deplorably ill-dressed. I cannot abide that, can you, Admiral?'

'No indeed, Your Majesty,' replied Slovo, favourably impressed by the lack of reaction shown by the Elfish troops. Drilling continued unabated around and over the deceased.

'Well,' said the King, as they passed through the soldiers and into the camp on the valley's opposite side, 'I suppose you must receive your reward.'

'If it's quite convenient,' said the Admiral, masking anticipation from his voice.

The King shrugged his mail-clad shoulders. 'It is all the same to me,' he said. 'But who is this Marcus Aurelius you revere so much as to betray your race for him?'

Admiral Slovo borrowed heavily from his ample reserves of patience. '*Was*, Your Majesty, was. He was a Roman Emperor of the second Christian century and a primary exponent of the Stoic philosophy to which, in all humility, I adhere. It was always thought that his writings survived in one volume only, the incomparable *Meditations*. However, it transpires you have in your possession a second book of equal merit . . .'

'Just so,' smiled the Elf-King mercilessly.

'. . . an eighth or ninth-century monkish copy of a hitherto unknown original whose title I do not know.'

'Because I will not show it to you,' said the King cheerfully.

'Indeed,' replied Slovo, knowing now how Tantalus suffered in Hades.

The King crooked his finger and from the chaos of cook-fires and horse compounds trotted an Elf-boy carrying a bundle wrapped in fine, scarlet Elf-silk.

'A page, I believe, was my promise,' said the King, withdrawing a wood-bound volume from the proffered bundle. With one long finger he flicked randomly through its crumbling contents, never shifting his gaze from Slovo. 'Of course, you could end up with a mere chapter heading or a blank,' he said, full of mock sorrow.

'There is that possibility,' agreed Slovo.

'But fate decrees you shall have . . . this!' The King's left hand halted its headlong progress and with thumb and forefinger seized a page by its top corner. 'A full page of writing – and a complete discussion at that: *On the cultivation of a bounteous harvest of Indifference*. Mother Fortune has smiled on you, Admiral: may this bring you much happiness – or indifference to happiness.'

The page was carelessly torn from the book and handed over.

Admiral Slovo scan-read it then and there lest, in a refinement of cruelty, the Elves straightaway snatched it from him. He had the substance of the matter committed to memory before he looked up again.

Like the children that they in some ways are, the Elves had suddenly lost all interest in him and abruptly wandered off. The book, the King, the Elf-boy were gone and Admiral Slovo was left alone and unregarded in the midst of their camp whilst the bustle continued all around him. It was his dismissal.

He re-read the page for safety's sake and then pocketed it lovingly. His horse was not far off, sheltering amidst the Arab stallions of the Elves, and, with luck and disregard for comfort, he could be back in Rome in five days. There was time to attend to his Vatican duties before he need worry about arranging death in Venice.

Everything was going supremely well – although he was careful not to permit himself more than moderate enjoyment of the fact. Admiral Slovo turned and smiled on the Elves training in the evening sunlight.

Acquisition of the whole book was an unrealistic aspiration. However, there was, he considered, every reasonable chance of digesting its substance, a page here, a paragraph there, before events resolved themselves. Perhaps the attack on Pisa would succeed and the Old Ways would rise as the King predicted. Then they would need fresh arms if mankind was to be finally swept from the scene. Alternatively, Pisa (judiciously forewarned by ... someone) might repulse the rising and force Elf-kind's first Over-King to fresh considerations. Time alone delayed the revelation that the guns Slovo had supplied could not survive (and were specifically designed not to survive) more than a few score firings. One way or another, the trickle of inducements to himself would continue.

Come what may, across the chasm of the centuries, Admiral Slovo would hear what the Stoic Emperor Marcus had to say; and in reading the book and taking its message to heart, he would be content with whatsoever transpired.

'Didn't quite work out that way, did it, Admiral?'

Back at the end of his life, Slovo was still talking to the Welsh Vehmist.

'Sadly no. When I next returned to the Over-King's camp, everything was gone as if it had never been. Oh – apart from one thing – one of my arquebuses was lying in the middle of the clearing, neatly snapped in half. I assumed that was for my benefit.'

'Correct,' confirmed the Vehmist.

'Well, I got the message,' Slovo continued, 'and never went back. In fact, that was the last I heard of the matter. I didn't get my book.'

'No,' said the Vehmist, trying to sound decently regretful. 'We didn't feel that you'd deserved it.'

Slovo toyed with a green fig, powerfully indenting it with his fingers. 'So it was another of your schemes, then?' he said, regarding the wounded fruit.

The Vehmist answered, 'We curtailed your little bit of private enterprise as a favour to ourselves and our allies. Mind you, your deviousness up to that point quite delighted us. The first we got to learn of anything was the attack on Pisa.'

'Oh,' smiled Slovo, 'so they got around to that, did they? How come I didn't hear of it?'

'Because,' the Vehmist replied simply, 'by then we were on the case. It was in the interest of all concerned parties – declared or not – to draw a veil over things. And the Pisans are an incurious lot, not given to history or recording. If they can't eat it or fuck it . . .'

'Yes, quite,' interrupted the Admiral fastidiously. 'So what happened?'

'I *said* you'd ask,' laughed the Vehmist, 'but my Master wouldn't have it – *not a man in his position*, he said. Good job I read the file right through for all the details . . .'

'I'm a military man,' said Slovo. 'I like neat endings.'

'Just so, Admiral, and I'm here to humour you in every respect. Well, it's easily told. They didn't do too bad, all things considered. Bear in mind, for instance, they were all separate peoples and tribes. Also, their last real experience of full scale infantry action was, what—?'

'A thousand?' suggested Slovo.

'Yeah, maybe a thousand years beforehand. Not only that, but they weren't using their preferred weapons, like the repeating crossbow and assassin's blades, but those guns you'd so kindly got them. Like I said, it was quite a creditable effort, really.'

'But to no avail, I take it?'

'No. They came on in pike columns, heading for the Town-Gate, covered by a skirmish line of your arquebus fellows. It was all rather neat apparently – given their undisciplined propensities. The Elvish cannons even scored a few decent hits, though how you'd miss a town wall I'm not quite sure.'

'You've clearly never fired a gun in the midst of battle,' observed the Admiral acidly.

'No, thank gods,' said the Vehmist, the gibe bouncing harmlessly off him. 'Well, the Pisans were surprised, of course. But they got some shots off, taking a few Elves out and – blammo – all order flees. Among the Elves it just turned into a mad scramble for the Gate and racial enemy, knives drawn.'

Admiral Slovo shook his head sadly. It didn't matter any more, but even at the remove of decades, displays of uncorseted emotion had the power to upset him.

'So they were all packed together like a mad mob by the time they neared the Town,' the Vehmist continued, trying manfully to conceal a modicum of amusement. 'Meanwhile, the Pisan militia had woken up, so to speak, and trundled a cannon or two to the spot and, after that, the Elf horde couldn't do a thing right . . .'

'After that,' interjected the Admiral, concluding on the Vehmist's behalf, 'they were torn asunder with grapeshot and fled, bewildered, each a victim of their own solipsistic individualism.'

'Neglecting to carry their wounded with them, I might add,' said the Vehmist reprovingly.

'Naturally,' said Slovo. 'They're *Elves*.'

'It doesn't excuse them,' the Vehmist persevered. 'We were quite inconvenienced by their left-behinds – living and otherwise. Still, it all got sorted out in the end: "bandits", was the official explanation, unusually ambitious ones. It suited all parties to swallow it.'

'And the left-behinds?' queried Slovo.

'A rather odd burial mound beside the City walls – a puzzle for antiquaries and grave-robbers to come: such long limbs . . . such elegant skulls. At their request, we left it to the other petty Elf-Lords to deal with their High-King. It was all done with consummate treachery.'

'I thought they might act sooner or later,' agreed the Admiral. 'He was premature – and bad publicity. His race do not care for undue attention.'

'Quite so,' said the Vehmist. 'Fen and fell and Downs folk

they must remain for a good while yet; till either their ambitions are modified or man's intolerance is moderated. Unless, that is, some reckless individual such as you, acts to fan their ancient grievance and deludes them once again into ruin.'

'I got impatient,' said Admiral Slovo, wondering why on earth he felt the need to explain any more. 'Quite aside from the delectable bait the High-King was holding out, you lot seemed to have abandoned me in the dusty labyrinth of the Vatican bureaucracy.'

'Sin, most grievous sin,' confessed the Vehmist. 'Apparently our attentions were particularly focused elsewhere during those years – although that hardly excuses our neglect. Your little project perforce drew our eyes back to Italy and made us realize there were blades we'd failed to sharpen back there. It was decided to tell you more.'

'Ah yes,' recalled Slovo, 'the international conspiracy annual dinner-dance . . .'

The Vehmist both smiled and winced.

⚡ The Year 1493

'I die in Germany. Afterwards, I am enrolled in a conspiracy.'

'You will sleep here, brother.'

Slovo stepped in. The first thing he noticed was the lack of a roof, the second the sound of the door locking behind him.

'You will sleep here,' came the voice of the Vehmic Knight from outside, 'and wake to life anew.'

Admiral Slovo did not answer. He was here at the Holy Vehme's pleasure and there was nothing to gain by vain protest.

The sea journey, a rarity for him nowadays, had revived old memories and forgotten tastes. All the way from Rome to . . . this place, where Germania merged into land disputed with the Turk, he had pondered the unnaturalness of his life, pushing a quill-pen, not a stiletto. The subtle and learned Vehmic courier (a friar in normal life) assigned to accompany him, and to subvert his every settled opinion, found little work left for him to do.

Everything had been arranged on Admiral Slovo's behalf, as neat and quick as a thunderbolt. The notice of leave of absence, signed by a Bishop no less, had arrived on his

Vatican desk just like any other piece of correspondence. That same afternoon, a clerk in his office, hitherto suspected of being nothing more than he seemed, confided to Slovo that a certain ship was sailing on the evening tide and that he must be on it. Admiral Slovo gladly surrendered to the equally pressing tide of events and let himself be borne along.

Now he found himself in an open-topped stone-built box observing the stars that shone down on him and the rest of the forsaken landscape. Even had he wished to escape, the constraining walls were too high and sheer to climb. The one and only door looked simple and sturdy enough to resist a siege. Slovo would be here just as long as the purpose of the Vehme required.

There was the very minor comfort of knowing that he was (technically) not alone. The brief night-time glimpse he'd been granted of the camp revealed at least two score similar cells. It was to be presumed that, for reasons of time-economy if no other, the Vehme initiated their recruits on a batch basis.

There were some minor furnishings in the cell but Slovo suspected there would be more than ample time to investigate them at his leisure. By forcing his mind to dwell on the writings of Euclid he caused himself to sleep.

In the morning, a hatch in the door opened and Slovo exchanged the cell's chamber pot for bread and wine. It had rained during the night but he did not complain or in any way converse with the invisible owner of the proffering hand.

Sitting on the muddy ground, he meticulously nibbled his way through the half-loaf and then sipped slowly at the wine. He memorized each mouthful's exact taste as solace in case there came a time of want – and so that he should know if and when his food was given that little narcotic or poisonous extra.

He had committed whole chapters of the *Meditations* and Epictetus' *Dissertations* to memory, and so had the faculty to wile away some hours in 'reading'. When this palled, as even the most sublime literature eventually must, he refreshed the body as he had the mind, with a period of vigorous exercise. The fierce glare of noon alerted him to the fact that the cell would never be more illuminated than now and it was thus an auspicious time to inspect fully the fixtures of his little world.

On the side opposite his chosen station there was a curious little table – perhaps an altar in intention – made of a stack of new-cut corn, levelled off below the head and made flat for a vase to rest on. This vase was also a direct gift of Nature, being made of cunningly woven green grass. In it stood a single stem and ear of bearded wheat.

Behind this on the wall were two images, paintings on wood, somewhat redolent of the icons Slovo had seen brought or pillaged from the schismatic Greeks and Rus. One was plainly of Zeus the Unconquered Sun – the second picture Slovo failed to recognize.

These items turned out to be the sum total of the diversions provided him and it took the calling to mind of his wife's sexual repertoire for Slovo to lull his mind to sleep.

After twenty-three days, the food stopped arriving. By then the wheatsheaf altar had dried and drooped towards the ground to which it would eventually return. Admiral Slovo had had more than enough opportunity to observe its slow demise. Made cussed by boredom and the attentions of sun and rain, he deliberately refused to enter a decline. Others undergoing the same test failed to bear up so well. Several times he heard voices raised in protest from nearby cells. The Vehme clearly had some means of rapidly silencing these weaker brethren for each remonstration was abruptly aborted within seconds. Slovo took the hint and kept his own counsel.

After a further week of a water-only diet, the Admiral grew light-headed and reconciled. All rancour and rebellion flowed out of him, hitching a lift atop his departing reserves of strength. At the very end of the week, after a day without even water, just before dawn, the disembodied hand offered a change of clothes in the form of shining white raiment. Slovo was glad to accept for reasons of personal delicacy, if no other.

Almost directly, the door was sprung and the transformed Admiral Slovo stepped out to rejoin the world. After initial difficulties with distance focusing, he discovered himself in the company of a dozen similarly hesitant figures. There were men of European race, some negroes, even one woman with yellowish skin and curiously arranged eyes. Still attuned to the discipline of the previous lunar month, no one spoke, and each kept even their visual curiosity under control.

Slovo was impressed by the organization brought to the occasion: the troops of cavalry which appeared served both to herd the initiates on their way and to explain how the camp remained unmolested. The horsemen were silent and answered to no orders but those already in their heads. Even so, they drilled and rode in perfect order as though they had been together for long and eventful years; brothers all, who knew each other's thoughts. Slovo wondered how this could be when they clearly came from each and every nation, race and army, retaining the dress and weapons appropriate to each. He could not conceive what force might cause *Gendarme*, *Stradiot*, *Reiter* and *Spahi* to act in such harmony.

Like bright-fleeced sheep the newly liberated prisoners of

the Vehme were shepherded away by these grim and speechless horsemen.

They were left at the mouth of an underground temple. There was no prospect of flight – the Vehmic cavalry would straightaway have ridden them down. This being so, Admiral Slovo boldly led the way forward, endeavouring, in so far as his weakened state would permit, still to appear the master of his own fate. A wizened Turk of similar fortitude joined him at the front.

They descended the sloping, torch-lit passage for quite some time, expecting at any moment to emerge into the high drama of a vaulted cavern or subterranean hall. However, this did not occur. To pay the Vehme their due, what they had to teach, true or false, had nothing of the petty or fraudulent about it. It did not require the assistance of showmanship.

At a point where the passage levelled slightly, Admiral Slovo almost bumped into a woman standing in the half darkness beside one wall. He surprised himself by his failure to adopt a fighting stance or to reach for an eye or throat with reflex malicious intent. Obviously his period of enforced preparation and contemplation had had some effect after all. Instead, he bade her good-day.

She was very young and quite exceptionally beautiful; her voice was sweetness itself, without being cloying. All but the last was, of course, largely lost on the Admiral, although he could academically acknowledge perfection when he saw it; particularly when it was revealed in all its naked glory.

'I beg your pardon,' he said, apologizing for the near collision once his survey was complete.

She giggled, one tiny hand courteously shielding her mouth from sight. 'That's all right,' she said, looking up at him provocatively. 'Welcome to the New Eleusis. Pray drink at the well.'

Then she straightaway turned to the old Turk and addressed him in his own tongue, presumably stating the same message. It was obvious Slovo was meant to move along.

He obligingly did so, allowing the Vehmic girl to greet each of the initiates. A mere score of paces on, he discovered the well referred to and dived his face into the torrent that splashed into a cup carved from the rock of the passage wall. The draught he swallowed was bitter, but mineral-rich and highly refreshing. He waited for all the others to drink and eventually the callipygian girl came to the fore to lead on. 'On' proved to be into a maze and in its dreary convulutions the party soon became separated. Then Admiral Slovo died.

At first he thought he was back at the tunnel's start, a flicking back of memory from future to past by no means uncommon to him. But then he noticed that this passage was radiantly lit and of infinite size, that his feet were no longer required to propel him forward and that the glorious light suffused his insubstantial body. The experience bore no relation to his previous trot down the tunnel to 'New Eleusis' and so Slovo was forced to more radical conclusions.

Looking down he saw the husk that had been Admiral Slovo, left behind, dead on the dusty floor. Meanwhile, the ... force that from sheer habit he still called 'himself' was called on by something that caused the great light and which drew all created things home to itself. Keen to make the light's acquaintance – or, wild notion, to re-meet his oldest friend – Slovo did not hold back. Surrendering like a whore offered a fortune, he barely noted the receding glimpse vouchsafed him of the maze in all its subtle and significant complexity. The supernatural, cut-away vision of the Vehmic mountain, with its wasp's-nest of rooms and barracks, chapels and thousands of swarming devotees, no longer had the power to amaze. Not even the confirmation of the globate nature of the world as it dwindled away, or the premature discovery of the existence of America, Australasia or Antarctica, particularly exercised him.

Admiral Slovo was exclusively interested in the distant figures he discerned at the heart of the summoning light. He could not see but devoutly believed that the beckoning couple were his mother and father. For the first time since childhood he felt entirely at liberty to water his face with tears.

There were other things as well to enhance and complete such unaccustomed high emotion. Something that might have been called music, but containing waves of empathy and intimations of wisdom, accompanied him courtesy of an invisible choir. Figures from his past, people he'd sent on before him, flashed into brief life to assure him, without the slightest guile, that there were no hard feelings. Admiral Slovo started to appreciate the things that previously would have cannoned off the dryness he'd cultivated. Suddenly these topics seemed of endless import – if only he could grasp what the light was trying to say . . .

Like a three-year-old newly introduced to the subtleties of Stoicism, Admiral Slovo wasn't ready for all that was being lavished on him; but he was growing by the second and very shortly he would understand all. And so forgive all.

And then someone forced a liquid down his rebelling throat and recalled him to life. Faster than man would travel until the invention of jets, Slovo shot back into his body and reoccupied the casing he had hoped to escape. In some inexpressible way, he didn't seem to 'fit' it quite as well as before.

The naked Vehmic girl was astride his chest, hammering

rhythmically on it with her fists until, after a lapse of seconds, he began to feel the blows. He also realized that his mouth was rinsed in something vile and he tried to spit it out. The girl smiled at him and ceased her efforts.

'Welcome back,' she said. 'They almost all do that, you know – try to spew the life potion out. It won't do you good, I made sure you swallowed a good dose.' She arched over him and pressed one ear to his ribs. 'No,' she said triumphantly. 'I've got it going properly again. You're back for good.' Then she skipped away.

Admiral Slovo didn't know what to feel – the first wrenching wave of loss proved to be bearable due to his revived Stoic capabilities, and that was good news. Less happy was the realization that he was losing full recollection of his journey into light. Like a sandcastle in combat with the tide, he felt more and more of the precious insights being washed away each second, until he was left with nothing.

It took him an hour to get out of the maze, for its twists and spirals had been designed by a mind of even greater deviousness than his own. Twice on the way he encountered the bodies of initiates who had succumbed to the poison in the well. Perhaps the Vehmic maid had been unable to call them back from death, or maybe she'd merely failed to find them. To Slovo, such carelessness with their charges only emphasized the profundity of the role his employers had arranged for *him*.

As he emerged from the maze into the blinding light of central stage, he entered a high-ceilinged circular room thronged with people, once again a highly cosmopolitan crowd, dotted here and there with initiates more maze-adaptive than he.

A corpulent man in a turban offered the Admiral a drink. 'Imbibe withour reservation, brother,' he said, in faultless Italian. 'This liquid contains no untoward additives.'

Slovo politely tasted the wine. It was fit for a Prince and rushed straight to his head.

Enver Pasha – Turk and Vehmist – courteously allowed Slovo a moment to look around and collect himself. He noticed the Admiral's attention was particularly taken by the great globe above, which illuminated the room. 'To some we explain nothing,' he said. 'To you, we are safe in confiding that it is an effect of the heating of steam. A minor part of our knowledge, it serves to impress either way.'

'I can see many uses for it in the outside world,' said Slovo. 'If you'll excuse the play on words, I wonder why you chose to hide your light under a bushel?'

The Turk shrugged and smiled with a flash of gold. 'There may come a time for its wider application,' he agreed, 'but by then it will be *our* time and we will have no need for concealment. In the interim, what we have, we keep.'

'Ah ... of course,' said Slovo, as though this was a damning revelation. He'd wanted to coax this confession of pettiness from the Vehmist.

'And that is the one lesson you must absorb today,' the Turk went on. 'From now on, you are we, and we are everything. Loyalty will come with the passing years but in the meanwhile let self-restraint, fear and respect serve the same ends.'

A steward offered them dainty refreshments, at which Slovo's starved taste buds leapt into vibrant life. He wolfed down three of the pastry envelopes before he was able to control himself and say, 'I recognize that man.'

The Vehmist turned and seemingly noticed the retreating serving-man for the first time.

'Doubtless,' he replied. 'He is a Bishop and often in Rome.'

'I hope,' said Slovo, reserving several options by temporarily casting his glance to the garish mosaic floor, 'that you do not expect me to wait on table like a lackey.'

Again Enver Pasha smiled. His voice had no kindness in it. 'No,' he said. 'You are higher in our favours than he, more pregnant with ... possibilities. However, if it were our wish that you should serve refreshments, that is what you would do.'

Slovo declined the implicit challenge by looking about. The party was becoming quite convivial and, as the Admiral's allotted host, Enver Pasha did not wish his charge to be a conspicuous abstainer from his communal spirit. He stepped in to mend the conversational thread.

'How was your near-death-experience, Admiral?' he asked politely. 'If you do not mind to speak of it, that is. Some people prefer not.'

'It was very interesting, thank you,' replied Slovo, both answering and rebuffing further enquiry. 'I take it that it was all your doing.'

'Oh, of course,' said the Vehmist. 'A mere matter of poison followed by an antidote, both in horse-doses. We find there's no equal to it in shaking a person loose from their foundations and making them receptive to new ideas. Naturally there's a wastage rate...'

'But you reckon the exercise worthwhile, even so,' Admiral Slovo completed the sentence for him, not wishing, for obscure reasons, to hear it from the Turk's own lips.

Enver Pasha looked for hints of criticism in Slovo's speech before replying, but could detect none. 'Just so,' he said. 'I presume that you saw the Universal Light – that's the commonest formulation for monotheists. I shouldn't attach any great importance to it, nor to any visions of loved ones coming to greet you. It is merely the last gambit of the dying mind, coping with its terror by recalling the passage to birth and freeing itself of the burden of memory. At least, that's what we presume.'

Enver Pasha suddenly noticed, by a stiffening of the Slovo

spine, that he had caused offence. He knew then that something Slovo had seen on the brink of oblivion had touched his heart. 'Still, it's over now,' he said hastily. 'Make of it what you will.'

'Thank you,' replied Admiral Slovo, more than usually stony-faced, not actually offended at all but simply ashamed at the recollection of his tears in the tunnel of light. 'So that's all, I take it. No dark secrets? No blood-curdling oaths?'

'No,' confirmed Enver Pasha. 'None at all. Some people will have them but in your case we don't feel it necessary. You already have the required reverence for the antique world, you are too self-contained to be impressed by blood vows and threats. We tailor each initiation to the individual. After what you have undergone, the orthodoxies of the outer world will seem even less attractive to you than hitherto, I assure you. You have been made receptive to wider sympathies and that is sufficient for present needs.'

'Though,' queried Slovo, 'you have told me nothing about yourselves. Surely I need to know *what* I am meant to be serving?'

Enver Pasha considered the point at some leisure. 'There's no need for it,' he mused at last. 'You're not one of those we'll drill and browbeat, because that would be counterproductive. In fact, you're free to go. However, it's your day, and I'm willing to humour you. Come with me.'

He waddled off through the throng and Admiral Slovo dutifully followed, taking the opportunity to snatch a further drink of wine and a handful of pastries en route. As they went, the Vehmist casually pointed people out, saying, 'Do you get the picture? We're anyone and everyone, a coalition, a family, an alliance of interests against the world.'

In this way they arrived at the wall of the great chamber, which was hung with tapestries depicting common themes from classical mythology. Clearly familiar to the point of contempt with the temple's layout, the Vehmist brushed one section of covering aside to reveal a door. Slovo coined the suspicion that it was not the only such concealed entrance or exit and that this vault was perhaps only one in a series.

Enver Pasha unlocked the door with a rusty key and waved Slovo in. Once the door closed behind them the noise of the party ceased with alarming abruptness. 'Well then,' he said, indicating the object holding pride of place in the antechamber. 'What do you think that is?'

'It's a large ball,' Slovo said in due course, 'with a cartography printed on its surface. I recognize the Middle Sea and Italia – but the curvature distorts reality and . . .'

Enver Pasha shook his head sadly and waved Slovo to silence. 'Observe,' he said testily, 'and learn something from this Earth-Apple. Here,' he pointed at a point on the globe, 'in Cathay, we have propagated the ultra-conservative Confucian philosophy amongst the bureaucrats of the Ming dynasty court. Liu Daxia, who is one of ours – and, incidentally, the War Minister, has ordered the destruction of the vital navigational charts that permitted Chinese junks to contact Asia, Afrique and Indonesia. He explained to the Emperor that contact with foreign "barbarians" can only dilute and weaken the Chinese culture. Accordingly, the home of that culture will stagnate and decline, lost in a dream of self-sufficiency and past glories. Therefore, when the fleets of the West – those lands you presently call Christendom – one day reach out to the East, they won't be barred from the Indian and Pacific Oceans.

'Further, look here. This is Songhay, the Kingdom of Gao and Timbuktu, a centre for caravans and trade in gold. We caused Sonni ali Ber, its most alarmingly able Emperor, to be drowned in the River Niger only last year. He was returning from great conquests in the South but there will be no more victories for Songhay. The Portuguese are being

... influenced into ambitions in North Afrique: Sonni ali Ber's successors will rule a land-locked, isolated territory that will fall sooner or later – spears and arrows against gunpowder. We have decided against the prospering of Afrique.'

Having fought against the Southern 'Horse Warriors' at the behest of Khair Khaleel-el Din, while resident in Tripoli, Slovo's indifference at this geo-political meddling knew no bounds. 'Are you quite sure you really need me?' was all he asked. 'Things seem to be going smoothly already.'

Enver Pasha idly span the globe, trying to avoid sight of his Turkish homeland, knowing full well what the Vehme had in store for that. 'Individually, no, of course not,' he said. 'Although some of our elders claim to discern strange destiny in you. However we do require numerous talented men, and women, our wonders to perform.'

'And how will I recognize them?'

Enver Pasha caused the globe to cease its revolutions, something he occasionally wanted to do in reality. 'You won't,' he said. 'Not unless they wish you to. All I would say is that you may look for us amongst the high and wise.'

'The two conditions are not often combined,' said Slovo wryly.

'Then perhaps,' countered the Vehmist, 'that will be their identification.'

'There are one or two other things; may I?'

'You might as well, Admiral. I doubt we'll meet again.'

'Well, primarily, what *is* it that you want?'

The Vehmist looked up at Slovo. 'We are a coalition of ambitions, as I have told you,' he said. 'However, there has emerged a consensus in aims; we all of us hope for the restoration of older and better days, and ways.'

'Elf-days, Imperial days, Pagan days?' queried Slovo.

Enver Pasha smiled tightly but refused to be further drawn.

'Well, are you sure it's all worth it?' said Slovo, trying another tack.

Enver Pasha had apparently never considered that point. 'Possibly not, Admiral,' he said eventually, 'but the project has achieved a momentum of its own after such a time. And besides,' he added cryptically, 'we are guided by *The Book* . . .'

'Which is not Holy Scripture or even the Qur'an, I take it?'

'Nothing so prosaic, Admiral. This is our own book; we wrote it and we observe, with joy, its prophecies fulfilled page by page. Do not exercise your curiosity too much, however, I doubt you will ever do more than glimpse its cover.'

'That good, eh?'

'Beyond all attributes of praise, Slovo, it is the story of times from misty past to equally misty future. All the same, I don't wish to send you forth entirely unappeased; you would only undertake private research and bring our investment in you to ruin. It has the summation of the ancient Delphic and Amun Oracles, the Eleusinian and Dodonan Mysteries and the Cumaean and Sibylline Books, I will tell you that much. Within living memory it has been added to by the blessed Gemistus Pletho – and since you've failed to ask – yes, it was he whose image decorated your initiate's cell. It is possible for you to acquire some of his less radical, openly available, works and thereby see the merest ghost of our project. Consider that as your homework.'

It was pointless trying to conceal the awakening of interest at the mention of bookish learning and so Slovo did not bother to try. 'I shall do so,' he said. 'What else must I do?'

'Nothing and everything, Admiral, you are not one of our aimed missiles. We expect benefit from whatever field you may cultivate. Simply go out and live, Slovo. Make friends and influence people.'

With that the Vehmist indicated that their conversation was at an end. He gently guided Admiral Slovo back into the Great Chamber where the reception was still in full swing. A black-clad servant was awaiting them bearing the Admiral's discarded clothes, now neatly laundered and folded. Slovo was not to know that they had also been cunningly loosened, if only by a stitch or two, and then expertly resewn. The Vehme would spare no effort, however painstaking, to ensure that their initiates departed home feeling that, in some indefinable way, they were not the same person as before.

Confident that all his other needs – transport, food and weaponry – would be equally met before he was dismissed, Admiral Slovo let himself be led from the Hall.

At the upward sloping exit, sister portal to that from the maze, stood two vast colossi from ancient times, marble effigies of Mars and Horus-Hadrian, one to each side. On a night of such abundant wonders, Slovo barely noticed them and walked through, burdened with thoughts of history-in-the-making.

He was alone in such carelessness, however. Even the other initiates now knew enough to study each departure through the living sentinels with intense interest. So, when yellow light flared in the eyes of neglected god and dead Emperor, and each stone titan groaned as though straining to track the Admiral's path, it did *not* go unnoticed.

Throughout the great Council Chamber of the Holy and Ancient Vehme, though there was so much of great import to talk about, every conversation died.

❧ The Year 1497

'A STAB IN THE DARK: I apply liberality to the dispensing of Justice and assist a soul in torment.'

'To my mind,' said Juan Borgia, Second Duke of Gandia, Prince of Teano and Tricarico, Duke of Benevento and Terracina, freshly appointed *Gonfaloniere* of the Holy Church, 'the realm of Venus is, more than any other, ripe for . . . conquest.'

'For taking – and despoilment!' agreed his sycophantic, masked friend.

'Just so,' said the Duke, licking his lips. 'Its frontiers are invitingly open, its forces so weak as to invite violation. As a youth I probed its outer provinces; now, as a Prince, I am invading in force!'

'I bear witness to this,' said the masked man. 'Duke Juan's three-pronged thrusts against the orifices of womankind advance on and in every day!'

They both laughed heartily and then Juan snuffed out his amusement as if it were a candle, resuming his normal vicious disgruntlement. 'And what think *you*, Admiral?' he said sharply. 'What is your opinion of my military metaphor?'

The small group in the vineyard set aside their drinks and delicacies and turned to regard Admiral Slovo.

'I have been a most infrequent visitor to the land of which you speak,' he said equably, unconcerned by the general scrutiny. 'Its scenery can be beguiling, I grant you, but extended stays are, I feel, a greatly overrated pastime.'

'The Admiral feels,' said Cesare Borgia, hitherto silently vigilant, '—and I tend to concur with him, that Queen Venus does not merit the diversion of a whole campaign. She does us no harm, poses no threat and pays tribute and lip service to our efforts. I cannot understand the spirit of aggression towards her.'

Duke Juan, ever on the precipice of malevolence, sulkily adjusted his gaze from Slovo to his own younger brother. 'Is that so . . .' he said icily.

Cesare considered the question with exaggerated care. 'Yes,' he said at last, 'that is my opinion and also, I suspect, that of our Father. It strikes me that he would prefer his *Gonfaloniere* to concentrate his energies elsewhere: for example, on the campaign which is the pretext for this party.'

'I am ever indebted for your advice, little brother,' said Juan, wearing a smile that was worse than any sneer. 'You know how I hunger and thirst to live up to *your* expectations. Ah, here is Mother come to quiet us.'

The conversational rack suddenly relaxed two or three notches as Vanozza Dei Cataneis approached them.

Cataneis had never been accounted beautiful or witty. However, she bore sons and, rarest of all qualities in her time and place, was loyal and discreet. For nearly thirty years these virtues had endeared her to Rodrigo Borgia (latterly Pope Alexander VI) although his more urgent affections now wandered elsewhere (and everywhere). The lady also possessed the preserving sense, innate to noble Roman Houses, of knowing, before even the participants did, when talk was turning deadly.

'Sons, gentlemen,' she said softly, 'I have detected a certain tension in the air, dispelling the evening calm and the scent of the vines. Surely that cannot emanate from this vicinity?'

'Absolutely not, Mother,' said Duke Juan, so profoundly dissembling as to shock Cesare and Slovo, inspiring new respect in them. 'We were discussing martial stratagems; a matter most relevant in the context of my imminent departure to war.'

Even the most skilful deceit is wasted on a man's mother. Madame Dei Cataneis was unconvinced. 'Then how fortuitous, Juan, that a military man is present to make informed comment on your opinions: Admiral Slovo, how are you?'

Slovo bowed graciously. 'Well, my Lady. And my eyes remove the necessity of enquiring after your own health.'

Cataneis favoured him with a frugal smile. 'And do you still kill Turks on the seaways, Admiral?' she said.

'But rarely, Madame – the occasional foray from my native Capri...'

'I thought you were a Florentine,' said Duke Juan, interrupting instantly as the information mismatch registered. 'Or was it Milan?'

Admiral Slovo's expression did not change. 'On one side,' he said, 'yes, possibly – however, to answer my Lady's question, nowadays I sail less predictable waters.'

'So one hears,' said Cataneis. 'You have been a most useful right hand, I gather, first to one Pope, then another...'

'They come and they go, Popes do,' said Joffre Borgia, the youngest present – and then coloured up, realizing what a stupid, perhaps even dangerous comment that was.

However defective their morality, the manners of those present were exquisite and they passed over the teenager's gaffe in decent silence.

'One endeavours to be useful,' said Slovo, 'and adaptable.'

It was a complete explanation for everything. Nobody of

the company's time and class would have dreamt of disputing such a statement.

'A universal maxim!' agreed Cesare, draining any feeling from his voice. 'We all aspire to its demands, do we not? Take my brother, Juan, for instance; one day, Duke of ... some place or other in Spain; the next, *Gonfaloniere* sent to re-educate the Orsini and Umbrian kinglings for past mis-judgements.[3] It is but the merest wheel of fortune and we must bow to its turns.'

'Whilst wishing Duke Juan every good fortune as you do so,' said the Lady Cataneis firmly, staring blankly into the middle distance.

'Just so,' agreed Cesare smoothly, thereby returning his mother's powers of focus.

Admiral Slovo was impressed. The venerated Lady had quietly established mastery in this potentially disruptive corner of her vineyard – or almost so.

'And your companion, Juan,' she said, 'his festive mask is *most* amusing, but seems a little too permanent. Tonight we celebrate with family and friends – and those that they can vouch for. There is no need for concealment.'

'Alas not so, in his case,' replied Juan airily. 'My Spaniard acquired a blade's kiss in my service and he now fears to distress gentle ladies and children of the quality with its aftermath. I retain him for his loyalty – and besides, he amuses me.'

This last, the Duke added hastily as he detected a slight communal shiver of disapproval at his display of sentiment.

There the stream of conversation ran underground and could not be found again. Cataneis was content in her victory, just as Duke Juan was discontented by his feeling of defeat. Admiral Slovo had long ago trained himself to relish silence, and anyway no reading of Cesare Borgia's chilly nerve circuits was humanly possible. Joffre, being inadequate, and the masked man, being a servant, were not entitled to contribute to the progress of intercourse – or lack of it.

Duke Juan's nerve broke first. 'Mother's mention of amusement prompts my memory,' he said, with all due show of confidence. 'I recall a provisional appointment. Would you therefore excuse me?'

'If the sap is rising, you rascal,' said Cataneis, 'I can do no else. This is a party given in your honour and there is therefore no reason for it to outlive your leaving or change of humour.'

'I am obliged,' said Juan, bobbing his ringleted head to show the required respect. 'Come, gipsy – life awaits us!'

The masked man bowed to all present and followed his master out.

'Who is he?' asked Cataneis, sharply.

'A Spaniard,' replied Cesare, 'called Sebastiano.'

'You have checked this? He can be vouched for?'

'Yes to both, Mother.'

'Then I am at peace on the subject.' The Lady Cataneis nodded to Admiral Slovo and swept away.

Evening was well advanced and in Rome, particularly in a Roman vineyard, such an hour is unusually charming. The fading light and the heat of the day were diffused by the vine-stacks, and the politically correct statuary caught and trapped the roving eye. It had been a most discreet party, designed, like the mild refreshments, as a respite from the social hurricane beyond the walls. Admiral Slovo detected something of the Stoic spirit in the whole concept and was pleased.

'Brother Joffre,' said Cesare quietly, 'I espy that Lord Bondaniella of the Palatine is slobbering down your wife's cleavage once again. This is a slight on our family and our Mother's hospitality. As is her acquiescence, might I add. Go and deal with the matter.'

With an oath, Joffre rushed away as he was bidden.

Alone together, Admiral Slovo and Cesare Borgia studied just about everything but each other. The Admiral nevertheless saw the flash in the Borgian eye when his companion eventually spoke.

'A man should honour his Father and Mother, Admiral.'

'*That you may live long and prosper in the land*,' agreed Slovo cautiously. 'Yes, it is divinely ordained as a binding mechanism for human society.'

Cesare nodded. 'And yet how much easier it is to obey that noble call, Admiral, when one finds oneself in total agreement with parental views.'

'Indeed,' said Slovo.

Cesare stretched forth his hand and plucked one grape from a bunch overhead, rolling it between his gloved fingers. 'So I find myself in pleasing accord with Mother,' he went on, ' when she says Juan's departure will be excused.'

For the first time – and for a second only – their eyes were permitted to meet and in the ensuing data exchange they both found the information they sought.

'I believe,' said Admiral Slovo, slowly, 'that I may be in your debt.'

'If that is so,' replied Cesare, 'then you will find me an easier usurer than those Jews you fraternize with.'

'I say thus,' continued Slovo, hurrying on, alarmed by Cesare's knowledge of his affairs, 'suspecting that, prior to your intervention, Duke Juan was minded to ... dispense with me: that is to say, with my services.'

'Such notions,' said Cesare, with as much casual significance as he ever permitted his voice to bear, 'ever fly about, Admiral.'

Indeed they do, thought Slovo, more than normally careful not to let his thoughts inform his face.

He had good reasons for so thinking. When he had watched Duke Juan ride forth that night, with his groom and the masked man, there had been a certain *fuzziness* to his image; a doubleness in the vision. It was as though his soul were preparing to leave him.

'So you found Duke Juan's body then?' said Rabbi Megillah. 'Well, there is merit in that, surely?'

'To a degree,' affirmed Admiral Slovo. 'But with His Holiness urging me on an hourly basis, I could do no other. For all my belief that some mysteries are best left unsolved, I had no choice in the matter.'

The Rabbi looked up from his goblet of water but swiftly controlled his eyes, purging them of the embryo of suspicion. '*Ecclesiastes* 9, 5,' he said to cover any misunderstanding. '"The dead know nothing." Therefore, what do they care?' He need not have worried for Slovo seemed not to have noticed the slip.

'That was only half of my commission,' the Admiral continued resignedly. 'The balance is more problematic.'

'Alexander insists on a culprit?' hazarded Rabbi Megillah.

'Precisely: justice even!' Slovo confirmed.

'He is of a class that can demand such exotica, Admiral. If it were you or I—'

'Or any of the dozen other ex-people today resting in the Tiber,' said Slovo.

'Just so. Few would enquire, fewer still would care and none would demand explanation from a world that is answer enough for any enormity. Some might question the Almighty (blessed be His name) but with little hope of satisfaction. In these times, such lightning strikes are all too common.'

'Though one can avoid travelling in storms,' said Admiral Slovo. '*Taanith* 25: Rabbi Eliezer said: "*Some dig their own graves.*"'

'But a bolt can seek you out, whilst safe at home, should it so wish.'

'Should it be so ordained,' Slovo corrected, realigning the conversational metaphor on to strictly natural phenomena.

Rabbi Megillah accepted the well-intentioned rebuke and pointedly steered his talk on to a new course. 'I'm told the wounds were savage,' he said, with decently feigned sympathy.

'As these things go, yes,' said Admiral Slovo. 'Certainly they were delivered with passion and commitment. There were nine entries in all; one in the neck, the others on his head. Any could have been the killing blow.'

'A shame,' said the Rabbi. 'He was a handsome man – for a Spaniard.'

'But no longer. When we dredged him from the sewer outfall area, little of the charm you mention was left.'

'We are but bags of blood, belted in and animated by the word of the Almighty (blessed be His name),' intoned Rabbi Megillah, as though Slovo would not know this simple truth.

Slovo left off his study of the table top and stared at the Rabbi. 'I do not recognize the quotation,' he said with interest.

'It is my own, Admiral.'

'Pity: composed by a Christian it might have found publication.'

Megillah shrugged, enviably untroubled by such considerations. 'Duke Juan's groom can tell you nothing?' he asked.

'He is dying,' said Slovo, smiling gently, 'but will not accept the fact. Thinking to collect his earthly reward, he says nothing, remembers nothing. Even His Holiness's rages have not shaken his memory.'

'Torture?' suggested the Rabbi.

'It would kill him within minutes. His Holiness's operatives in that field are so unimaginative, and I am too fastidious to offer the suggestions that might do the trick.'

'What of the masked man, Admiral; has he been located?'

'Gone, Rabbi: never existed, not known in the world of men.'

'Then there is your culprit!' smiled Rabbi Megillah, glad to be helpful.

'As well present the smith who made the dagger,' said Slovo, shaking his grey head. 'The Pope does not want the killing tool, but he who wielded it; not the assassin, but his patron.'

'He expects a great deal of this life,' said Rabbi Megillah in surprise. 'But what a Pope wants, he must have.' The Rabbi had ample, sad evidence of that law in his own short experience as ghetto leader.

'That or an acceptable substitute, Rabbi. Regrettably, what I presently have for His Holiness is very far from acceptable – to him or me.'

'You have a perpetrator!' exclaimed Megillah.

'Oh, yes.' Admiral Slovo smiled for the third or fourth time that evening (possibly a record). 'Let us just say,' he mused, 'that I had a word in someone's ear.'

'Thank you for agreeing to this interview,' said Cesare Borgia, 'and for maintaining a suitable reticence regarding same.'

Admiral Slovo bowed and graciously accepted the thanks.

'Would you care for refreshment, Admiral?'

'I think not, my Lord.'

'You need not fear poisoning, Admiral; my reputation is exaggerated.'

'As is my thirst for intoxicating drink, my Lord. Besides:

113

I recognize that there is currently no advantage to be accrued in my removal.'

Cesare, Protonotary of the Church, Treasurer of Cartagena Cathedral, Bishop of Pampeluna, Archbishop of Valenzia and Cardinal-Deacon of Santa Maria Nuova, sat stock still, quietly reviewing something in the ultra low-temperature conducting machine he had made of his mind. 'Ah yes,' he said in due course, 'I recall now; you're the Stoic, are you not?'

Admiral Slovo signalled his indifference to that or any description.

'If such serves to distinguish me from His Holiness's other investigators, I am happy with the tag,' he said. 'You might be judged likewise – if you will forgive me – by anyone noting your sombre black garb.'

Cesare smiled. 'Yes, I will forgive you. I acknowledge the connection. There are advantages in the self-control appertaining to your philosophy but the reasons for my habitual choice of dress run deeper.'

'As does my philosophy,' riposted Slovo.

Cesare abruptly shifted his direction of advance in the manner that, militarily, was later to make him famous. 'And how deep do your present investigations run, Admiral?' he said.

'River deep, mountain high, my Lord,' replied Slovo. 'But that is not something I should discuss before any other than His Holiness – or possibly close family.'

'Ignore Michelotto,' said Cesare, indicating the swarthy and similarly black-clad man sitting at his side. 'He is mine; I trust him with life and death.'

Admiral Slovo looked at Michelotto and the long-haired, bulky retainer politely inclined his head. His wide and innocent eyes deprived him of the look of an assassin – which must have been of some advantage in that trade.

'Very well,' said Slovo. 'I can inform you that my investigations are complete, that my presentation is prepared and my provisional conclusions drawn.'

'And would it be a culpable betrayal,' said Cesare, weighing each word, 'to prematurely reveal those conclusions to any other than His Holiness, the Pope?'

'Most certainly it would.'

'But nevertheless?' prompted Cesare, the very rarest sliver of doubt embedded in his voice.

'Nevertheless,' confirmed Slovo, 'all things being considered . . .'

'I will not insult you with offers of gold and patronage,' said Cesare swiftly, not wishing to snatch defeat from the jaws of unexpected victory.

'No, do not,' said the Admiral. 'There are motives for betrayal other than the mundane – but you, of course, know that.'

Cesare Borgia modestly waved the compliment away and economically used the same gesture to urge events on.

'Your brother,' said Admiral Slovo, leaning back in his chair, 'I need hardly remind you, left your Mother's party saying, in effect, that the night was yet young and other pleasures awaited him.'

'In effect,' agreed Cesare, allowing a modicum of contempt to surface. 'The regions below the belt-line controlled Juan's life; that was well known.'

'So the most cursory enquiries revealed,' said Slovo, equally dismissive of such weakness. 'Now; he was accompanied on the occasion in question by a groom and the masked Spaniard who had been his constant companion and buffoon for the month previous. He left us; a night passed and then the Duke's household reported his absence from home. His Holiness did not take alarm, reasonably assuming that he was holed up with some other man's wife and reluctant to be seen leaving her abode by daylight.

'After the succeeding day and another night passed, His Holiness appointed me master of all things relating to the issue and by late afternoon of that very next day, I had located Duke Juan's body.'

'You are a most perspicacious man,' said Cesare in an absolutely neutral tone. 'Any Pope – or Prince – able to retain your services would be fortunate indeed.'

'I could not term the task pleasurable,' Slovo continued, 'but it was most certainly educational. To illustrate this, permit me to recount one anecdote from my investigation.'

Cesare warily waved him on.

'In the continued absence of Duke Juan, I turned naturally to the Tiber – it being the conduit for every kind of unwanted thing. I interviewed a timber merchant who, on the night in question, had kept watch on his water-side yard from a boat on the river. In response to a certain memory-jogging, he remembered, in increasing detail as my patience wore thin, how a group of men had brought a body to the river bank and disposed of it near the sewage outfall. I asked him why he had not reported the occurrence and he told me that in the course of his brief tenancy he had seen upward of one hundred such short-shriftings. No one had troubled him concerning those, he said, therefore why should he think this one any different? Such is the world we live in, my Lord. I thought the man's point a reasonable one and so let him keep his left ear.'

Cesare indicated his approval of the Admiral's liberality.

'We dredged the area,' Slovo continued, 'and Duke Juan was revealed, all cut about and gory, as the street balladeers already say. Thus rewarded, I turned to the matter of responsibility and was spoilt for choice for candidates with personal or political motives. The body had thirty ducats on it, and therefore I knew Juan was not the victim of some thief. Actually,' said Admiral Slovo, in unchanged voice, 'to my surprise, your own name was mentioned. For example; as a rival with Duke Juan for the favours of your younger brother's wife, Donna Sancia.'

Cesare laughed. It sounded like distant cannon shot.

'Precisely,' said Slovo. 'I knew that the lady's favours are too widely and generously given for anyone to fight over them. However, another whisper portrayed Juan and you, together with His Holiness, your Father, as incestuous competitors for the hand – and other parts – of your sister, Lucrezia. That rumour I will pass over in silence other than to say I traced its origin to one Giovanni Sforza, formerly married to your sister but divorced on the humiliating grounds of impotence.'

'I will note that,' said Cesare, smiling again.

'And assuming you have at least the barest familiarity with inheritance laws, I discounted the notion that you sought to acquire your brother's Dukedom,' granted Slovo.

'Which passes to his eldest son,' agreed Cesare.

'Just so, my Lord. But to sum up, none of these proposals *satisfied*. So I was accordingly driven back to my own resources and deductions.'

'Which were?' said Cesare, as if he set little store by any expected answer.

'Which arose,' persisted Slovo, 'from forcibly preventing the immediate washing and laying out of your brother's corpse – as strongly insisted upon by certain Borgia servants. I was therefore able to detect the tiny token of blood present in Duke Juan's right aural cavity and postulate from that the entry point of the professional assassin's needle-stiletto. Such a blow putting the matter beyond issue, it became clear that the other visitations of the blade were post-mortem, designed to mislead.'

Cesare nodded appreciatively whilst making private calculations.

'And my deductions were confirmed,' Slovo went on, 'by today re-meeting Michelotto – or Sebastiano, as was – in your employ. He has altered appearance, posture and manner most convincingly; but a mask worn for one month in the fierce Roman sun leaves indications not easily erased. I also note, in passing, it transpires he has no scar.'

'No,' said Cesare. 'My brother thought there might be advantage in the employ of a masked servitor and so concocted a pretence.'

'But he is a businessman,' said Slovo.

'. . . and therefore open to alternative offers, yes,' confirmed Cesare. 'Yet he remains a person of sensitivity and has been much troubled by his previous meeting with you. I believe he wishes to apologize.'

By way of rare indulgence, he indicated that his servant might enter the conversation.

'My Lord Admiral,' said Michelotto in a dead, dull voice. 'I want to broaden your understanding of our encounter in the vineyard. I desire to convince you that I am not always thus. May I say that my sordid speech was dictated by Duke Juan's company. In matters of the flesh he was a very degraded man and in certain roles, one has to make . . . accommodations that can be distasteful.'

'I quite understand,' replied Admiral Slovo. 'Men are driven by the storms of circumstances and, unable to stand alone against them, are hardly accountable for the course of their little ship.'

Michelotto stood and bowed in apparently genuine appreciation of the Admiral's generous spirit.

'If I take your meaning,' said Cesare, 'it prompts me to suggest a possible explanation of Juan's death.'

'Really?' said Slovo, counterfeiting surprise.

'Could it not be, Admiral, that he was removed by an ambitious member of his family, say a younger brother, anxious to secure the secular honours that would otherwise ever be showered on Juan? Might not such a ruthless and resourceful man infiltrate the Duke's household with a killer and then disguise the murder as an all too plausible crime of passion?'

'It is entirely possible, my Lord,' agreed Slovo. 'In fact, such is the favoured solution detailed in a number of letters written by myself to His Holiness; presently secured in places various and intended for delivery only in the event of my unexpected demise.'

'Then may that day be long delayed,' said Cesare solicitously.

'But that eventuality aside,' Slovo continued determinedly, 'I detect the very brightest future for you now that you are the senior of your clan. And since that is so, I would welcome your guidance on my report to His Holiness. In short, my Lord, and to be plain, the bill of fare being before you, would you care to make a selection? I'll call it suicide if you wish . . .'

Cesare sighed with pleasure and sank back into his chair. 'What all too rare a joy it is,' he said, smiling and savouring the moment, 'to meet with such clarity of vision.'

Admiral Slovo woke from sleep – and then wondered whether in fact he had. Instead of being bedded and in his night attire, he was fully dressed and out and about. Quite *where* he was about he couldn't say, but from literature and elsewhere he recognized a labyrinthine cave system when he saw one.

The tunnel walls were high and irregular, disappearing up out of sight, beyond the reach of the diffuse and flickering yellowy-red light whose point of origin he could not detect. Looking round for same, he found he was not alone.

'I want a word with you!' said a rather cruel voice, whereupon a tall, dark and sodden figure stepped out of the shadows to the Admiral's side.

'Good evening, Duke Juan,' said Admiral Slovo politely. 'How are you?'

'Dead – and covered in indescribable things,' replied Duke Juan, gesturing angrily at his gaping wounds, 'as you can well see! Otherwise I'm fine. Start walking.'

He pushed at Slovo's shoulder and they set off together down the gently sloping tunnel.

'How do I come to be here, may I ask?' said the Admiral. 'Am I dead too?'

'Sadly no,' said Duke Juan. 'The explanation is that my anger, being so great, is able to fetch you hence in the hours of the night, when the tide of man's spirit is at low ebb.'

'I see,' said Slovo, clearly fascinated. 'And this word you wanted with me?'

'Humanity's ingenuity has not yet constructed a word of the required ferocity. Therefore I am obliged to resort to whole sentences.'

'Oh dear,' said Admiral Slovo, sounding remarkably unperturbed all the same. 'That sounds rather unpleasant.'

'It does and it will be,' said Juan, showing his fine white teeth through the muck of the Tiber. 'I would prefer to kill you but, that not being permitted, will settle for driving you mad.'

'How so?' asked Slovo. 'Your company is not appreciably more repugnant than in life and this place is marginally tolerable. Purgatory, by definition, has to be so. Incidentally, which route do we take at this junction?'

'It makes no damn difference which path you take,' growled Duke Juan. 'The tunnels are all the same and go on

120

for ever. You never meet anyone, you never see anything different or interesting. That's Purgatory for you!'

'I'm prompted to mend my ways so as to avoid it,' said Admiral Slovo.

'Oh, but avoid it you will not!' crowed Duke Juan. 'I shall keep my fury at boiling point and fetch you here every night to walk with me. Each morning you will wake tormented and drained, and eventually your sanity will depart. Then you may linger on awhile, deprived of all dignity in some inferno of an asylum and breath your last done up in chains with fine ladies laughing at you. Or perhaps you will throw yourself from your villa roof, driven beyond endurance or, fondly imagining you can fly, smash into fragments on the hard pavement below. Either way, I'll have you treading these tunnels in your own right before long.'

Admiral Slovo obligingly looked suitably impressed. 'I tremble at the prospect,' he said and Duke Juan smiled like an evil child. 'However, as a matter of curiosity, might I enquire why your resentment is focused on me? It was not me that caused the needle to be inserted in your ear; not me currently usurping all the honours bestowed on you by a proud father. It is your brother, Cesare, who is now *Gonfaloniere*, out doing the subduing and conquering that you might have done. Isn't picking on me a trifle unjust?'

Duke Juan spat at the tunnel wall. 'Of Cesare I expect nothing! What he did was predictable and in accordance with his character – I just didn't anticipate him moving so soon. But you, Admiral, I'm shocked! Entrusted by St Peter's heir to seek out the killer of his eldest son, and what do you do? Don't think that I haven't been watching. *I'll call it suicide if you wish* – disgraceful! You let Cesare get away with it!'

Slovo having no reply, they trudged on in silence for a while, choosing paths at random. Even in the pre-industrial fifteenth century, Admiral Slovo had never encountered such profound *quiet* and he was beginning to enjoy it. Until he recalled that he had an early appointment with the Pope that morning and he needed his rest.

'Duke Juan,' he said apologetically, 'I hesitate to mention it but there may be something you've overlooked . . .'

❧

'So the rest of the night you slept well?' asked Rabbi Megillah.

'And every night since,' confirmed Admiral Slovo. 'Though my conscience has scant right to it, I continue to sleep the sleep of the just.'

'From what you say,' mused the Rabbi, 'it would appear that His Holiness, did he but know it, has grounds for thanking Cesare. The Borgias need someone to purge their line of stupidity.'

Admiral Slovo agreed. 'I'm almost tempted to feel that Cesare sees it that way,' he said. 'If Duke Juan had been the better man, by Borgian standards, I honestly believe that Cesare would have stood aside.'

'Duke Juan *was* a most unreasonable young man, wasn't he?' said Rabbi Megillah.

'Indeed,' replied Slovo, 'and a good thing too. His unreasonableness was my salvation, if you'll excuse the term. As I pointed out to him, making demands on those of us still in the wicked world; requiring justice in a society he well knew to be far from just; expecting higher standards of behaviour than those he practised whilst alive: it was certainly unreasonable. Worst still, it was sinful – and that could only prolong his Purgatorial perambulations. Ditto the anger required to drag me to him – and his desire for revenge from beyond the grave. He was in a self-perpetuating dilemma. Either he could renounce his quest for what he called "fair play" or face an eternity of wandering, never fully purging himself of sin and thus gaining release.'

'And from your continued nocturnal bliss,' said Rabbi Megillah, 'one must assume that he has taken the path of wisdom.'

'So it seems,' nodded Admiral Slovo. 'And speaking of paths, I also kindly pointed out that he should be following the pathways sloping upwards rather than the contrary. "It might well be easier to go down all the time," I said, "but what's the merit in reaching the wrong destination by however an easy route?" He whined a great deal about that and bewailed the ground he would have to retrace.'

Rabbi Megillah tut-tutted. 'Young people these days,' he said. 'You do everything for them and they're not the least bit grateful.'

'You're right,' said Admiral Slovo unselfconsciously. 'There's no justice, is there?'

❧ The Year 1498

'I offer hospitality, but for which Notre Dame *would become a Mosque.'*

'They think you did well,' said Fra Bartolommeo della Porta, looking over the top of his sketching board. 'I suspect they have high hopes of you.'

Admiral Slovo, irked by standing still so long, was not minded to accept compliments. 'My primary concern was survival,' he said, 'rather than advancing the career of Cesare Borgia – whatever store the Vehme might set by him.'

'I'm not so sure they do,' replied della Porta, continuing with his furious sketching. 'You hear rumours he's just a temporary protégé to be ditched later on. The word is they're more keen on this Florentine chap called Machiavelli, who's going to write a book inspired by Cesare. You never know with them, do you?'

'No indeed,' answered Slovo civilly.

'Keep your head still, damnit! Anyway, whether you intend to please them or not, you always seem to end up doing so. I've found that time and time again. They manoeuvre you into positions where your interests and theirs align. You wanted to live and Borgia wanted to skip the murder rap, see? Left arm up a little higher.'

'I hear they gave you a close shave with Savonarola,' countered Admiral Slovo. 'Is that why you have that facial twitch?'

Della Porta glared at Slovo.

'Presumably,' he said, applying the charcoal stick with extra vigour. 'I didn't have it before I was in the Convent di San Marco when the mob stormed in to get him out. Even now, I'm not sure how I survived.'

'Be thankful you didn't end up like your master. They hanged and burnt him, didn't they?'

'What was left after the torture, yes,' agreed Fra Bartolommeo, with a vigorous twitch. 'I got off with painting a load of nobodies in the Florentine State. "*We shall look for your famous perception of the ideal in forms*," they said. I ask you, Admiral, how do you depict the "ideal" in a collection of politicians and porcine bankers?'

Admiral Slovo intimated, as far as a stock-still man can, that he didn't know.

'Possibly,' he said, 'in the same way that you are foisting grace and poise on to the dry old stick currently posing for you.'

'Oh no!' laughed Fra Bartolommeo. 'You're going down just as you are. I'm going to use you in my great *The Last Judgement* as one of the damned in torment.'[4]

'Many thanks,' said Slovo dryly. 'And for what sin am I to be shown as suffering?'

Fra Bartolommeo looked impishly up at the Admiral.

'Can't you guess?' he said. 'Though it's boys *and* women for you nowadays, I hear ...'

Admiral Slovo looked out of the window over the endless roofs of Rome and, choosing his moment, slid in the *coup de grâce*. 'And what is it you've been told to do now?'

Della Porta grimaced. 'They want me to be a monk – a real one – in Florence. I mean, I've been very good about the celibacy thing so far but now they want me to make it life-long. Apparently I've got to go the whole hog, be genuine and everything. It's not much of a reward for supervising the whole Savonarola episode.'

Slovo smiled consolingly. 'Perhaps your painting will blossom when it is the sole outlet for your energies.'

Apparently della Porta still wasn't impressed. 'Mebbe so,' he conceded insincerely. 'They're very keen for me to go on painting.'

'There you are then,' concluded the Admiral. 'Now, before you go—'

The monk-designate at last got the message. 'Oh, so there's no meal then? So much for Roman hospitality . . .'

'I'm not a Roman,' said Admiral Slovo guilelessly. 'And besides, I should have thought, with the prospect of the monastery stretching before you, you'd be wanting to make the most of your time. I recommend you make your way to that network of alleys we call the *Bordelletto*. Alternatively, if your purse is even more meagre than your costume suggests, there is always the *Ponte Sisto*, near the Hebrew ghetto.'

'I take it that's not a *personal* recommendation,' said della Porta waspishly, grunting with the effort of hefting on his pack.

'You may take it which way you like,' answered Slovo, 'as will the denizens of the Bordelletto. Is there anything else?'

The painter turned back at the door, glad that the Admiral had provided the excuse to do so. 'Yes. They want to know what you thought of *The Laws*,' he said.

So, the Vehme were aware that he had acquired a copy of Pletho's most celebrated work. Presumably they had an eye upon – or even within – his household. It could not be prevented and what cannot be cured must be endured. Slovo therefore ignored the revelation.

He would have liked to say that he had been ... enthused by the Greek philosopher's prescription for Utopia. However, that would not have seemed like him and would have aroused interest.

'Tell them I was convinced,' he said, and Fra Bartolommeo, by the moving of his lips, showed he was committing the reply to memory. It was positive enough to allay doubt.

'Oh, one other thing, Admiral. Do you know of a Turk, a Prince apparently, resident at the Papal Court?'

'There is one,' advised Slovo, 'Alamshah, son of Sultan Bayezid the Second. He's a hostage here whilst His Holiness and Daddy conduct some high-level funny business together.'

'Yes, that must be him. Well, the Vehme say they want you to buy him a drink.'

'Then, with Italy burnt and conquered, we'll re-invade Spain, consolidate there for a few years, convert the Christians and include them in our forces. After that we could invade France in a pincer movement. Two more years would see us at the Channel Ports, and a year after that in London. Peace and the Crescent would reign from the Atlantic to Indian Oceans.'

'I think you've missed out a few countries, Prince,' observed Admiral Slovo politely.

'There'd be some mopping up to do, I grant you.' conceded Prince Alamshah, nodding his bristly black beard. 'The odd island here and there like Malta and Sardinia, a few insignificant outposts like Hibernia or Iceland. They would have to wait a little longer for the blessing of the Prophet's rule. It's their loss.'

Admiral Slovo considered the outline of Armageddon laid before him and wondered which side he would wish to prevail. There was much to admire within the Prince's faith, an equal amount to deplore. Against its attractive simplicity were to be weighed some of its more arbitrary prohibitions.

'A worldwide empire without the solace of wine would be short-lived, I fear,' said Slovo.

The giant, energetic Ottoman had anticipated any number of objections from his latest chaperon but not this one. 'Wine?' he said, somewhat puzzled and brushing an imaginary blemish from his rainbow silks. 'The stuff people drink here so they can fall over and vomit down the front of their clothing? No, I can't see that its lack would topple what I seek to construct. We'll uproot the vines of Europe and put their owners to honest work.'

'I see,' answered Slovo, unselfconsciously taking another sip at his cup and considering whether his might be the last generation able to imbibe so freely. It was a thought to conjure with certainly – the price of wine would rise astronomically and smuggling it would make certain men rich . . .

'All I wish,' continued Alamshah, 'is that my father would get on with whatever it is he's up to with your Pope-person. I want to go home and prepare for the struggle to come.'

'You are a very single-minded young man, if I may say so,' commented the Admiral.

The Prince took that as a compliment. 'Islam has been compared to a sword,' he said. 'It is as simple and shining and useful as that. I make myself just such a sword in Islam's service. What you call mono-mania, we call conviction: that is why we will win.'

'I'll grant you,' Slovo said, 'that the tide seems to be running in your favour. You captured Constantinople shortly before I was born; Otranto was sacked when I was a young man and now you draw near to Vienna. Christendom is riven with dynastic and doctrinal division, whereas you are happily united and eager to press on.'

'Don't stop,' said the Prince, closing his eyes and basking in the flow of good news from the enemy's lips.

'I'm afraid that must suffice,' said Slovo, spoiling the moment.

'Well, Admiral, even so, if I ever appear at the Gates of Rome with an army, it would sadden me to separate you from life – particularly since you would be unsure of Paradise. So why don't you convert and save me from the dilemma?'

Admiral Slovo managed to look suitably grateful. 'That's very kind, but no thank you,' he said. 'I'm happy as I am.'

'Well, there you are then,' said the Prince in a two-plus-two-equals-four voice. 'You are not blind but you do not see. I tell you, Admiral, it is time for a new dispensation to sweep the world. And since there is nothing better for me to do during my period of Papal *hospitality* – I like to dream aloud of it. There's no harm done.'

Admiral Slovo smiled. 'You like to dream, do you?' he asked as innocently as he was able.

'I do,' maintained the Prince stoutly. 'Each of my best notions have been harvested from periods of contemplation.'

'And your dreams of conquest and conversion derive from this, I take it?'

'I cannot remember a time when I did not entertain visions,' said Alamshah, obviously recalling fond memories. 'However, it is thanks to this present holiday that I conceived my most exact plans. Before you are dead, Admiral, should you perchance live a natural span, you might hear a finer sound from the spires of your churches and cathedrals, your Oxford and Sorbonne; something more wholesome than the dead clanging of bells: *Hayya alas salah* – Come to prayer. *Assalatu Khairum minan naum* – Prayer is sweeter than sleep! I really think I can achieve that!'

'I'm almost minded to agree with you,' said Slovo encouragingly, and he signalled for one of his servants to attend him. A boyish maid in a short red doublet and tights swiftly appeared in the garden and bent forward to receive her master's whispered instructions. After departing in haste, she was back within minutes, struggling with two large sealed amphorae.

'Take these as a gift from me, I insist,' said the Admiral to the Prince. 'And think kindly of me when your day comes.'

Alamshah scowled. 'If the contents of those jars are what I suspect,' he said brusquely, 'I should prefer to have the girl.'

'In Christendom, Prince, our servant's virtue is not ours to command,' answered Slovo quickly, almost convincing himself. 'What I *can* offer is a container of the very best vintage that my estate in Capri has ever produced. You will never taste better.'

'I will never taste it at all!' protested Alamshah. 'And tell the girl to begone!'

With a flick of the fingers, Admiral Slovo did so but as instructed, she left the amphorae behind.

'I know of your religious scruples,' said Slovo, 'but believe me, Prince, there is no wine in the world like this for the promotion of reverie and dreams – '

'Admiral,' interrupted Alamshah wearily, 'you are entirely aware of the Qur'anic prohibition and . . .'

'Perhaps, Prince, since your scheming is all to Islam's advantage, the rule need not be strictly applied in your case – if all you seek is to enhance your speculative faculties. Such was my reasoning at least . . .' Alamshah half smiled, as if to say he appreciated the Admiral's tender concern. 'Besides,' the Admiral continued, 'not all of your brethren have been so consistent. Al-Motamid, poet and last Moorish King of Seville, went so far as to mock in his verse all those who forsook wine for water. I further call to mind the great poet Principe Marwan – also a Moor – who found sunshine in the fruit of the vine.'

'I am familiar with the *Diwan of Principe*,' said Prince Alamshah, the merest fraction, it must be said, less convinced and adamant than before. 'He was a heretic, Admiral.'

'It's true,' said Admiral Slovo sadly, 'that your Holy Book appears to exhort forbearance from the fruit of the vine. With that in mind, I arranged that the second of the two amphorae contain nothing but the finest Roman beer. You will permit, I trust, that that at least is quite innocent of any contact with the forbidden grape.'

'Mere sophistry, Admiral,' said Alamshah. 'Our religion denies us all reason-depriving intoxication, and reserves such pleasures for Paradise alone.'

'All that may be so, Prince,' said Slovo. 'I had only your interests at heart in making the proposal. It just occurred to me, up to now you've only dreamed of entering Paris as a conqueror. But after consuming just a part of these two jars, you'll think you're actually *there*!'

A week later, Admiral Slovo received a discreet note at home. Purely in the interests of plotting Islam's ultimate triumph, Prince Alamshah wrote, did the Admiral have any more jars of *haram*?

'Like a fish!' said the scholar from the Morean Platonic Institute. 'His father Sultan Bayezid appointed him governor of Manisa, which as you doubtless know is a very important slice of western Turkey, but the responsibility didn't reform him. His mother, who is worse than a she-bear with ten headaches, attends him constantly and is executing people all over the place – but he still manages to find drink. He'll be dead within two years.[5]

131

'Which is presumably why the Vehme arrange his smuggled supplies of wine,' commented Slovo.

'Exactly,' agreed the spindly Greek. 'He had to go, preferably by his own shaking hand, if the verses were to be thwarted.'

The Admiral accepted the scroll handed him.

'Oh, indeed yes,' said the scholar, confirming Slovo's enquiring glance. 'They're from *The Book* – transcribed, of course. Your star rides high, you're very honoured.'

Curiously unmoved, Slovo studied the two scrawled and crabbed quatrains.

> *The Troubles of Israel*
> *will come to Po, Tagus,*
> *Tiber, Thames*
> *and Tuscany.*
>
> *The cruel sect of the Moslems will come,*
> *hiding weapons under their robes.*
> *Their leader will take Florence and burn it twice,*
> *sending ahead clever men without laws.*

'And this was going to be him?' asked Slovo, handing back the verses.

'It was thought so. With his energy and burning belief he would have brought the world under one faith.'

'Which didn't suit?'

'It wasn't *our* faith, Admiral. We had you find his Achilles' heel and then prise him open. The Arch-Sultan Alamshah will never be now: you've done well again. In fact, we reckon that you are ready for bigger things. Accordingly, the Pope thinks likewise.

*

132

'Childhood's end,' said the Welsh Vehmist. He stood at the edge of the summerhouse, his attention caught, his comment prompted by the noisy games of the Slovo infants down in the villa below. 'Once shown a portion of *The Book*, there is no way back. It marked a new stage in your career. You were ours in a new and deeper way.'

'To where could I have retraced my steps?' asked the Admiral. 'The only way seemed onwards.'

The Vehmist nodded at such sagacity. 'It was as well the two judgements concurred,' he said, his back to Slovo. 'When our faith in one of the *illuminati* dies, it all becomes very messy.'

'I can imagine,' answered Admiral Slovo. 'Not only he or she, but everyone they might have confided in – and everyone that *they* might have confided in . . .'

'. . . has to go,' completed the Vehmist, 'yes. We hate such large-scale and noticeable necessities. Fortunately, it's rare indeed. The last I know of nigh wiped out a town. We had to blame the plague.'

'And doubtless the Jews or lepers who "caused" it.'

The Welshman chuckled. 'Yes,' he said, 'that one always finds a ready audience, especially in Germania. Make up some nonsense about compounds of pus and spider-juice, stuck to church pews with baby-fat, and it goes down a storm. Credulity's a great ally.'

The Admiral could hardly disagree, but neither could he be expected to approve. 'It is a brave or foolhardy man,' he said, with an edge to his voice, 'that meddles with popular belief.'

The Vehmist swivelled on his heels to address Slovo, a smirk adorning his pale face. 'Precisely!' he said. 'That's why we chose you to work our will on a myth.'

✥ The Year 1499

'GREAT EXPECTATIONS: I save a dynasty, dabble in racial politics and have my portrait painted.'

> *'... the king hath aged so much during the past two weeks that he seems to be twenty years older.'*
>
> Report of Bishop de Avala, Spanish Ambassador to Scotland, on the situation in England, 1499

'Wotcha, stony-face! What's the problem?'

Admiral Slovo turned his chilly gaze to see a crop-headed docker.

'Cheer up mate, it might never 'appen,' said another.

For Slovo 'it' had already happened. He had been ordered forth from his sunshine, books and comforts, out into the wild North and the company of barbarians with bad teeth and manners. 'It' was personified by the human slab who had mocked him, a person now the merest impulse away from stiletto-time.

'Slovo, ho!' shouted a mildly more cultivated voice, breaking the spell.

The Admiral swivelled round to find himself hailed from the far end of the quay by a small group of horsemen. The one thing he *really* hated was having his name bellowed out in public – a deplorable breach of security, enough to set nerve endings ablaze. It was a bad end to a bad trip.

Their obvious leader, a red-faced military type, trotted up to within polite talking distance, only now taking the trouble to wipe some odd white-ish foam from his spade-beard.

'Slovo?' he barked again. 'The Roman? Is that you?' His Latin was as bad as his manners.

'I am he,' said the Admiral quietly.

'Sorry we're late: been waiting long?'

'A matter of a few hours, three or four at the most. There has been opportunity to study Pevensey's Roman *Castilia* and its surrounding hovels. The rain was almost refreshing.'

The military man nodded absently. 'Still, you had your baggage to sit on, eh?' He pointed to Slovo's sea-chest. 'And good old England to look at. Only we got delayed on the road, see.'

'The English beer, it is so good and irresistible,' offered the second prominent horseman – as clearly an alien as the others were obviously English. 'We had to stop and indulge.'

The old soldier gave his plump companion a blackish look. 'Yes, well ... anyway,' he said, 'this is de Peubla, Spanish Ambassador sort of chap; as to me, I'm Daubeny – Giles – Baron. The rest are your escort. Are you fit?'

'Reasonably so,' answered Slovo. 'Why do you ask?'

'I mean are you ready to go? We're paying you by the hour I understand.'

'Few things would give me greater pleasure than departure from here, my Lord.'

'Well, you're easily pleased then,' said Daubeny. 'We've brought a horse, so jump up and say farewell to Pevensey Port.'

Admiral Slovo mounted up, earning his first plus points in the Englishmen's eyes by his ease of doing so. He looked round at the rain-damp little houses, the ruinous castle, and dull, copper sea, suppressing a shudder as he did so. 'Farewell, this side of the grave, please God,' he muttered.

But from his new prominence on the war-horse, Slovo caught sight of the surrounding and sombre marshy levels, and suddenly English domestic architecture possessed new-found attractions.

'What of my sea-chest?' he asked briskly for fear his opinion of the view be sought.

'Oh, it'll be sent on I expect,' said Daubeny airily. 'The dock artificers will deal with the matter.'

Slovo looked dubiously at the swarming dock workers and in a valuable Stoic spiritual exercise forced himself to bid farewell to his possessions.

'Best hoof forward then, Roman,' said Daubeny, leaning close. 'There's no time to lose.'

'No, indeed,' confirmed the Spanish Ambassador, shaking his head sadly. 'King Henry can't afford to mislay another army.'

'To the little mayde that danceth ... £12/0s/0d'

> From the personal account books of
> King Henry VII of England

'A whole bloody army, boy,' said the King to Slovo. 'Vanished off the face of the Earth, so it did! By my leg of St George, it can't go on!'

The Admiral had heard of this most prized of the King's possessions and treated the oath with appropriate gravity.

'Ahem!' coughed De Peubla. 'Your Majesty . . .'

King Henry VII and Admiral Slovo returned their attention to the little tot who had been dancing before them. Now disregarded by dint of their serious talk, she had stopped and was tottering on the precipice of tears. Henry, though slight of build, proved he could shift when he wanted and was instantly up and away across the table like a nobleman offered a crown.

'There, there,' he hissed, crouching down to the little girl. 'Never you mind the silly big-people and their problems. There's nice dancing it was, wasn't it lads?'

A ragged chorus of *oh yes* and *absolutely* sprang from the assembled aristocracy and courtiers.

'Off you go to your mumsy,' suggested the King of England, 'whilst we are so daft and preoccupied. And here's a shiny farthing for you.'

The three-year-old, now on the up-stroke of her emotional see-saw, took the gift with a smile and retreated from the room, face front as she had been taught.

'It's funny,' said Henry to Slovo as he returned to his seat by the slower but more dignified route. 'I don't mind the odd execution, not if it's strictly necessary, it's hurting people's feelings I don't like.'

'Quite so,' agreed the Admiral politely, recognizing that Kings must be allowed their eccentricities.

'It's in my pockets my feelings are, you see,' Henry went on. 'Not the best place for them to be, the Church would say – but rather there than in my pride or lustful impulses like some I know, that's what I say.'

'Indeed,' answered Slovo.

'And it's in my pocket I'm being hurt, boy!' said Henry, with real feeling. 'Taxes, dues, levies, they're all being lost – along with the taxmen in some cases.'

'And now an army,' offered the Admiral.

'Ah yes. *Ruinous* expense: prepaid mercenaries, German *landsknechtes*, Venetian *stradiots* and English bowmen, all with my – their – advance wages in their nasty little purses. Horses, cannons, silk banners, all gone! Disgraceful, I tell you it is!'

Admiral Slovo covertly studied Henry's jewel-encrusted

doublet and reflected that times were not perhaps as bad as all that. Most impressively, the King didn't miss a thing.

'Oh yes,' he said, patting the brooches and emblems covering his chest, 'there's still enough for the occasional treat. I risked my head for this country and if I should like a bit of shine and sparkle about my person, why shouldn't I indulge myself? I deserve it!'

Slovo's taste in princely attire ran more to the plain black of the fighting Borgias but he had long ago embraced the endless variety of mankind. He smiled and nodded tolerantly.

Meanwhile, his shot-across-the-bows delivered, Henry lapsed back into his previous lilt. 'I'm an easy-going sort of King,' he said, leaning back and surveying the window-view of the Tower through narrowed eyes, 'just what this land needs. There's been too much Civil War. A little is good for getting rid of bad blood but too much breeds poverty and other such nastiness. The English need a spot of peace and prosperity and I'm the boyo to give it 'em. It's true I'm a Celt but I'm a *desiccated* Celt and that's an important difference. All the nonsense has been wrung out of me by life. That means I can pass for English – at a distance – and makes me tolerable to them: for they're a dry bunch of bastards, Admiral, I tell you that in confidence.'

'Dry' was not the term that would have surged into Slovo's mind to describe the jolly-brutal, cudgel-wielding race he'd encountered en route from Pevensey Port to the Tower of London. From his fastidious perspective, the whole culture needed at least another five hundred years of development and suffering before polite judgement could be passed.

'Mind you,' Henry pressed on, 'for bowmen and pragmatic traders, you couldn't want for better – and there's precious little tax to be had out of a Kingdom of poets. No, England's what I always wanted and it's what I got.'

'The ancient prophecies, Your Majesty,' mused de Peubla from beside them. 'It was all the preordained will of God.'

Henry grunted dismissively. 'Didn't seem that way when the clothyard was flying down at Bosworth, boy,' he said grimly, 'and that big bastard Richard was hacking his way ever closer. "*The Armes Prydain*" sounded pretty damn thin then, I can tell you – not many!'

'A versified Celtic vision, Admiral,' explained de Peubla helpfully, 'predicting the union of the scattered Celtic peoples to defeat their Saxon enemy.'

'"*The warriors will scatter the foreigners as far as Durham...*"' recited Henry. '"*For the English there will be no returning ... The Welsh will arise in a mighty fellowship ... The English race will be called warriors no more ...*" and so on and on. A load of old bardic guff, if you ask me. It's the same as all the King Arthur stuff ...'

'Ah yes,' interrupted Admiral Slovo – who had only a passing, say, one-night-stand, relationship with modern literature, 'your lost King and his Holy groin ...'

'Er ... yes, in a manner of speaking,' confirmed Henry, only momentarily disconcerted. 'Well, I'll *use* all this, you see; like I named my first born Arthur just to get the Cymru vote, but don't expect me to believe in it, man – that or the "*Prydain*". It's for footsoldiers only, like all this national-consciousness business.'

Slovo signalled his agreement. This was getting pleasantly cynical.

'I mean, you'll hear it recited five times a day,' Henry went on, 'from the tribe of Cymru and Cornish nobles who have somehow ensconced themselves at court in my victorious wake. And all because their mother's cousin's friend lifted a blade on my behalf – or would have done if it hadn't been so rainy that day. Ah! I've not much time for them, Admiral; they rub me up the wrong way, so they do. Besides,

I know the English are mostly either ambitious or a bit slow, but if these idiots taunt them too much they'll wake up! There's six times as many of them as there are of us, even if every man-jack Celt combined – and who ever heard of that? We'd all get our throats slit that day and no mistake. No, as to these boasting Welsh boyos, I'll disabuse them of their great expectations before too long, you wait and see.'

Admiral Slovo smiled in concurrence.

King Henry returned the favour with an appraising glance. 'Come with me,' he said eventually, as if some inner debate had been resolved. 'I'll show you what this is *really* all about.'

Admiral Slovo allowed himself to be guided around the table and to the nearby window.

'There!' said Henry triumphantly, indicating the courtyard bustle below. 'The Tower of London! It has a ring to it, don't you think? It *means* something in the counsels of the mighty. Now, that could not be said of, for instance, the "Tower of Llandaff" or the "Tower of Bangor", could it?'

'Perhaps not,' replied Slovo meaninglessly, whilst actually occupying his mind with thoughts of his wife and where she might have fled.

'It's like a bull's-eye, Admiral,' Henry explained. 'The very precious centre of a target that any man might care to hit. This is where it starts from – power and control. Now, in the ordinary course of events one would deal with outer rings of the dartboard as and when convenient. But what do I find? I find that someone or something is extending these zones by stealing parts of my sovereign realm and pushing back in towards the very centre, look you. That is why I've called you from your Roman employ – and paid His Holiness a pretty penny for the privilege too, I might add.'

'I shall not see a coin of it, I assure you, Your Majesty,' said Slovo, fearful of association with the Borgia Pope's rapacious ways.

'No doubt, more fool you,' replied Henry, closely supervising the off-loading of a haycart for signs of wasteful practices. 'Still, you'd think I'd get a discount, loyal son of the Church and all that.'

'I couldn't say, Your Highness,' said Admiral Slovo, miles away. 'I have no knowledge of the world of commerce.'

Henry looked on the Admiral as he would one afflicted. 'Oh, I *am* sorry to hear that,' he said. Then, he swiftly retreated from compassion and resumed business as normal. 'Just sort it out, will you, Admiral,' he said briskly. 'Leave tomorrow and get things back to normal. What I have I hold, that's the name of the game, and what I hold I intend to pass on – intact – to my two fine sons.'

Slovo nodded, 'They are handsome-looking youths.'

'What d'you mean?' snapped Henry, suddenly all sharp-edged suspicion. 'How would you know? Arthur, Prince of Wales, is at his court in the Marches and young Henry is with him.'

'Then who,' said Slovo calmly, 'are the two golden youths below who have been smiling up at us all this while? They surely know you, and such familiarity I attributed only to Princes . . .'

In fact, their smiles seemed more akin to triumphant smirks to Slovo's mind but this had only reinforced his guess as to their princely origins.

Henry went to look in the direction indicated but corrected himself just in time. His bejewelled hand flew up to cover horror-struck eyes. 'Come away from the window, Admiral,' he said in an anguished voice. 'And leave this very night; not tomorrow, do you hear? This very night! And just get things back to bloody normal, will you boy? Please?'

*

'You weren't to know,' said Daubeny. 'His Majesty doesn't encourage discussion of the subject.'

'Although, of course,' said de Peubla delicately, 'he has nothing to answer for in respect of . . . that matter.'

Slovo's sight of the two 'Princes', where none should have been, had caused a disproportionate fuss. There was the matter, he gathered, of previous young claimants to the throne meeting untimely ends – the merest commonplace of court life in his own native land. Here, though, it was a touchy subject and the parade ground for troubled consciences. Blame had been successfully attributed to some dead King and it was evidently bad form to revive the issue. Slovo had swiftly taken the hint and pleaded poor eyesight, the deceptive evening sun and so on. Nobody believed him but the gesture was regally appreciated.

'Well, this is where we broke 'em,' said Daubeny. 'What more do you want to know?'

'I've no idea,' replied Admiral Slovo with brutal honesty. 'I'm awaiting inspiration.'

'Could be a long wait then, mon-sewer Ite-eye,' said the baron resignedly and reached into his saddle bag for his ever-faithful flask of fire-water.

Stretching to his full height in the stirrups, Slovo surveyed the battlefield. Since it was, for the most part, the Celtic peoples that were seceding willy-nilly through King Henry's fingers, it had seemed sensible to visit the scene of their most recent trial of strength. Here, a mere two years before, Henry had methodically massacred an insurgent Cornish army. Today however, Blackheath, Kent, appeared to have nothing further to teach the curious other than, by dint of the burial-pit mound, the old perennial that rebellion is folly.

'It got a bit tasty down there by the bridge,' pointed Daubeny with a shaky gauntlet. 'A fair few of my lads got turned into pincushions. Mind you, after that, as I recall, it was all pretty straightforward.'

'They had no cavalry, no cannon, no armour,' said de Peubla in a knowing voice. 'It was like harvesting wheat so I am told.'

This struck Admiral Slovo as frightfully unnecessary. In the Italy of his youth, before the grim incursion of the French, tens of thousands of well-paid mercenaries could strive in battle all day long at the cost of a mere handful of deaths per side. The dispute was still settled but with so much less waste.

'And it is the same "Cornshire" that most frequently departs from King Henry's realm, is it not?' he asked.

De Peubla nodded. 'Along with Powys, Elmet, Cumbria and other such long-gone entities.'

'And ones we'd never even heard of,' laughed Daubeny. 'The army we lost was in Norfolk – or somewhere called *logres* as it briefly became. Not a man jack has come out yet and don't suppose any will: all been eaten by now I shouldn't wonder!'

'I have never read of the Celts as displaying cannibalistic traits,' said de Peubla, clearly racking extensive mental files. 'There was once the distinctive cult of the severed head, it is true but—'

'Oh shut up, you Iberian ponce!' barked Daubeny, and de Peubla obediently did so.

'It's like this,' said the Baron to Slovo, his patience likewise strained to the limit. 'Bits and bobs of the place keep drifting in and out of bloody history. You can never be sure when you send out the taxman or a travelling-assize, they won't come up against a "Free Kernow" or resurgent "Elmet". Then they either disappear, never to emerge, or, the natives being more confident than they've any right to be, they get driven off with a barbed yard of arrow in their backside.' He paused to take another reviving swig. '*Then*, shortly after, even a few hours in some cases, everything's back to normal and the nice, peaceful inhabitants don't understand what the hell you're on about when you question them – hot pokers or no. So, you can't take reprisals against innocent people (well, you can – but His Majesty forbids it), else you'd have a real rebellion and for no good reason either.'

'How interesting,' judged Slovo, musing that in their rough equal division of initial territorial advantage, all battlefields looked much the same.

'Indeed so,' agreed de Peubla, bobbing up and down on his pack-horse with the intellectual excitement of it all. 'If it wasn't for the urgent problem it presents, and the needs for such secrecy as can be mustered, oh how I wish I could investigate these glimpses of other worlds!'

For the first and last time, Admiral Slovo and Daubeny saw eye to eye and their glacial glances froze de Peubla to silence. His enthusiasms, his bourgeois origin, Slovo could forgive; his doctorates in Civil and Common Law commanded respect (or caution). Even the irregularity of his Spanish salary and consequent impoverishment might have been points to solicit sympathy. It was common knowledge that de Peubla was obliged to lodge in a London inn of low repute and that the timing of his visits to Court were prompted by a simple desire to eat.

All this was enough to make even dry-hearted King Henry like the little fellow – in fact their friendship had grown to be quite genuine by regal standards. But not so Admiral Slovo and Daubeny. To the Baron, he was a foreigner: enough said. To the Admiral, well, his Stoic ethics could not accept the man's conversion to Christianity. If someone was granted the surpassing gift of Judaic birth, he believed they should accept that life would be painful and stick to their guns. Humanistic thought, quite the rage in certain circles at that time (and ever since), did not play a large part in Admiral Slovo's life.

'Well, that's it,' said Daubeny, already bored. 'Not much to see, is there? All the deaders and body-bits were gathered up and the local proles doubtless gleaned all else away. Learn anything?'

'No,' said Slovo without inflection.

'Better if you'd seen the battle,' added the Baron glumly.

'Unhappily, I was otherwise engaged,' the Admiral replied, his conversation in free fall as he pondered. 'The Duke of Gandia, Juan Borgia, was murdered that day.'

'Not Cesare's brother?' whispered de Peubla, as though the Beast of the Romagna himself might be eavesdropping.

'The same; their joint father, His Holiness, Pope Alexander, requested that I investigate the murder and so . . .'

'Yes, yes, yes,' interrupted Daubeny, spluttering his way out of a long pull at his flask, 'I fully understand why you couldn't grace my battle with your presence. And I do wish you'd keep that "m" word to a minimum – particularly in the context of the Princes?'

'Your forgiveness,' asked Slovo insincerely.

'Not that we've anything to hide, mind,' added Daubeny, now more than a little tipsy. 'It's just that we don't want the evil eye put on our own two jewels in the crown.'

'Arthur and Henry, oh yes,' smiled de Peubla, moving charitably in to rescue the Baron from his self-made quicksand. Daubeny remained appropriately quiet and still as it was done. 'Two fine prospects for the English nation to gaze upon and wish long life to. Even the most fleeting thought of harm to them is painful.'

'Absolutely,' said Slovo, apparently with great seriousness.

'Arthur's the one they make all the fuss about,' bellowed Daubeny. 'Prince of Wales and Lord of the Marches. Got his own little Court he has and a name calculated to get the

British all expectant. If you were to ask *me*, well, there's more chance of finding a book in his hand than a sword – or anything else interesting and rounded.'

'A reference to horse-flesh, doubtless,' commented de Peubla primly.

'Whatever!' laughed the Baron. 'Tall and serious, that's what he is. Very interested in chivalry – ha! Give me Prince Henry any day: a real little Englishman: rosy-cheeked, stocky little chap and already very sound on the Celts. Hates anything to do with poetry and prophecy!'

Daubeny sadly observed his flask was now empty and, with the uncanny facility Admiral Slovo had already noted in the rough-as-coal-bunkers nobility of this land, sobriety instantly returned when he next spoke.

'Still, it's all in God's hands. We shall see what we shall see.'

It was seeing what they saw as they turned the horses for home, the new and marvellously changed prospect of London now spread out, that halted them in their tracks.

'Sod this,' said Daubeny quite calmly. 'I'm not going down there. Where's London?'

De Peubla did not answer, being too busy fixing the scene in his mind as a solace for the disappointed old age he fully expected.

'London is still there,' answered Slovo, waving his black glove towards the transmogrified metropolis below. 'But no longer, I suspect, known by that name. What would you hazard, Ambassador?'

De Peubla rocked his head from side to side in a charmingly hybrid Hebrew/Iberian gesture. 'I do not speak any of the British tongues, Admiral,' he replied. '*Londres* perhaps? *Londinium* possibly?'

Slovo noted that Sir Giles Daubeny was dumbfounded, but then the poor man *had* just lost his Capital City. He turned to smile on him. 'Some foreign name like that, I expect,' he agreed with de Peubla.

'It may not have lasted long,' said de Peubla as they trotted along slowly, 'but I am most glad to have seen it.'

'Speak for yourself, Hispaniol!' growled Daubeny. 'I like my severed heads in their proper places – on battlefields or adorning spikes at the King's order; not all over a City Wall dangling on chains with bells on 'em! What sort of a welcome do you call that?'

'An instructive one?' suggested Admiral Slovo, gamely entering into the spirit of things.

'It's that all right,' replied Daubeny with a bitter laugh. 'Likewise all the idols and symbols – all those curls and swirls – not a blasted straight line or plain picture to be seen: fair made me nauseous it did! Oh yes, it spoke pretty clear to me: *Saxons not welcome!* Praise God that it faded!'

'Just so,' agreed Slavo (though actually his indifference knew no bounds). 'And none that we questioned were aware of their brief transformation. One can only surmise therefore that some twist in the skeins of fate permitted us a glance of what might have been . . .'

'Hmmph!' snapped the Baron.

'Or what might *be*,' continued the Admiral implacably.

'Enough!' said Daubeny, chopping the air with his metal-clad gauntlet. 'It is *not* going to be. You heard His Majesty's words – *sort things out* – so get sorting. That's what we're meant to be about, isn't it? Why else would I allow you to drag me down to this god-forsaken tail-end of nowhere?'

'Why indeed?' answered Slovo politely. 'Cornshire is, I agree, impermissibly barren and stark. Why, I wonder, do people persist in living amidst such extremes of Nature?'

'Habit?' postulated de Peubla, endeavouring to be charitable.

'Some such strong force,' agreed Admiral Slovo. 'And I do apologize to you both for so exposing you to the very outer fringes of the World. It is merely that I somehow sense that we are tracking the mischievous shift-phenomenon to its lair.'

'Good,' sighed Daubeny. 'So let's kill it and go!'

'Would it were so simple,' murmured Slovo, schooled in a more ancient culture and thus aware that murder was but the beginnings of politics.

The little party with its most curious of missions should have been acting in all urgency. Each day brought a fresh dispatch from King Henry, urging them on by news of further outrages. The North had been raided and there had even been an insolent proclamation received from 'Free Surrey' (*Libertas Suth-rege*, if you please!), and His Majesty had estates there. Henry's Celtic powers of fancy and invention were being fast exhausted by the explanations he was having to concoct. Dark hints were dropped in his letters about Slovo's fee and the current state of the Royal coffers.

However, the Admiral would not be rushed. 'We do not have enough time to hurry,' he grandly explained in a reply to the King – thus causing a Regal headache and a spoilt banquet. To Henry's considerable but unspoken distress, Slovo was methodically tracing the zig-zag of his thoughts across the shifting map of barbarian England: there had been musings in St Albans, a glimpse of devastation where Winchester should be and '*Dumnonian*' resurgence at the Gates of Cirencester. Each time he and his group, plus escort of soldiery, arrived just that instant too late to experience for themselves immersion in the 'shift'. It could not however escape a mind so subtle as Slovo's that each encounter was closer and closer, and that their steps were drawn inexorably west. Only too able to empathize with spiders, he recognized a web when he saw one.

The Celtic land of Cornwall had seemed a good place, just sufficiently off-centre, from which to pluck the cobweb and see what stirred forth to seize its prey. In purely aesthetic terms, though, Admiral Slovo had to agree with his comrades: he had had better ideas.

'Take that island, for instance,' said Daubeny, pointing at St Michael's Mount across the bay. 'What good is it? Soil you couldn't grow weeds in and fortifications fifty years out of date – even in Scotland!' (This last with particular venom.) 'And as for . . . what is it we passed through?'

'Ludgvan,' prompted de Peubla, wary of the Baron's brandy-borne torrents of temper.

'And as for the . . . village, if one may so dignify it, of that name,' Daubeny spluttered on, 'I've pulled down better houses than those. No wonder the poor wretches invaded England in '97 – anything to see a bit of decent countryside. And another thing—'

The sea breeze across the bay played with the Admiral's fashionable basin-cut hair as he tuned out the rant-frequency to hear more subtle whispers – from both within and without.

On the presently submerged causeway to the Mount, the two young Princes were clearly visible, more solid, though unearthly still, than ever before. At that distance even Slovo's sea-trained eyes could not be sure but he nevertheless felt certain that they were smiling at him – as before. The water broke over their feet in ways it should not, the wind did not disturb their golden locks. Mere additions to the scene for Admiral Slovo's benefit, they looked at him, a distant matchstick figure, and he likewise looked at them.

'Do you see something, Admiral?' asked de Peubla, who under his assumed clumsiness was as watchful as a cat.

'Nothing that has not been my constant companion on this

journey, Ambassador,' came the unhelpful reply. But, in fact, sudden enlightenment dawned like a storm-laden day over Slovo, a revelation sufficiently dark to make him smile.

When he raised his eyes again, the fort on St Michael's Mount was no longer obsolete or quaint. Storey upon storey, crammed with cannon, rose into the sky above a tessellation of the very latest Dutch-Italian style fieldworks.

Even Daubeny could see that this was no longer a place to be laughed at, its black and white flag of St Piran not a subject for mockery. Only the suspected smiles adorning the Princes on the drowned causeway remained as before, though perhaps a little broader now, to Slovo's favoured eyes.

Enquiring at the church in Ludgvan, at the Admiral's request, they were welcomed to 'Free Kernow' in most uncertain English by a priest called Borlase. When the foreigners' business was confidently demanded, Admiral Slovo casually killed him at the presbytery door with a stiletto.

'I needed to see if my theory was correct,' protested the Admiral to his shocked companions later.

'They ask me to investigate something,' said Admiral Slovo, 'to "sort it out", and then cavil at my methods!'

'I agree,' sympathized his fellow countryman. 'You never know where you are with the English. Mostly they're as rough as a Turk's lust and then suddenly they've gone all mushy on you.'

'*Pre*cisely,' said Slovo, warming to this young man and more glad than he could, of course, decently show, to run into such a compatriot. 'And their sense of humour . . .!'

'Nothing but toilets,' nodded the young man. 'Yes, I've run into that – and even that would amuse them – *run*, do you see?'

150

Admiral Slovo had come to Westminster Abbey with the intention of hearing mass and offering up a prayer for his speedy delivery home. At the door, however, his eye had been caught by a lithe figure with a sketch-book and charcoal-stick, whose evident grace and taste in dress proclaimed him a non-native. As it turned out he was a Florentine, but the Admiral could forgive him that for the sake of civilized conversation – and a possible pick-up.

'Your sketch shows no small talent,' said Slovo, 'Master . . .?'

'Torrigiano – Pietro Torrigiano. And so it should after all my schooling.'

Admiral Slovo studied the artist from head to foot but received no satisfactory answers to the silent questions he posed. 'Your style betokens tuition,' he agreed, 'but the residual stigmata of humble origin suggest insufficient funds for such luxuries.'

Torrigiano smiled wryly. 'What I do not owe to God, I owe to the Medicis,' he conceded, and at the second half of his tribute spat heartily on to a proximate headstone. A passing chantry-priest looked blackly at them but thought better of any other protest. Foreigners were best left to their own damnation.

'Duke Lorenzo, dubbed "The Magnificent",' continued Torrigiano as he sketched furiously, 'rescued me from my peasant destiny and placed me in his sculpture school. We were taught by Bertoldo, you know, and he was taught by Donatello!'

'Most impressive,' commented Slovo (who was actually self-trained to indifference in all matters artistic).

'It was also Lorenzo who expelled me from both school and Florence and into my present penurious exile. I altered another pupil's face; we couldn't both remain, so Lorenzo made a decision as to who showed most potential and . . .'[6]

'That is the way of Princes,' said Slovo, trying and failing to offer consolation. 'Difficult choices.'

'Difficult to live with possibly,' answered Torrigiano with a mite less respect and tact than he should have shown to an elder and better; the very cockiness that would ensure his death, many years on, in the prisons of the Inquisition in Spain. 'Mind you, I have made a life of sorts here in this land. The odd commission does arise.'

'None odder than this, I suspect,' said Admiral Slovo. 'Draw me now against the background of the Abbey – or whatever it may be called at present. Use all speed whilst the effect lasts.'

Slovo had been starting to lose interest in his young find and thus looking about, thinking of Kings and Crowns, discovered that the world had changed whilst they talked.

Torrigiano gaped in awe, even as his hand tore madly across the new canvas. 'Mother of Sorrows!' he gasped. 'Where are we?'

'London,' replied Admiral Slovo, considerately remaining as still as he could, 'or some substitute for it. Do not slacken your efforts, Artist, we may not be here long.'

Torrigiano shook his head sadly. 'This is for a life-time study,' he said, 'not a tantalizing browse. Is it still a church?'

Unable to turn and observe properly, Slovo shrugged. 'Possibly; though not, it seems, a branch of the Christian faith I've yet encountered.'

'The gargoyles,' enthused Torrigiano, 'the domes; such a torrent of flowing colour. I could worship here.'

'But who?' smiled Slovo at his chilly best. 'That is the question. Now, be sure and feature my best side ...'

'It's disgusting,' said King Henry. 'Take it away!'

Torrigiano's face fell at this savage review of his efforts.

152

'His Majesty is not alluding to the verisimilitude of your depiction,' said Admiral Slovo to him. 'I can vouch for that. It is the effect he finds distressing.'

'All that bloody ivy and carving,' confirmed Henry. 'It makes me heave, so it does. Who would have fashioned Westminster Abbey like that?'

'No one of, or to, your tastes, that seems certain,' said de Peubla in a manner intended to be soothing. He got a regal glare for his pains.

'I can see that,' said the King. 'It is not the sort of place in which Kings of England are crowned.'

'Though maybe Kings of another sort,' said Daubeny, looking bemusedly at the picture held by Torrigiano.[7] The eye-borne volley of royal ill-will was worse even than that just received by de Peubla.

'Bit of a cheek, isn't it?' the Baron blundered on, unaware of his present disfavour. 'I mean, kidnapping the centre of the realm like that. It'll be the Tower next!'

As King Henry's eyes widened and he was about to say something he would regret, Admiral Slovo stepped into the breach.

'That is entirely the point,' he said, with all the brusqueness that etiquette would permit. 'The process is becoming more frequent, and of wider reach. It was for the proving of this that I conducted my Cornshire experiment about which so much unpleasant fuss has been made . . .'

'He was a *priest*, boyo,' muttered Henry darkly. 'You just can't do that here.'

Slovo waved the protest aside. 'Not only was the Borlase person dead in his "free Kernow",' he went on, speaking slowly, anxious that these mere shallows of trouble be properly traversed prior to the really treacherous deeps in store, 'but on our "return", he was also found to be similarly deceased – mysteriously struck down in this, our own, *real* world.'

'So?' snapped Henry, thinking of the gold he'd had to throw at the Lords Spiritual to buy their grumpy peace over that little matter.

'*So*,' answered Slovo, 'this was a progression. The "real" and the "projected" worlds were becoming interactive. One might even suspect they were in the process of merging. Up to now, Your Majesty, you may have mislaid the odd taxman—'

'Or army,' added Daubeny.

'But,' continued Slovo, 'they were lost into fleeting visions, leaving behind no lasting effect. What my much maligned experiment showed was that the two possible worlds were coming together and joining as one. These "alternatives" are maturing into reality. In short, one version will ultimately prevail.'

'And if people begin to retain memories from the period of crossover,' said de Peubla, entirely enthused as he caught on and raced ahead, 'then the spirit of independence and rebellion could blossom with a profuse abundance such as never seen before!'

'It'd make the Wars of the Roses look like a wench's kiss,' said Daubeny, smiling broadly.

'Yes, yes, yes!' roared Henry. 'All this I understand – dammit! Now when are you going to tell what there is to *do*!'

Suddenly all the bluster evaporated and the King looked on Admiral Slovo with plaintive eyes. 'I want *my* version of history to win,' he added sadly.

'It can still do so,' replied Admiral Slovo confidently, signalling that Torrigiano should place his picture strategically in the King's view. 'But I warn you, stern measures will be required.'

Henry visibly brightened. 'Oh well,' he said, 'I'm no stranger to *them*. Needs must and all that. Tell me more.'

Admiral Slovo looked at the two Princes standing, invisibly to all bar him, behind King Henry's throne. They beamed back at him angelically.

'Then,' he advised, seeking to minimize his own part in the reckoning to come, 'might I respectfully refer you to two passages from Holy Scripture: namely *Genesis* 22 and *Luke* 10, 37.'

Henry looked puzzled but, in his freshly optimistic mood, was willing to go along with the game. 'Come on then, Wolsey,' he called to a loitering cleric, 'here's your chance to shine, boy.'

The priest screwed up his face, mentally travelling back to the days when he had learnt his trade. 'The first,' he said eventually, much relieved to find the requisite mental cupboards stocked, 'is the story of Abraham and the abortive sacrifice of his first-born son, Isaac. The second is a quote of Our Lord's: *Go and do thou likewise*.'

'Whaaat!' shouted Henry, leaping to his feet.

'A drastic remedy, I agree,' said Slovo defensively, whilst pondering the correct form for brawling with Kings, 'and you are not obliged to take my counsel.'

'I should hope not, Ad-mir-al,' said Henry, now quiet and deadly.

'Oh dear,' gasped de Peubla, full understanding falling on him like a shroud. 'Oh dear . . .'

'I fear, however,' continued Slovo, conscientiously mindful of a commission accepted, 'that the gradient of the . . . slippage is against you. If nothing is done, then very soon some visitor to these shores will find a most radical – and permanent – change. They will assume, I suppose, a rising or some such has taken place and there will be none left to

155

gainsay them. As to where you and yours will be that day, I cannot say.'

'Nowhere perhaps,' suggested de Peubla, still in shock.

'Perhaps,' nodded the Admiral. 'A version of events superseded, a history that just didn't happen.'

Henry went white and scowled. 'And what brought it all on?' he asked, quite reasonably in the circumstances. 'And what's it got to do with my boy?'

'Such things have laws entirely their own,' replied Slovo disarmingly. 'If forced to explain the phenomenon—'

'Which you will be, if necessary,' said Henry, less than gently.

'. . . then I postulate the freak convergence of two trends – each separately harmless, but together a mighty tide to overwhelm the sea-walls of normality.'

'Speak Latin, man!' spat the King, his Welsh accent ranging wild and free.

'I speak firstly,' said Slovo, stoically swallowing the insult, 'of a thousand years of longing and expectation by a set of emotionally incontinent peoples: sustained by prophecies, engrained by endless defeats, and marvellously revived by your victory at Bos-worth. Now, met and enflamed by the choice of name and ceaseless promotion of your first born, the age-old wishes are coming true.'

'And it's all my fault, is it?' asked Henry, his face worryingly impassive.

'You are your own nemesis, albeit unknowingly,' Slovo confirmed. 'You have benefited from, fed and upheld the very alternatives which are superseding you. However, none of this would be so were it not for the second factor, the vital additional force which permits this terrible violence to the way things are.'

'And what might that be?' asked Daubeny, looking for a chance to be helpful and pointedly loosening his sword.

156

'It is not a matter for promiscuous discussion, I fancy,' said the Admiral, as quietly as clear diction would permit. 'Suffice it to say that what I propose, namely the Abraham option minus Jehovah's intervention, is the cancelling balance to some similar act so horrendous that it has wounded the fabric of the Universe's propriety. Through this wound, the other gangrene affecting your Kingdom has effected its entry.'

Silence settled on the Tower throne-room as some thought furiously and others just as furiously strove to avoid doing so. The spectral Princes looked, unseen, at King Henry as grim and confident as advancing glaciers.

'So . . . if Arthur goes . . .' croaked Henry.

'Some other, equal, act will thus be answered for,' agreed Slovo, 'and propitiation is made to the scales of Justice. The decision to act alone should be sufficient: you need not move precipitately. Then, with the deed done, the bubble of your aboriginal races will be burst with their Arthur the Second no longer feeding false hopes. And I would also suggest some judicious oppression.'

'Annexation? Suppressing the native gobbledey-gook?' offered Daubeny in joyful tone.

'Something like that,' agreed Slovo in a neutral voice. 'Then I suspect you will have no more trouble from them for some hundreds of years.'

'By which time we shall be safely in our tombs,' said Daubeny to the King, as though relating a great stroke of luck.

Once again a humid silence fell. Admiral Slovo presumed Henry was debating as to which he wanted most: his son or his realm. No one else dared speak. It was only then that Slovo realized with a delicious shock that Henry perhaps saw more of the murdered Princes than hitherto suspected.

'I shall be in my tomb, yes,' said Henry at last, in a voice

157

of pure lead, 'but not, I fear, at peace. Do you do tombs, Master Sculptor?' he asked a dozing and bemused Torrigiano.

'I can turn my chisel to anything, Sire,' came the blurted reply in richly mutilated English. 'I was trained at the—'

'You'll do,' interrupted the King, boring into the foreigner with his eyes. 'I'll make you rich and famous, which is the entirety of what men want from life. May the two bring you more happiness than they did me.'

Enraptured and blissfully ignorant, Torrigiano bowed deeply.

Henry almost broke down but recovered and ploughed on. 'I want it to be in the Westminster Abbey that cruel fate wanted to take away from me,' he said. 'Money – ha! Well, that's no object. Let us see vast amounts of good black marble and granite, anything nice and soundproof.'

'Why so?' asked Admiral Slovo, his professional curiosity titillated beyond prudence.

'Because,' answered Henry, 'I suspect I may be screaming through eternity.'

The Princes vanished.[8]

❦ The Year 1500

'In which some stony-hearts confide that I am important.'

'In the absence of guidance, I did what I was asked. His Holiness does, after all, pay my wages and provide a roof over my head. That's more than the Vehme have ever done.' The Admiral's voice was transformed into a sinister whisper by the subterranean chamber's acoustics. It was considerably less crowded and well lit than on his last visit during his initiation.

The Tribunal looked suitably shocked at such an explosion of ingratitude.

'Brother Slovo,' said the presiding judge in her gravest tones, 'the Holy Vehme has given you a life!'

'I had one of those already,' answered Slovo. 'I thought your powers were restricted to taking life away.'

He was not minded to be deferential. He did not take kindly to being summoned, under threat of death, into the wilderness of the Germanic fringe so soon after his arduous return from England and a frosty farewell from its King. He had been looking forward to a period of spiritual recuperation with his book and the stiletto collections in his Roman or Caprisi villas. Moreover, a Genoese woman had moved in adjacent to the former and gave every indication of being able to accommodate his particular fancies in the manner for which ladies of her City were infamous. Now, instead of being amidst such rich stimulations, he was once again in a part of the world that thought civilization an optional extra. It really wasn't good enough.

What, after all, was the worst thing the Vehme could do to him, he reasoned? Hang him from a tree at some lonely crossroads? Stick a sword in his heart? Well then, if such was their wish, let them get the hell on with it. He couldn't stop them.

The panel of three spent a moment in whispered conference. 'We find that there may be some justification in your lack of charm,' said the female judge at last. 'It is regrettable that some of our messengers have but one manner of summoning in their repertoire.'

'The scroll was affixed to my pillow with a dagger,' agreed Slovo. 'Like a spider on one's face, it's a disgreeable sight to wake up to.'

'You should lose such developed sensitivities, Admiral,' said another judge, a pale-fleshed northerner, as far as his black cowl and the inadequate light revealed. 'Life would be easier for you.'

'Starting from scratch,' countered Admiral Slovo, 'with all the disadvantages of being employed as a pirate, I have on the contrary sought to cultivate such sensibilities.'

'As you wish,' came the riposte. 'It's your choice. I merely sought to advise.'

'Which happily touches on your real purpose here, Admiral,' added the third judge, a cold-eyed condottiere if ever Slovo saw one. 'We wish to give you our thoughts.'

Slovo was going to say that they could just as well have written, but felt that he'd already over-expressed his outrage. 'Then I am at your disposal,' he said, turning to look purposefully at the great chamber's shuttered doors and guardian statuary behind. 'Aren't I?'

'Yes, you are,' admitted the Tribunal leader, showing that they too were not afraid to state brutal truths. 'A closed session this may be, with no other brothers or sisters present, but you may rest assured that we are not without resource. No meeting of the Vehme is ever held unless its precincts and the surrounding country are first fully secured. But why this sour spirit of rebellion? When will you make your full submission to our great undertaking?'

'When you confide what it is, perhaps?'

The three judges simultaneously voiced brief sounds of exasperation.

'We tell you what is fit for you to know,' said the condottiere. 'Where is your *faith*?'

Admiral Slovo had no wise or safe answer to that and so remained silent.

'We hear,' said the female Tribunalist, 'that you are "convinced" by the Laws of the Blessed Gemistus: does that not presently suffice?'

'Frankly no,' said Slovo. 'It is a thin thing on which to found a life of altruistic action. Why should I go among the English barbarians or risk the company of the Borgias for a book with which I may intellectually agree? There are any number of such writers in my library.'

'Name them,' commanded the northerner. 'Aside from the *Meditations*, of course.'

'I don't doubt your spy or spies have already itemized my possessions,' said Slovo, 'but if you insist—'

'We do,' said the condottiere.

'Well, I would name the Greek Heraclitus, who holds that fire is the basic stuff of the universe and that all things are in eternal flux between light and dark, hunger and satiation, war and peace. Truth is the harmony of these opposites.

Then there is Socrates who teaches that life must be experienced direct and not be filtered second-hand through reason or learning. Plato proposes the rule of philosophers, and Philaenis the Leucadian's Tribadic manual serves to excite my carnal lusts in an imaginative manner. Is that enough?'

The Tribunal indicated it was.

'That's sufficient,' said the lady in judgement, 'to confirm that our first thoughts were correct and that your journey here was not wasted. Once again we have neglected you, Admiral; we confess the fault. In the absence of the expression of our favour and confidence in you, your enthusiasms – should a Stoic have such – have drifed where they will. Where we would now wish you to be a single shot, you've become a wild volley. We would not have you so diffuse, Admiral, so unfocused. You will not find us negligent or careless again. We want to take you into our counsel.'

Having made himself master of his will to live, Slovo was both willing and able to stake all on a supposition. 'Why?' he asked. 'What are you afraid of?'

Instantly he knew he had struck home. For the merest second the faces of the three Vehmists were not their absolute slaves to command – as should be the case in all who attempt great things. The momentary display of fallibility told Slovo more than anything else he'd heard that night. The Tribunal's craven failure to address his question, even after yet further whispered consultation, also spoke volumes.

The lady Vehmist 'answered', her sophisticated Roman voice now well under control, 'For instance, should you wish to speak of your recent service to us, we will speak freely to you. It is our intention that henceforth, you be a sentient tool in our employ.'

Slovo looked within and acknowledged that there were a few matters that trailed free and unresolved from his recollection of the English adventure. 'Very well,' he said. 'Let me put our new relationship to the test. Am I to presume from your lack of alternative guidance that you shared Pope Alexander's concern to preserve the English Tudor monarchy?'

'You may,' replied the condottiere. 'Although we think the Papacy may one day repent of that policy. It was our wish that the Britannic Isles be subject to the firmest and most centralizing of regimes. We have plans for that particular race and our requirement is that they be welded into a modern nation state.'

Slovo's neck was beginning to ache with craning up at the Tribunal on their raised dais, but he bid his protesting body be silent. 'Then that is strange,' he said. 'At initiation I was told that you stood for the restoration of older and better ways. The resurgent Celts indisputably represented a revival of the antique.'

'You should not always look for consistency in us,' said the lady Vehmist, smiling falsely. 'Consistency is the handmaiden of rationalism and leads to predictability. Not all that is older is better, not everything better is yet born. We pick and choose. Sometimes it is necessary to go forward in order to come back.'

'But what are your plans for me?' asked the Admiral.

'They are ... fluid, Brother Slovo,' replied the condottiere. 'Merely continue as you are for the moment.'

Slovo looked at the Vehmists and they looked at him. It should have been an unequal contest, three against one, a conspiracy of unknown size and mighty ambitions versus one short-lived man – but somehow it was not. Slovo sensed that the Tribunal were deprived of some ultimate sanction against him; that in a curious way he was their master, sitting in judgement on them.

Pondering on this paradox, he let the silence stretch

163

uncomfortably until he made another intuitive leap and landed in a very interesting landscape.

'I'm in your Book, aren't I?' he said, first ensuring there was no trace of triumph in his voice. '*The Book*.'

The Tribunal looked saddened.

'We suspect so,' their leader confirmed after a brief pause. 'There are allusions that could refer to you.'

'May I see them?'

'No, that might pervert the prophecies they detail.'

'Did you always think thus? Is that why I was recruited?'

'No again. It is only lately that our analytic scholars, our hidden universities, have seen the concordances between your career and what is written. At your initiation here, the stone gods into which we have drawn down some of the essence of the divine, recognized you. We always watch for it but such a thing occurs at intervals of centuries. That was when we were first alerted.'

'I recall the antique colossi,' said Slovo, looking back at them, 'but . . .'

'Mostly they are silent, Admiral,' said the northerner. 'Using the magic bequeathed us, we can preserve some fraction of those gods who linger on and we store their god-head in stone to wait out the Christian-Islamic monotheist era. They are duly grateful and assist us as best as they can.'

'Gods with no worshippers,' commented Slovo. 'How terribly sad.'

'We aim to change all that, Admiral,' said the condottiere with quiet confidence. 'We may ally ourselves with atheists and Elves, radical humanists and Roman-Empire nostalgists – in fact anyone who rests uneasy under the present dispensation. However, we never for one moment lose sight of our ancient objective. So there you are, Admiral. Now you know our "great secret"! We wish the old gods to burst their bounds of stone, empowered by the prayers of millions!'

Slovo contrived to look appropriately impressed and honoured, but did not believe a word of it. 'And I have a role in achieving this – according to your predictive Book?' he asked.

'It seems so,' agreed the lady Vehmist. 'Possibly a crucial one. However, to be more specific might subvert the lines of fate traced by the Blessed Gemistus. Rest content in the knowledge that mighty events, things even we cannot yet clearly discern, seem to hinge upon you.'

'So you'll take good care of me?' he said, unable to resist the temptation to tease.

'For the moment, yes,' agreed the Vehmist with commendable honesty. 'At least, we'll ensure that destiny is able to have its way with you. If, as our Holy Book suggests, you are going to be the world's salvation, we can hardly do otherwise.'

There was a violent noise from behind the Admiral. He looked round just in time to see the two great effigies they had spoken of slowly topple forward and crash – miraculously intact, he noted – to the ground. When the dust had abated, he saw that their heads and upraised arms pointed directly towards him, as though in homage.

'And so,' said the condottiere, remaining in his seat with admirable cool, as the thunderous noise echoed round the chamber, 'it seems, say all of us.'

The Year 1506

'BE ASSURED, HE IS NOT THERE: I commission a masterpiece of Western art and learn the key mystery of Mother Church. A friend is glad to hear he has not wasted his life.'

In high summer, the streets of Rome could be distressing in a thousand subtle ways. Admiral Slovo, experiencing them all, looked over the side of the carriage and coveted the cool green salad being eaten by a poor man. In his ignorance, he also envied the man's undoubted innocence, his air of 'tomorrow I'll up and go elsewhere' – but mostly he envied him his solitude.

'It is unpleasantly humid, Admiral,' said Madame Teresina Bontempi. 'The various forks of my body are suffering great discomfort.'

'It *is* unpleasant, my lady,' Slovo replied, holding his smile rock-solid.

The Lady Bontempi's coach, he thought, was as big and ornate as that of a conquering Sultan. And its present mistress was of a parcel with it – an over-filled, pink-and-white strumpet sitting beside him, riding the vehicle as she did her lover, Pope Julius II – that is to say, often but for short distances only. In another close parallel, Slovo suspected that the mere act of being seen to be riding was the thing; regardless of any point to the exercise.

However, in contrast to her nocturnal forays into Venus's jousting field, on her carriage rides Teresina Bontempi demanded both noble company and genteel conversation. The idea was to deter the catcalls of those too debased (or free of social restraints) to keep their moral judgements to themselves.

Slovo found that she was free with herself in a manner that depressingly failed to stir him. The opinions of the populace he could quell with a glance of his renowned stone-grey eyes, but his own inner verdicts were more ungovernable. In short, Madame Teresina Bontempi drained the well of his duplicitous diplomacy, a spring hitherto through inexhaustible.

'... and at San Giovanni Laterano, Admiral, just beside the statue of the bemused man on a horse ...'

'The Roman Emperor, Marcus Aurelius, madam,' prompted Slovo, his eyes narrowing with sudden weariness.

'... a group of what I can only assume to be escaped apostate galley-slaves, danced around my coach and called me "whore!" as I passed. "Whore!" – can you imagine it?'

Admiral Slovo nodded sagely, modifying his smile to signify sad appreciation of human depravity.

'I can believe it, my lady,' he said slowly. 'You have my sympathy – and my understanding, for I am in the same case.'

'You are?' said Bontempi, shocked for the first time in memory.

'Indeed, madam,' said Slovo, favouring her with a charming show of teeth. 'It is a full five years since I commanded a warship, yet still they call me Admiral.'

'Most Blessed Father, I have been turned out of the Palace today by your orders, wherefore I give you notice that from this time forward, if you want me, you must look for me elsewhere than at Rome.'

Michelangelo Buonarroti, in letter dated 1506, to
Giuliano della Rovere, Pope Julius II

'You have incurred our gravest displeasure,' said the Pope. 'It is in our thoughts to have you dispatched.'

'To Capri?' asked Admiral Slovo.

'Pray banish the Island of Capri from your mind, Admiral. To put it plain, my proposal is to send you on your way by means of an inserted blade. Do you now grasp my ... thrust?'

'Entirely, Your Holiness.'

The Pope looked wearily at Slovo, resting his over-burdened head on one gaunt hand. A moment of rare silence passed in the state room and ebbed out to quieten the entire Vatican.

'Admiral,' said Julius, at long last, 'do you recall when you first put on that invisible mask?'

'Not with any precision, Your Holiness: my study of the Stoical tradition started early.'

'I can well credit it. But rest assured, Admiral, I will provoke you to a show of emotion one day.'

'I am at Your Holiness's disposal.'

'That's right; you are. Meanwhile, whilst one finds much to commend in these ancient Stoics and dead Pagans, I must remind you that there is no *fullness* in them. If, on that "one day" I have referred to, I should actually proceed to shorten your years, for say ... abusing my companion of the moment as a "whore", or perhaps killing an over-witty Perugian poet of our acquaintance (oh, yes, we know of that), then,

168

Admiral, on that day, you may find yourself short of the price of salvation. I should be distressed to think of you in Hell.'

Admiral Slovo bowed his grateful thanks for this display of concern. 'Even that, Your Holiness, I could bear,' he said, 'for our parting would be but brief.'

An English Cardinal tittered behind his jewelled hand – alas, too loud – and thus earned himself, one year hence, the Primacy of the 'Mission for the Conversion of the Turks'.

'*Meanwhile*,' said Julius, with furious gravity, 'some wretch of a Florentine sculptor has fled our employ without discharging his commission and having learnt what he should not. The details of contract and correspondence are with one of my tribe of secretaries. Take a Swiss captain to back up your silver tongue and fetch back this—'

'Michelangelo,' prompted the English Cardinal, vainly hoping to escape the martyrdom he somehow sensed in store.

'—the same,' said Julius.

'Alive?' asked Admiral Slovo.

The Pope considered the matter. 'Yes, I think so,' he said eventually. 'If it's not a lot of extra trouble.'

※

'There was something else I do not wish to communicate; enough that it made me think that, if I stayed in Rome, that city would be my tomb before it was the Pope's. And that was the cause of my sudden departure.'

Michelangelo Buonarroti, in a letter sent from
Florence, dated Spring 1506

'And after the mockery of the "Disputation", said Rabbi Megillah, 'they formally burnt the *Torah* scroll in front of the

169

Ghetto gates. I could hold my tears no longer – but what is this to you; forgive me for troubling . . .'

'*Job* 32: "I will speak of my troubles and have more room to breathe",' said Slovo. '*Taanith* 15: "A worthy person must not be crestfallen."'

The Rabbi, in the midst of revisiting his sorrow, found a smile. Especially when Slovo spoke again.

'*Proverbs* 31, 6 to 7: "Give strong drink to him who is perishing and wine to those in bitter distress. Let them drink and forget their poverty and remember their misery no more."'

'*Ecclesiastes* 10: "Wine makes life joyful",' echoed the Rabbi, studying the wine flask but making no move towards it.

'There is no need to restrain the joy referred to,' added Slovo. 'The vintage is *kashrut*; purchased from the ghetto by my servants this very day.'

As they ate and drank sufficient to be sociable, Rabbi Megillah told Admiral Slovo about his recent doings, his family and the razor-edge life of the ghetto. Slovo listened carefully and chatted back.

'And your wife, Admiral; how is she?'

'Quite well, I understand. A mutual acquaintance brought me news of her quite recently. However, *Sanhedrin* 7 remains applicable: "When love was strong, we could lie on the edge of a sword; but now, when love has diminished, a bed of sixty ells is not wide enough for us."'

A little pause followed this conversational derailment until the Rabbi coughed to clear the air and said, 'Well, my old friend, I am indebted to you for your hospitality. Is there anything I can do for you?'

Stretching his smile to the appropriate length, Slovo named his price. 'Since you mention it, might I allude to *Yebamoth* 122?'

'"Do not bar your door to the borrower,"' recalled Megillah. 'Of course, it is not right or politic for me to refuse you but ... well, remember *Baba Metzia* 75, Admiral: "One that complains but finds no sympathy is he who lends money without witnesses." To so extend my credit to one especial Christian, well – it marks you out, you know.'

Admiral Slovo acknowledged gravely that this was so.

'And it also jangles my last thoughts of the day, Admiral. You ... extend me: my position grows tenuous. Tomorrow, I and my people might be banished beyond the sea ...'

'Or be called home by the Messiah,' suggested Slovo.

'Indeed. That may be so, although it occurs to me that money will be of no account on that happy day.'

'This is possible,' said Slovo. 'Meanwhile, Rabbi, I am called upon to deal with some *artist* type on behalf of His Holiness. Money will do the trick, in that I find it is often the case that the true hunger firing creativity is a desire for gold and the security it brings. Such is my plan with the fellow in question. I'd rather pay your usury, dear Rabbi, than listen to any more wearying talk of "art".'

'As you say, Admiral,' concurred Megillah, slipping gladly into the old, familiar coinage.

'And,' continued Slovo, 'it occurs to me, in the circumstances, that your reluctance might be overcome; your interest rate acceptably low ...'

Rabbi Megillah expressed surprise at this presumption. Then Admiral Slovo explained his meaning to him awhile and, at the end, the Rabbi gladly, happily, extended him unlimited credit.

'Michelangelo, the sculptor, who left us without reason, and in mere caprice, is afraid, as we are informed, of returning, though we for our part are not angry with him, knowing the humours of such men of genius. In order then, that he may lay aside all anxiety, we rely on your loyalty to convince him in our name that if he returns to us he shall be uninjured and unhurt, retaining our apostolic favour in the same as he formerly enjoyed it.'

Final of three briefs from Pope Julius II to the
Florentine Seigniory 1506

'And,' said the Swiss Captain, Numa Droz, as they rode along, 'when the Turks captured Otranto in the August of 1480, they tortured and killed half of the twenty-two thousand souls within and enslaved the rest. There were really *interesting* piles of bodies, you know: not just the usual ones you find on battlefields. Then the Archbishop and the Town Governor got publicly sawn in half so as to awe the infidel.'

'And did it, Master Swiss?' asked Admiral Slovo, feigning interest.

'Did me! I apostatized then and there; made the profession of faith to their top turban and was put on the strength.'

'Indeed,' observed Slovo dryly, 'and yet you seem passing young for a man present at such a long-ago event.'

'It was my first venture out of Canton Uri, my Lord Admiral. I was a mere stripling. I ended up as a Master of Artillery and Janissary Procurer for a Macedonian frontier fort, and that was quite a nice time. The Mussulman religion is also ... interesting ... but nothing like the real thing,' added the Swiss, part sincere, part in sudden recollection of his present employer. 'So I deserted, made full restitution to Christ in Ravenna ...'

'And how expensive was that?' enquired the Admiral, for his own reference purposes.

Numa Droz looked shocked.

'The price, Admiral,' he said firmly, 'was long hours on my knees – and the hard acquisition of true repentance. Money is weightless; mere base metal in questions affecting the soul. Contrary to what you might think, I'm a true son of the Church; albeit prone to lapses.'

Slovo managed to keep his surprise to himself – there was a need for care. All Swiss met outside their natural boundaries were controlled mass-murderers, specially exported for that reason. The two of them were alone together on the Florentine road and Numa Droz could at any time surrender to his national passion for blood. Slovo discreetly loosened the stiletto concealed in his saddle.

'And then I took employ with Ferdinand I of Naples,' Droz continued, the little difficulty apparently forgotten. 'Now, there was an interesting man. He kept a sort of gallery of his dead enemies, stuffed and mounted, and all dressed in their finery, for him to promenade around from time to time, musing on the shortness and vagaries of life. One day, when I was in special favour, I was given a private viewing . . .'

'So was I,' said Admiral Slovo. 'The Duc' de Praz-Ridolfi of Romagna looked better than he did in life, I thought. I complimented Ferdinand on it and he actually smiled!'

'Ridolfi?' said Droz. 'The slim one, hooked nose, yellow doublet?'

'With jewelled dagger poised in left hand, yes, the same,' confirmed Slovo.

'Oh ... well, we have that much in common then, Admiral.'

'And also service with his Apostolic Holiness,' added Slovo, quietly mortified to find even two points of similarity with this barbarian.

173

'Oh yes, I should say so! What happy days, Admiral. I can tell you; as soon as I heard the stories that he was unchristian, warlike and intemperate, I said farewell to Naples and sped to Rome. There's not been a peaceful day since, I'm glad to say.'

'My recollection is much the same,' said Slovo crisply.

'He's been a good father to mercenaries everywhere – for and against him. I was put on the strength right away, you know; full pay from day one whether you kill or not – and you don't get that sort of consideration just anywhere. Oh look, there's a strangled man in that ditch.'

'So there is.'

'And Julius even got that Michel-angel fellow to design us Swiss lads uniforms. Do you like it?'

'No.'

'Me neither. Still, I expect it'll grow on people. Mind you, before then, I'll have earned and stolen a packet and be back in Uri with the wife.'

Admiral Slovo studied the sky without much hope of consolation and, finding none, pressed on.

'You are far from home, Master Swiss. Suppose your wife has not waited?'

Numa Droz shrugged and flicked at his horse's ear.

'Then I'll kill her and marry afresh. Her sister's quite juicy, now I think of it. Either way, there's a wife at the cabin door.'

Far along the road, Admiral Slovo's constantly roving eye had detected a lone horseman. Numa Droz spotted him at the same time and suddenly all thoughts of home were forgotten.

'A demi-lance, riding hard, alone,' Droz said in clipped tones. 'We stand.'

The two men, forged in different but equal fires, did not visibly prepare to meet the rider but *adjustments* were made

174

all the same. Most encounters on the road were innocence itself but mistakes could not be undone.

'Admiral Slovo?' said the man when he drew near (but still politely far enough away).

Slovo smiled whilst remaining inscrutable. 'Possibly,' he replied.

The rider did not take offence. He was familiar with the etiquette of the time.

'I am Peter Anselm,' he said, with as much of a bow as his armour would permit. 'Or Petro Anselmi to you, condottiere in the service of Florence, sent to greet and hasten you.'

Admiral Slovo raised one inquisitive eyebrow, confirming nothing, but signifying the very slightest interest in pursuing the 'Slovo' identification.

'This Michelangelo business – it draws to a head,' explained Anselmi, 'the Seigniory see cause for speed.'

Admiral Slovo did not approve of qualities like speed; cousins as they were to the unforgivable: carelessness. 'And what is the news, Condottiere?' he asked pleasantly.

'All good!' the man replied. 'There could be a war!'

> *The Seigniory sent for me and said, "We do not want to go to war with Pope Julius because of you. You must return; and if you do so, we will write you letters of such authority that, should he do you harm, he will be doing it to the Seigniory." Accordingly, I took the letters and went back to the Pope.'*
>
> Michelangelo Buonarroti. Private letter. 1507

'The Republic of Florence,' said Admiral Slovo, breaking the news as gently as he could to someone he suspected of naïvety, 'will not risk the losses incumbent in war, solely for you. The strong order the weak, who in turn direct the powerless. I invite you to speculate on your own position within that hierarchy. In short, the Seigniory will at our request, charmed by a little money, spew you forth to whatever fate has in store.'

'That is the way of the World,' added Petro Anselmi with a grin. 'My little son knows that and he's only three! Where have you been all your life, Artist?'

Sheltered from the gales of reality by two small but talented hands, thought Admiral Slovo – but forbore to say as much as he watched Michelangelo look from Slovo to Droz to Anselmi. *Bags of nerve*, judged the Admiral, *or maybe just bad temper allowed free rein.*

'I disagree with the Admiral,' said Michelangelo, his agitated voice going up and down the scales like a monkey on a stick. 'I doubt Florence can ever afford to defer to such an aggressive Pontiff for fear of the demands, yet unformulated, that would follow in train. It is *my* belief that the Seigniory have chosen a field on which to stand and fight.'

Admiral Slovo smiled and leant forward to replenish his goblet with wine. Numa Droz remained impassive, his gaze shifting lithely back and forth between Anselmi and the Sculptor – thus passing the little test Slovo had set him.

'I detect the echo of another's voice behind your own, Master Sculptor,' said Admiral Slovo patiently. 'May I be so bold as to enquire whose?'

Michelangelo's ugly young face coloured. 'I have taken counsel with a certain officer of the Republic,' he said briskly.

'A certain Second Chancellor?' enquired Slovo. 'Perhaps a certain Master Niccolo Machiavelli?'

Michelangelo confirmed the suggestion by shrugging noncommittally and suddenly finding the ceiling very absorbing. 'And what of it?' he asked angrily. 'People seek me out for their statue requirements; I seek his advice on the subtleties of statecraft. This is an age of specialists, Admiral.'

Slovo concurred. 'Ordinarily, yes – but in this case, no. In my friend Niccolo, we have a man sadly attended by Madame Misfortune in his every endeavour. His thoughts are trained, drilled and marched boldly out to battle – to be routed at reality's first charge. His long-planned Florentine citizens' militia will come to nothing.'

'Good,' said Anselmi, his professional feelings outraged. 'Amateurs spoil trade.' Numa Droz wholeheartedly agreed.

'His foreign missions,' Slovo continued, 'have spread vigorous ill will and throughout his life he will unerringly change sides from Medici oligarchs to the Republic and back; at precisely the wrong times.[9] If I were you, Master Michelangelo, I would not hazard *my* already short existence on Machiavelli's advice.'

Michelangelo glared at him, fright and frustration boiling up into bravery. 'Well,' he said, 'I'm obliged to you for your fatherly words. But, given the choice, I'll cleave to his opinion, not yours.'

With one black-bejewelled finger, Slovo waved Numa Droz forward.

'I don't know much about art,' said the Swiss, 'but all I've heard indicates that an artist needs his HANDS!'

Before his last words had ceased, Droz's sword carved a silver arc, its proposed termination the joint of Michelangelo's right wrist.

Its speed was such that there was no time for the Artist to disgrace himself with a scream, or, in fact, to react at all. He therefore maintained the most commendable Stoic calm and watched as Anselmi somehow parried the blow with his short-sword.

'Very sorry, Master Swiss,' said Anselmi with courteous regret, 'but I can't permit that: orders, I'm afraid.'

'You're very good,' said Numa Droz, one craftsman to another as they disengaged blades. 'Nice and fast.'

177

Anselmi permitted himself a modest smile. 'Thank you – but you made it possible; there wasn't full force in your blow. You didn't intend the complete job, did you?'

Droz further indicated his spirit of professional fellowship. 'You're right; I confess – but not many could have told.'

'Just a life-long scar, not a hack-off, am I right?'

'Precisely!' said Numa Droz, wreathed in sunny smiles. 'Just an indication of what could be.'

'I'm off!' shouted Michelangelo, regaining his powers of speech and coordination, but halted one second into his progress in order to avoid impaling his throat on Anselmi's sword.

'You stay where you are,' said the condottiere, expertly using the tip of his blade on the Sculptor's Adam's apple to guide him back to his seat, 'and listen to what these kind gentlemen have to say.'

'I am indebted, sir,' said Slovo graciously, slightly cheered by this economical display of skill in a world of so much wasted energy and emotion.

'Florence is all for freedom,' said Anselmi, his barbarous Italian only slightly spoiling the effect, 'but my understanding is that the sentiment is conditional upon Florence's perceived present interest. Now, if it were down to me, Sculptor, I'd let you stay in the City and then we'd have war with His Holiness – excellent! It would do my free company's trading figures a power of good. However, sad to say, my employer is of a more reflective mind. Accordingly, you'll sit this meeting out, attend and digest. At the end, if you remain obdurate, I'll escort you safely home – comprehend?'

Michelangelo nodded obediently. The sword slowly withdrew.

'Cutting to the root of the matter,' said Slovo, choosing the phrase advisedly and watching Michelangelo pale afresh, 'I am willing, of my own funds, to offer you three hundred ducats to return to Rome and complete your commission. My personal lines of credit with the Florentine goldsmiths guild, via a Jew of Rome, are easily verifiable.'

'Already done,' commented Anselmi efficiently. 'Sculptor: this man has what he says he has.'

There was just the merest whisper of a slight in thinking such a confirmation necessary, but Slovo passed over it with magnanimity. Numa Droz, awaiting a signal to act, took his cue and appeared to relax.

'What use is gold to a dead man?' asked Michelangelo reasonably enough. 'I would not survive my first night back in Rome. Please explain to me the seductiveness of being the richest garrotted corpse in the Tiber.'

So there it was: Slovo had made persuasive appeals to the three great motivations: firstly reason, then fear, then avarice. Thrice rejected, unable to tempt the rabbit from its Florentine burrow, he now had to exert himself and exercise ingenuity.

'I think,' he said sadly, 'this issue might be resolved if the Sculptor and I were to speak alone.'

'Conceivable,' said Anselmi, as politely as his cultural background would permit. 'Possible even: if you were to surrender the stiletto concealed in your right boot and perhaps the curiously large, probably spring-loaded, ring – yes, that one with the jet-stone.'

'Don't leave me!' shouted Michelangelo, turning to the condottiere as his protector.

'There are deeper tides at play in this episode, Sculptor,' said Slovo, in an even tone, like a good father to his child, 'as you well know. That being so, if I were to say that I mean you no harm; if further, I was to swear to that effect *by all the gods*, would you not then change your mind?'

Michelangelo swivelled to look at him, his face emulating the paleness of his marble creations, and was obliged to swallow a sudden excess of saliva. 'Yes, I would,' he said, abruptly calm again. 'Please leave us, Anselmi; I wish to speak with the Admiral.'

'For all your present differences,' said Slovo, 'may I first say that I do admire your *Pietà* . . . and the *David*.'

'So you do have artistic sensitivities?' asked Michelangelo with keen interest.

'No. Not as commonly defined.'

The Sculptor looked at Slovo as if starting his assessment afresh and a lengthy silence fell on them. Slovo was happy to let it live its natural span.

'Admiral,' said Michelangelo eventually, 'I find it hard to trust a man such as you. Without a lively appreciation of art, a human is the prisoner of his fallen nature.'

'Offhand,' replied Slovo, 'I might counter that it is only His Holiness's most lively appreciation of your art that brings us to this meeting.'

'He is an exception. Cold and rigid in his grave, he would still be untrustworthy. What alternative token of faith can you offer me?'

Admiral Slovo twirled the tip of one gloved finger in his wine, watching the resultant whirlpool pass from birth, through vigour, into nothingness. 'Well, he said, 'I might say that I find the Stoical teachings (tempered with certain Old Testament insights) most persuasive . . .'

Michelangelo waved a dismissive hand.

'But mainly,' Slovo continued, 'I would pick upon the word "faith" in your question – which was undoubtedly a test, a reference to the real reason for your reluctance to return to Rome.'

Michelangelo twisted his irregular face into the distant

relation of a smile. 'As was your "by all the gods", Admiral,' he said.

Slovo showed his own facial travesty of human pleasure. 'Indeed,' he confirmed.

'I should have guessed,' said Michelangelo, absent-mindedly rending apart a small loaf, occasionally popping a morsel of the soft bread in his mouth. 'There were so many clues in the design of Julius's tomb. His Holiness was practically telling me the secret...'

'I think not,' answered Admiral Slovo very slowly, as if afraid of being misunderstood. 'You have a subtle and discursive mind, well stocked by interest and education. Pope Julius is likewise when sober – and calm – but differs in thinking himself alone in being so. One starts off not tolerating fools gladly and ends up thinking all men fools; that is the way of it. You see, normally, the secret passes from Pope to Pope, and a very few select others, and hitherto there has been wisdom and modesty enough to maintain discretion.'

'Even with a Borgia Pope?' exclaimed Michelangelo.

'Rodrigo – that is to say, Alexander VI – was capable of good sense and virtue,' said Slovo defensively, 'although he found the world such a playground that he saw few occasions for either. But yes; he kept the trust. Even Cesare did not use the information to his advantage.'

Michelangelo was clearly impressed.

'And that was wise,' Slovo continued, 'for wilful and promiscuous employment of the knowledge could lead to only one end. Mother Church, much as we may mock or neglect her as we might our earthly mothers, is a mother still. The one thing she cannot tolerate is the questioning of her marriage's validity in front of her children. Do you follow me?'

'The other people who've found out ... from time to

time,' said Michelangelo, putting what he already knew, but couldn't accept, in the form of a question, 'they were killed, weren't they?'

'Well, of course,' said Slovo. 'What else? These are not soft times. Even from a gospel of love, a certain robustness of response is bound to be encountered.'

'I *should* have guessed!' snapped Michelangelo, his anxiety coming round full circle. 'When he summoned me last year and showed me the plans for St Peter's, I should have guessed something.'

Admiral Slovo's hand gestured meaningless sympathy.

'... a titanic marble tomb,' Michelangelo rambled on, 'a testimony to his perceived greatness; that I could understand. One almost expects it of the modern sort of Pope, albeit on a lesser scale. But what he wanted was more than that. It was a slap in the face to decency. Moreover, it was entirely unchristian. Actually, I rather liked it!'

'For which reason, you accepted the commission?' said Slovo.

'Oh yes, the sheer monstrousness of it appealed to me. In constructing it, I would share in the immortality of its intended occupant. A shocked world would not lightly forget the creator of the Hecatomb of Julius. And lasting fame is my one unvarying desire.'

'Then I now see a way out of your present predicament, Sculptor – but pray continue.'

'It was to be three storeys high, studded with forty massive statues. I even finished one of them – the Moses – and made it look like Julius when he's drunk and itching with the "French disease".'

'But he didn't recognize himself,' said Slovo. 'Fortunately for you.'

'No, I didn't think he would. Anyway, there were to be these friezes depicting the travails and death of antiquity, and their gods bound and tortured by the new revelation. The allegorical statues touched on that as well but mostly they were of personified virtues – the fierce, martial ones – representing the qualities of the man within. They were to wind their way around and up the tomb, alongside all the victories of Rome, past and present, all the prostrate cities and captive nations, right up to the final storey where—'

'Where Julius himself . . .?' hazarded Slovo.

'That's correct. Encased in a marble effigy, thrice life-size and thirty times as handsome: topped by a mob of angels exulting over their gain, and the Earth deploring its loss.'

'Rather than a wicked old soul about to meet his maker,' observed the Admiral.

'If you say so. I'll give him this though; funding was limitless: I've never had such quantities of marble at my disposal. Not only that, but I had the go ahead to put red and gold tongues of fire up and down its entire height – and onyx to create deep internal shadow. There was even a requisition for five hundred skulls to be brought up from the catacombs to decorate the base. I tell you, Admiral, it was the greatest project I'm ever likely to have.'

'Possibly not,' said Slovo, trying to employ the tone of kindness, 'but go on.'

'And then I had to go and make sure of things, to guarantee my work's survival by deepening its foundations beyond that agreed. My workmen broke through an old floor level and summoned me, they're all dead I suppose . . .'

'I'm afraid so, Sculptor. They sleep with the Tiber fishes.'

'As shall I, because of what I know,' conceded Michelangelo in deep despond.

Admiral Slovo re-attracted his attention by tapping the table with the pommel of his (spare) stiletto. 'Not necessarily,' he said. 'If His Holiness required your presence in Paradise, it would have been effected before now. In common with all mankind, you must eat and drink, and walk in the streets – there is no escape from the desire of a Prince should it and he be sufficiently strong. The deed could be done even now, with this blade which was overlooked by your Englishman's search.'

'Oh!' said Michelangelo, studying the needle with rapt fascination and recommencing his attack on the bread.

'But it shall not,' said Slovo comfortingly. 'In the event, I now see a tunnel through which you may scamper to survive and prosper. His Holiness has cancelled the tomb project in St Peter's. Naturally, he wishes no more attention drawn to *that* spot. But Julius – and the Church – may be served in more ways than one . . .'

'I am overjoyed,' said Michelangelo, sounding far from it.

'Whilst at the same time ensuring both your current life-span and the immortality you so crave.'

Michelangelo suddenly revived and cast the maimed loaf over one shoulder. 'You have my undivided attention, Admiral.'

'Then listen, with infinite care,' said Admiral Slovo.

And so Michelangelo did, gradually growing more cheerful and expansive.

'Still,' he said, after an hour had passed, 'it is quite a sight to have seen, Admiral, do you not agree?'

Slovo shrugged noncommittally. 'I only had the barest glimpse,' he said, 'through the tiniest of approved peep-holes. Pope Julius permitted it so as to bind me to him for life.'

'They were all there,' continued Michelangelo in a voice of wonder, 'spread out for me to see. Of course, when the workmen broke through, I had them widen the hole – to get a good view. I think I spent a day and night observing, forgetting all about food and sleep. I yearned with my artist's heart to paint that scene – I still do – though I know I never shall. All the sketches I made are safely burnt.' Swallowing his emotions, he queried, 'How old do you think that chamber is, Admiral?'

'No one knows. Certainly as old as Rome itself. However, since I saw representatives of the Hittite and Assyrian pantheons down there, I suspect that the vault's history may long predate Romulus and Remus.'

'Or,' mused Michelangelo, 'possibly they were brought there from similar prisons in previous Empires.'

'Maybe so,' conceded Slovo. 'Assyria defeats Egypt; Babylon defeats Assyria and so on and on through Persia, Greece, Parthia and Rome – the booty of one passes to its successor.'

'And the new Rome marches on,' said Michelangelo, warming to his subject as his inner vistas lengthened. 'Such a teeming crowd of many shapes and colours. I saw gods from the New Americas, freshly arrived[10] and bickering with a Thor and Odin more accustomed to captivity. Oh yes, Admiral, they're all there – Mars and Mithras, Serapis and Set – the whole lot. Jupiter the Unconquered Sun (only he is conquered now) conversed with Osiris; all the glorious portrayals of antiquity were made flesh. It was a complete convocation of every deity that human fear and society's needs ever gave birth to.'

'And yet St Peter's power holds them all fast,' countered Slovo. 'Curious, is it not?'

'It is,' Michelangelo granted. 'They jumped and flew at me but some force held them back. Likewise, their constant assaults on their prison's single door failed before its flimsy lock and Papal seal. Tell me, Admiral, who conveys the captive gods there and who sets that door fast?'

'Special troops?' offered Slovo.

'Remarkable,' said Michelangelo, shaking his head. 'I shall never forget it.'

'Oh, you shall,' said Slovo quietly, no longer hiding the

naturally icy and uncharitable note of his voice. 'That is part of the deal. The Church brooks no competitors, not even talk of them.'

'I have forgotten,' said Michelangelo earnestly, 'completely. Forgotten what?'

'Not so fast,' said Slovo swiftly. 'Hold on to your recollection just a little longer. I have a question for you: there is one detail I require from your hours of observation – that is also part of the deal.'

> *'The Pope was still unwilling that I should complete the tomb and ordered me to paint the vault of the Sistine. We agreed for 3000 ducats. I am still in great distress of mind . . . God help me.'*
>
> Michelangelo Buonarroti – private letter
> dated 1509

'So, as I suggested,' said Admiral Slovo, 'Michelangelo made his return, discreetly, reverently and with the appearance of due reflection. Julius received him at Bologna – or rather he was apprehended sidling into Mass at the Church of San Petronio.'

'Offering prayers for his deliverance, one presumes,' hazarded Rabbi Megillah, combing his patriarchal white beard with his fingers.

'If so, they were efficacious. Some of Julius's grooms who were present recognized the Sculptor and dragged him to His Holiness – who happened to be at dinner. Fortunately it was a dry repast and the Holy Father's temper was coiled and at rest. Of course, there was thunder and lightning but Michelangelo recalled my strictures and curbed his own mercurial propensities, merely bending the knee and praying for pardon.'

'As well ask for mercy from a rabid lion, Admiral.'

'Normally so, but two factors intervened in the Sculptor's favour: one, the Cardinal Francesco Soderini spoke on his behalf...'

'And how is the Cardinal's health?' enquired the Rabbi politely.

'He survives, albeit with person and dignity bruised. "Your Holiness might overlook his fault," was what he said. "He did wrong through ignorance. These artists, outside their art, are all like this." At which Julius exploded and had his servants kick the Cardinal from the Palace. It was a useful diversion, breaking the brunt of the charge. Secondly, and more importantly, in a world where mercy must justify its existence, the Sculptor was able to offer something in return for his pardon.'

The Rabbi nodded, looking at and through Slovo into some future, kinder age.

'We discussed the matter with infinite care,' explained Slovo, 'and decided the most tempting offer was something that catered for Julius's aggrandizement, and then something for posterity. To be specific, Michelangelo offered a bronze colossus of His Holiness and then the Sistine Chapel ceiling.'

'That work which he has recently commenced?' asked Megillah.

'The same – supposedly the single effusion of his talent, all for Julius, all for the preservation of his name. The Pontiff forgets, of course, that it is the perpetrator, not the patron, that is honoured and remembered – but that is of no account to us.'

'We shall be safely dust,' agreed the Rabbi, picking at the dish of Venetian rice before him. 'But meanwhile, your forethought seems to have borne dividends, Admiral – the Sculptor still lives.'

'And looks fit to remain so until called home in the natural order of things. Michelangelo is putting heart and soul into his work and when the Sistine ceiling is complete, Julius will not wish to be remembered for killing its sublime creator. That is his long-term security. And with luck and ingenuity, I think he will see it through.'[11]

'And speaking of seeing . . .' asked Rabbi Megillah, giving up the struggle to restrain his curiosity.

'Ah yes,' said Slovo, idly playing with the sunbeams reflected on his silver goblet, 'my commission. I questioned the Sculptor closely; even to the point of writing an inventory. I can confirm Zeus and Apollo and Woden and Augustus and Lao-Tse—'

The Rabbi interrupted, his unfairly wizened face reflecting quiet confidence, modified only by understandable, forgivable, human doubt. 'But what about . . .?' he whispered.

'I am more and more persuaded that you may be right,' said Admiral Slovo. 'I pressed the Sculptor most assiduously on the question of JEHOVAH's presence. Be assured, Rabbi. He is not there.'

אַ

In Rome, Pope Clement VII was reading a letter from Henry VIII, King of England, *demanding*, no less, a divorce from his Spanish wife. The good and amiable Pontiff had thought that he'd got troubles enough already, what with the Luther business and all. He little dreamed that in less than two years, Rome itself would be sacked with a ferocity to make Alaric the Goth's visit eleven hundred years before seem half-hearted. Twenty-two thousand Spaniards, Italians and Lutheran German *Landsknechts* would occupy the 'Eternal City' for ten months and leave it gutted. From that day's perspective, Pope Clement would look back on 1525 as a golden age.

Meanwhile, Slovo, on the verge of suicide, was still wrangling with the Welsh Vehmist in his Caprisi garden.

'You might have *told* us about the prison of the gods,' said the Vehmist.

'It transpires you already knew, so no harm was done.'

'That's not the point, Admiral. Your feet should have run swift to inform us out of the love you bore us. But yes, as it happens, we knew long ago.' The Vehmist allowed his voice to mount with anger. 'We knew when your remotest recorded ancestor was not even a blob of semen. We have numbered Roman Emperors in our ranks, how could we *not* know?'

'How indeed?' replied Slovo, humouring him but concluding that their knowledge and infiltrations were not as extensive as they would wish.

'And because we knew,' the Welshman rushed on, 'the fire in our hearts became fiercer still. The long incarceration of our gods would merely make their day of liberation more sweet!'

'You merely had to work out how?' said Slovo in facetious support.

'Yes, it is a puzzle we are still engaged in,' answered the Vehmist, seeking vainly to conceal his deflation. 'It may be that we have a religion to dispose of before we can re-establish our own. If it does come to that and a thousand-year war, so be it.'

'So *that's* why . . .' prompted Slovo.

'Quite right,' agreed the Vehmist. That sort of challenge is complexity enough for a score of generations; so you found no dispute between Pope and Vehme when a new and deadly creed arose that was anathema to us both. We were content that he chose to set you on it.'

'I did my best to please you both,' said Admiral Slovo. However, I suspect that we're just putting off the evil day.'

The Year 1508

'PUTTING OFF THE EVIL DAY: In which I render a god homeless, mingle with Royalty, learning their dark and disgraceful secrets, and do the world a great favour for which it is not particularly grateful.'

'What we have heard is monstrous enough,' said Cardinal Treversari of Sienna. 'I do not believe anyone else should know.'

Pope Julius, troubled by his various bodily ailments and a naturally fuseless temper, smote the table with his little gold-and-steel wand. If the Cardinal had been within easy reach, he would have copped it instead.

'Damn your eyes!' Julius exploded. 'I've decided that this special *concilium* will agree on the additional disclosure. So why aren't *you* agreeing? Didn't you hear me?'

'I could hardly fail to, but—' replied Treversari nervously, not so old in years nor so steeped in virtue or despair as some of his colleagues around the table, as to be free of fear.

'Then clean your ears out!' bellowed Julius. 'Before I do it for you!' He indicated the attempt might be made with the wand's sharp end and thereby signalled the discussion period closed.

However, before responsibility, killer-stress and venereal disease had changed him, Julius had been a reasonable man. The spectral remains of this youth bade him try once more to justify matters to his inner retinue of approved (but, alas, not trusted) Cardinals.

'Look,' he said, begrudging the waste of time that even this form of consultation represented, 'we need him. This is his sort of thing; perhaps the Almighty designed him for it.'

'I hope that is so,' said Cardinal Guicciardini of Florence. 'For if we or our times created him, then what judgement would await us?'

That was indeed a thought to conjure with – and then to be forcibly thrust aside. Pope Julius frowned.

'But the knowledge he would have ...' protested Treversari, pushing his luck too far. 'How will he react?'

'No one will ever know,' answered the Pope in a tone that the more perceptive realized meant a grim and perhaps short future for the Cardinal. 'He is as inscrutable as the back of a corpse's knee. Merely consider that if there should be problems, we can always kill him; I do not think he would mind unduly.'

'Oh ...' said Treversari, plainly discomfited.

'I am so happy that *you* are, at last, happy,' smiled Julius. 'Now, with your kind indulgence, may we ring the bell and get him in here – and the other monster too.'

On hearing the summons, Admiral Slovo entered the Council-chamber from its anteroom. Accompanying him was a nun, a woman so ancient that if he'd had a bare shred of chivalric feeling and if propriety had allowed, he would have felt obliged to assist her.

'Your Holiness, your eminences,' he said, bowing economically.

'Slovo,' said Julius, just as concisely, 'we've another of those damn things (begging your pardon, Sister) in the best-not-discussed areas of life you've come to specialize in. Go and deal with it, will you.'

'Certainly, Your Holiness,' replied Slovo straightaway so

that the Pontiff might not lose face by unjustified faith in his servants. 'Might this be something of sufficient moment to be beyond those duties covered by my salaried remuneration? Will I be obliged to recruit assistance?'

Julius sympathized with such anxieties, for he too had eaten the bread of exile in his time and so knew the true joy that financial security supplies.

'Yes to both,' he said tersely. 'Now remind me, what is it you usually require for overtime?'

'One: freehold land in Capri,' Slovo counted off on his black-gloved hand. 'Two: a pardon-in-advance for "sins of temperament"...'

'Oh yes,' said the Pope, his bearded lip curling. 'I remember about you now – the Tuscan Vice—'

'Three: a choice item from the Vatican Library. Grant any one of these; and I will be pleased.'

'In view of your task,' said Julius, giving way to rare generosity solely in the hope of disconcerting Slovo's impassive mask, 'you may have all three.'

As experiments went it was an expensive failure and he henceforth resolved to take a leaf out of the Admiral's own book, impulse-wise.

'As to assistance,' he continued, 'that is being arranged. It is a mere matter of the Kings of France and Aragon, the Holy Roman Emperor, the rulers of Mantua and Ferrara; plus their respective armies, of course. They will render what little aid they can. I'll even throw in my own forces and bind all in a formal treaty, how's that? In fact, my people are arranging the details in some Franco-Flemish rat-hole even as we speak.[12] That should be just about sufficient, don't you think?'

'I'm not sure,' answered Admiral Slovo coolly. 'It all depends on what I have to deal with. Besides, the great men you have named are notoriously duplicitous, nationalistic and self-interested. I am inclined to doubt they would pay the slightest heed to what a mere Roman Admiral might say.'

'That all depends on *what* he might say,' countered Pope Julius significantly. 'Take it away, Sister . . .'

The aged nun was ready and waiting. 'I have had a dream . . .' She quavered.

'She has had a dream,' said Admiral Slovo.

'So what?' sneered the youthful Louis XII of France. 'I have them all the time.'

'Me too,' agreed Maximilian I, 'King of the Romans', feeling free to speak now that someone else had ventured the first opinion. 'Especially after I've hit the old cucumber brandy. The big difference, however, is that *I* don't set two-thirds of Europe to war afterwards.'

'But since we *are* all here,' said Alfonsi d'Este, Duke of Ferrara, rather too hastily for his own good, 'perhaps we should hear the story out.'

Ferdinand II of Aragon, a man much admired in that room for his duplicity (and deplored by history for the same reason), successfully waved everyone to silence. All being rulers in their own lands, they duly resented him for it ever after. 'So,' he said in a neutral tone, 'this League is not, after all, a crusade against the Turks . . .'

'No,' confirmed Slovo. 'That was to fool the Venetians.'

'And neither is it a covert arrangement for countering a century of Venetian expansion,' hazarded Louis XII.

'No,' agreed the Admiral. 'That was to fool you lot.'

'Therefore,' summed up Gianfrancesco Gonzaga, Marquis of Mantua, dangerously calm, 'it now becomes clear that we have invaded Italy, plunging Europe into war, risking all, on the say-so of a sleepless nun . . .'

'Not not just any old nun,' added Slovo suddenly. 'This is

the famous Black Lady of the Palatine; the one who predicted the fall of Otranto.'

'That was twenty-eight years ago!' barked Ferdinand. 'And the walls were notoriously ruinous. I could have taken the place with a troupe of dancing bears!'

'Who, moreover, foretold the death of Pope Alexander VI,' Slovo gamely continued.

The assembled monarchs burst into laughter. The noise issued incongruously from their care-worn faces.

'He was seventy-three!' roared Alfonso.

'And a behemoth of brandy consumption,' added King Louis.

'And related to Cesare Borgia!'

This last contribution by Gonzago brought the amusement to a sudden close. The Pope's famous son, the black-clad monster of the Romagna, might well be down but wasn't yet out.[13] Even though exiled from Italy and deprived of all power, he retained the ability to frighten.

Slovo smiled benignly, still master of the situation. 'A degree of scepticism was in fact anticipated,' he said. 'Accordingly, a number of further, highly specific dreams were commissioned from said "Black Lady". You may be interested to hear that the project was attended with astonishing success.'

The rulers looked on Slovo with suspicion.

'Is that so,' commented Louis in a sour voice.

'Yes indeed, Your Majesty. His Holiness went so far as to say that such favour must betoken Divine blessing on our little enterprise. Here, your Lordships, see what *you* think.'

As he spoke, Admiral Slovo distributed wax-sealed scrolls, each personally addressed to the great men present. They eyed them gingerly, like unfired cannon.

Ferdinand of Aragon, in keeping with his intrepid spirit, was the first to break the spell, ripping the roll open and scanning the parchment within. Despite practice since youth in keeping his feelings well hid, he was unable to prevent a widening of the eyes and a retreat, indeed rout, of blood from the face.

'How could she know?' he hissed. 'All my discretion . . .'

'Wasted against an all-seeing eye,' answered Slovo, trying to sound as non-judgemental as possible. It was not any of his concern how an over-stressed warrior chose to unwind.

Meanwhile, King Louis had opened his own missive – and gasped. 'It's not true!' he wailed.

Admiral Slovo turned his inscrutable eyes upon the youth.

'Well, OK, it is,' the King conceded sullenly. 'How many people know?'

'The Pope, the Nun and I,' replied the Admiral. 'One person with the power to forgive and two others who do not matter.'

'This is ... dangerous information,' said Maximilian, reading slowly and loosening his collar.

Gonzaga and Alfonso covertly stowed their letters away for future, private reference.

'Dangerous perhaps,' agreed Slovo reassuringly, 'but intended for only the most restricted circulation.' He gestured expansively in the way Pope Julius had specifically instructed him to. 'Besides, these predilections of yours, and the equipment and body parts used to satisfy them; they are concerns for yourself – and perhaps your confessor – alone. The same liberal sentiment applies to those of you who have seen fit to murder close family members. His Holiness does not seek to wield nefarious power over you. All that is sought is your faith; faith in what has been dreamed.'

Maximilian coughed uneasily, 'We have faith,' he assured Admiral Slovo. 'The faith of a saint in Christ. We are all ears, aren't we, gentlemen?'

There was a babble of assent.

Slovo bowed slightly.

'She has, as I've said,' he continued, 'had a dream . . .'

※

'It *really* is appalling,' said King Louis, at his most fastidious.

Slovo didn't feel strongly one way or the other but nodded sagely all the same.

'I could not live in such a world,' agreed Alfonso angrily. 'Where is the honour? Where the glory?'

'Locked away for ever in some bourgeois safe-box,' replied Gonzago of Mantua. 'Kept hidden by little grey men and laughed to scorn!'

The Kings and Princes were all agreed. The Nun's vision of the Year of Our Lord 1750, as recited by Admiral Slovo, had shocked them to their collective hollow core. Thoughts of an industrial Imperial Venice, awash with metal warships and studded with ack-ack guns, horrified them. It was bad enough that their date of birth obliged them to straddle the Medieval–Renaissance divide. That their posterity should be called on to embrace a future of slavery within Imperial Venice was the trigger to the release of powerful emotions.

'I'm not having it!' announced King Louis. 'Oh no! I shall put a stop to this!'

'How fortuitous then,' smarmed Slovo, 'that His Holiness should have arranged five of Europe's mightiest armies to be conjoined to execute your will.'

No one ever liked a Pope to be proved right – it had too many disturbing implications – but, for a man who had never been told No, the French monarch took the *I told you so* well.

'Yes, I suppose it is,' he snapped. 'Together we'll show 'em.'

Maximilian, the oldest present, had not been able to adapt to the news and was still in a state of shock. 'But I don't understand,' he said. '*Why?* Why would they turn the skies dark with their war-craft, why burn a dead hinterland for leagues around their triple-walled Capital?'

'It's a new religion,' said Admiral Slovo, as gravely as he could. 'Some fresh ethic has arrived in Venice – that being the summation of the Black Nun's dream and the cause of my Master's concern. A new revelation breeds the fanatic in those it first visits, leaving them not disposed to be gentle with those of an earlier dispensation.'

The rulers looked from one to another in alarm.

'Merchants can never rule,' spluttered Louis incredulously.

'*Must* never rule,' corrected Maximilian.

After five minutes of similar anti-mercantile diatribe, Slovo felt satisfied that the Monarchs were sufficiently inspired by fear to act in the desired way, and he spoke again, 'You need not *destroy* Venice,' he counselled. 'Europe needs someone to befuddle the Turk with trade and double-talk. What's required is the removal of its new inspiration, the source of its burgeoning energies.'

'This new religion?' queried Maximilian.

'The same,' answered Slovo.

'And how, pray, shall we do that?' said King Louis superciliously. 'Stick a sword in it?'

Entirely relaxed amidst these mere mortals, Slovo replied at once, 'Just leave it to me. All you have to do is clear the way and keep the Venetian army off my back. In some manner yet to be determined, I shall do the rest.'

The Kings and Princes exchanged puzzled glances, not sure whether to be impressed or offended.

Admiral Slovo turned to them with a humour-free smile. 'Don't worry,' he said by way of an explanatory aside. 'It's my sort of thing.'

*

'Oh, thanks *very* much!' said Numa Droz. 'How can I ever repay you?'

The Swiss's sarcasm could not be swept aside. Whilst conveniently absent-minded about favours, Droz never forgot anything considered an ill turn. Alone of all his debts, those he always settled in full.

Slovo's horse picked up the chilly vibrations and had to be quietened before the Admiral could reply. 'I thought you'd be pleased,' he protested. 'Would you have been happy to miss out on a career opportunity like the League of Cambrai?'

Numa Droz was not placated. 'Maybe not,' he said, 'but I was looking forward to a nice normal battle. *Now* I find it's your trademark spooky stuff!'

'May I remind you, Master Droz,' said Slovo evenly, 'that as my personal assistant you are the highest-paid mercenary in this army.'

'And what good is money to me, if I'm in no fit state to use it?'

Admiral Slovo's face became even more of a mask than usual. 'My patience is exhausted,' he said quietly.

Numa Droz then learnt the valuable lesson that wisdom (disguised as fear) could overcome even his own boundless ferocity. 'If I don't take this job,' he said, 'I'll be dead, won't I? Because then you'll have told me too much about this "new religion" business. And even if I take you out now, I don't doubt that orders for my death are already conditionally laid.'

Admiral Slovo frowned slightly in a pained *of course, who do you think you're dealing with?* gesture.

'On reflection,' said Numa Droz brightly, 'I'm delighted to accept this commission, Admiral, and am obliged for your recommendation.'

'Good,' said Slovo, giving the prearranged signal for the

concealed handgunners to stand down. 'So go over and sort out that bodyguard unit King Louis has forced upon us. Oh, and find out who's Commander-in-Chief and fit us into his plan of battle, will you?'

'It's done,' said Numa Droz, striding away.

Admiral Slovo had long observed that the safest course of action in a general engagement was to get stuck in. Those who remained aloof were asking to be selected as targets or easy pickings against unequal numbers. In due course, he therefore rode forward and charged with the French army, indulging in the usual hacking and stabbing of other mothers' sons who had in no way offended him.

Numa Droz, who had to watch his back against the French as well as worry about the enemy and the Admiral, was in his element and effortlessly efficient. Amidst the scrum, he saved Slovo's life countless times and cleared the necessary space for his Master to observe and ponder. The King's elite troop of Scottish archers performed the same function as an outer circle of expendables.

As luck would have it, it all worked rather well. Self-tuned into a high state of awareness, the Admiral's mind picked up the air-borne vibes before the coarse and licentious soldiery, before even the well-bred nerve endings of the metal-covered Gallic aristocracy. He bravely embraced what was seeping invisibly through the ether, then painfully managed to claw free from its grasp. How wise, he reflected, was Pope Julius – or the Providence which directed him – to select me for this task. So few other men could have done it.

Despatching a *stradiot* by a simple parry-feint-blade slide (they didn't seem to teach that basic move or its counter any more), he looked about for the source of his sensory experience. It was soon located and full comprehension thereby gained. He reined his horse back and sought the ear of Numa Droz.

'It's all sorted,' he said, his natural dignity marred by all the jostling and a flesh wound on the face. 'I know what's going on now. Cut me a way back. We'll need to be quick.'

It soon became clear that Slovo was right about the need for expedition. What he had already felt now began to affect the grosser sensitivities of the Allied army and, in turn, their professional performance. Before long they would cease to fight; soon after they would start to flee.

In the memoirs of his old age (acquired, read and then burnt by a Sicilian Bishop in the eighteenth century), Admiral Slovo's account of the Battle of Ghiaradadda (14/5/1509) refers to an alien sensation that began as calm but soon mellowed into an indifference disguised as tolerance. It then intensified (a contradiction in itself) into a loss of vivacity and ended, most horribly, in the featureless but enduring grey plains of boredom. If Admiral Slovo had not already been on first-name terms with philosophical misery, he could not have fought off, even temporarily, so terrible a foe.

Slowly, but surely, it was this very foe that was leading to the unravelling of the Allied army. As the last determined man in that army, Admiral Slovo made it his business to take charge of the artillery.

'Do you see that obelisk I'm pointing at.'

'Behind the Venetian lines – with all the people round it? The grey thing beside the Officers' latrines?' checked the gunner. 'Yes, I see it.'

'Desist fire on all else bar that until it is destroyed,' ordered Slovo. 'There could be monstrous gold in this for you, you appreciate—'

'I don't need bribing,' said the cold-eyed man. 'I take a pride in my work. That box is bloody *dead*: you watch!'

Such myopic stupidity inspired confidence and sure enough, soon after, the guns spoke united and deadly, like the voice of God.

Admiral Slovo turned to address his remaining colleagues. 'The obelisk to which I referred is presently departing this vale of tears,' he said. 'Our troops will then regain their confidence and the Venetians will run away. You will proceed to the obelisk's remains and convey to me as prisoners those remaining about it.'

And that's just what happened.

When Numa Droz and the Scots returned with their prisoners, the Swiss looked furtive and guilty.

'It's like this,' he said, avoiding the Admiral's eyes. 'We could have been back sooner but I stopped to get some heads.' He held up a damp-bottomed canvas sack. 'All those running people – just too tempting. There'll be a quarter off my invoice for the lapse – I insist.'

It meant nothing one way or the other to Slovo since Pope Julius was picking up the bill. He didn't even acknowledge the confession, being too busy studying the crop of serviceable captives, yet he stored it up as possible future ammunition against the Swiss.

There were a dozen of them, some a little damaged in transit but basically of merchantable quality, all dressed from head to foot in grey. One was distinguished by the paler grey of his robes, but otherwise this was a brotherhood, united even in defeat, that glared wildly at Admiral Slovo.

'I think I know you,' said Slovo in a kindly tone to the one man singled out by his clothes.

'Murderer!' spat the grey man in return.

'And knowing you,' Slovo continued unperturbed, 'I suspect I now know all. I apologize for the largely wasted errand, Master Droz, but would you kill these others please? It transpires they are incidental.'

The process brought a little more reasonableness to the

man Slovo had selected. Wide-eyed, he rushed away from his companions as Droz and the Scots moved in.

'I'm very sorry,' explained the Admiral to him, 'but my instructions were very clear: "root and branch" were the words – and so it must be.'

'You do not understand what you are destroying!' said the survivor, half angry, half placatory.

'On the contrary, Master Pacioli, I am only too well aware,' replied Slovo. 'But if it is any comfort I suspect that I have destroyed nothing, merely postponed something. By the way, whilst unable to actually admire your great book, I appreciate the power and thought within and, of course, the illustrations by Da Vinci.'

Despite the circumstances and the bodies piling up, Luca Pacioli, author of *Summa de Arithmetica* (Venice 1494), the world's very first accountancy and double-entry book-keeping primer, was fanatic enough to enjoy the pseudo-compliment.

'It is the start of great things!' he said excitedly. 'It was the reason I was chosen. And it can still go on, it is not too late! Despite what you've done, we can still cut you in.'

Admiral Slovo smiled his thanks for the offer but declined. 'Not my cup of sherbet, I'm afraid,' he explained politely. 'I'm rather partial to being on the winning side, you see, and your ... persuasion's time is not yet come. It will soon, doubtless, but today's work will set you back until well after I am safely dust.'

'That cannot be!' answered Pacioli, calmer and more rational now that the screaming round about him was over. 'We have logic on our side.'

'A commendably austere ally,' agreed Slovo, 'and thus not in keeping with the spirit of the age. Incidentally, who chose you? What did it call itself?'

'Just such a *spirit* as you speak of,' said Pacioli, with all the fervour of a true believer, 'but not that of this untidy, ungoverned era. The spirit that called to me was of a glorious time to come! There will be an ending of history when man will speak, rationally, to man – but only as much as is necessary and only of solid, tangible subjects. Life will be sensible and capable of prediction and . . .'

'Yes, yes, yes, spare me,' interrupted Slovo. 'The name if you please, sirrah.'

'It called itself the Te Deum,' replied Pacioli, winding down again. 'I do not pretend to understand that – perhaps some play on the Latin or the Church service of that title. Still, with all it promised for mankind, I felt that this initial irrationalism could be overlooked.'

'Indeed,' said Slovo charitably.

'I was its chosen prophet and it called me *Gateway*. My humble book was its prompting, the invitation and portal into our world, I was told, and I would be accordingly blessed. I was honoured to receive its precise instructions for the building of its dwelling place, its tabernacle – just like Moses the Hebrew and the old, now superseded, spirit of Jehovah.'

Numa Droz and his company, all devout Christians in so far as their career would permit it, made menacing signs of disapproval at this blasphemy. Admiral Slovo silenced their growls with a gesture.

'Which was the grey obelisk with drawers, I take it,' said the Admiral.

'"The Filing Cabinet" as we were told to name it,' confirmed Pacioli. 'Therein its spirit would dwell. The Doge, inspired by the vision vouchsafed me, spared no effort in its construction, but the Te Deum was unassuming and its requirements modest; mere sheet metal of grey with trays of lighter fawn – a humble house for so universal a benison.'

'But sadly vulnerable to the brute force of cannon balls,' commented Slovo.

'Yes,' answered Pacioli bitterly. 'You have sundered the House of the New god and killed his priests. It and I and history will never forgive you.'

'Fortunately, I care nothing for the judgement of all three,' said Slovo.

'Yet you have nothing of the emotional about you,' said Pacioli, making a last valiant effort. 'You could easily be one of us. When we opened the drawer of the Filing Cabinet to allow the spirit of the Te Deum to go forth and disconcert its enemies, its calming breath must have touched and inspired you.'

Admiral Slovo smiled as if gently declining an invitation to a party.

'But you refused the call of the New Way and broke its tabernacle,' said Pacioli in a crushed voice. 'And now its spirit wanders I know not where.'

'I AM HERE,' said another voice, crashing into Pacioli's mouth like a guillotine. It sounded deceptively mild, the voice of a man outlining something dull but inevitable. 'And though now homeless, I will never again go away.'

The soldiers all about crossed themselves. Pacioli seemed fully aware of his occupation by extraneous forces and tears of joy began to roll down his annexed face.

'I could have given you so much,' continued the voice. 'First, the Venice-of-the-million-Office-workers, and then on and out to the greater world. Think, Admiral, you might have had fast-food by 1650; kalashnikovs and motorways by 1750!'

'Sorry,' said Admiral Slovo. 'My bosses didn't go for it – whatever it is you're talking about.'

'Well yes, you should always do as your superiors direct,'

conceded the voice. 'I just wish they'd been a little less short-sighted.'

'Thank you for being so understanding,' said Slovo and then stabbed Pacioli in the eye with a stiletto.

The proto-accountant died instantly but the Te Deum's animating force lingered on, causing the body to remain limply upright. It seemed an appropriate stance, all things considered.

'You're not rid of me,' the voice went on from Pacioli's gaping mouth as though nothing had happened. 'This carcass was my gateway and such I named him. He may be gone but I'm through the gate and here to stay. He and I have planted a seed. It will assuredly flower in some other time and place.'

'A grey bloom will surely hold little appeal,' said Slovo.

'Oh, you'd be surprised!' snapped back the voice. 'My disciples pay a high personal price, it's true, but what I teach holds the key to power. There will always be consumers for my product.'

'Balls!' said Numa Droz, obscurely offended by this talk and holding aloft his sword. '*This* is power!'

Pacioli's dead eyes beheld the blade and his slack mouth was twisted into an ironic smile.

'For a little while longer,' the Voice agreed. 'But one day, and it will not be long delayed, my disciples in grey with their calculators and briefcases will each command the power of ten thousand such . . . swords.'

'Sounds good,' said Numa Droz eagerly. 'How do you make these *kal-cool-ators* and *bre-cases*? Are they single or double-edged?'

'You couldn't handle them,' replied the Voice, dismissing him. 'You are the past. So is Venice, so is Italy. They have failed or rejected me and will thus decline. Romance and interest they may well retain, but power will migrate and then return to conquer them. I shall fuel, inspire and then accompany that power when the day comes, and imagination will have to bow its knee. Meanwhile, I must bide my time and await the inevitable call from elsewhere – perhaps from the lands of the North. We shall see, shall we not. *I'll be back.*'

To Slovo, these threats were like growls from sheep – insulting rather than fearful. With a nod of the head, he indicated the troops should move in.

They hacked with their swords, bringing the ex-Pacioli down, but their grievous blows, a leg off here, a cloven head there, did not deprive the Te Deum of speech.

'There *will* be accountancy,' it bubbled and spluttered. 'And insurance and statistics, audit and risk-analysis. I *will* bind the world and make it safe. Tomorrow belongs to me!'

At that point Pacioli's interconnected body parts gave way and the spirit fled. Slovo and the soldiers saw a smoky shape skim over them and away. As it passed, it turned a Scot's prized red locks grey. A final message perhaps.

And that was the last Admiral Slovo knew of the matter.

A century or so later, an Antwerp cloth merchant woke up one morning and found that, out of nowhere, his head was full of startling new business ideas (a bit *grinding* maybe but very sound even so). By then, of course, Admiral Slovo was dead and gone.

ꝗ The Year 1509

'In bed with the Borgias. Cannons and cuckoldry in Northern Italy. An ordeal not entirely in accord with my tastes.'

'So, how was it for you?'

Admiral Slovo propped himself up in bed and considered the question. 'Very interesting,' he said at length.

'But nothing like the real thing, I suppose.'

'Merely different,' the Admiral corrected. 'A little ... crowded perhaps – especially so, now that passion is spent.'

Lucrezia Borgia, Duchess of Ferrara, was loath to dismiss the bevy of handmaidens, especially since the one trained in Sapphic verse was sleepily lisping her favourite lines:

> Some say a cavalry corps,
> some infantry, some again
> will maintain that the swift oars
>
> of our fleet are the finest
> sight on dark earth, but I say
> that whatever one loves, is.

She waited until the last moving words were said and then shooed all the painted hussies from the giant bed. Admiral Slovo stoically endured being clambered over by young female flesh and was polite enough to utter his thanks as each body passed. They moved as swiftly as they could, for fear of Lucrezia's whip – there'd been enough of that in the night.

In private at last, the Duchess offered the Admiral a compliant smile. 'There,' she said, 'I don't suppose you always get such a warm welcome from the Vehme.'

Admiral was leaning over the side of the bed, ensuring that his boots (and thus the concealed stiletto) were still in easy reach. Only then could he relax sufficiently to frame a reply. 'No indeed,' he said. 'Imposition on my own hospitality and bulk consumption of my wine is more the norm. Therefore I thank you for a night of quite exquisite diversion, not to mention surprises.'

'How so?' asked Lucrezia, intrigued. She had seen the Admiral as a challenge, a grand test of her bedroom skills, little expecting such a return in physical and mental stimulation.

'I don't refer to the extension of my erotic range, as you might think,' he mused – and Lucrezia looked disappointed, 'but to the revelations about your status. I must confess that I never suspected you of leadership of the Borgia clan, let alone membership of the Vehme. I am getting old and unobservant.'

Lucrezia was thinking her own thoughts about the passing of years and, at the advanced age of thirty, had been hopeful of a compliment on her continuing loveliness and her mettlesome performance in bed. However, she kindly overlooked the Admiral's incivility. Those same years had provided ample opportunity to become hardened to the selfishness of men.

'The deception was fully intentional,' she said. 'I am only too gratified to hear of its success. In each Borgia generation one member is pre-eminent by virtue of their ambition or drive. Daddy, I grant you, was a good Pope – religious considerations aside – and poor dead Cesare was excellent at frightening people. Juan and Joffre, whilst not much use for anything else, could at least breed and restock the line. I was the one chosen to lead, although forced to dissimulate and adopt a secret guiding role by my sex and the prejudice of the age. We haven't done so badly out of it, all things considered, and the Vehme seemed to concur with the family's appointment.'

'Is that general Borgia knowledge?' asked Slovo, rearranging their scarlet sheets to protect his modesty.

'Oh no!' said the Duchess, uncovering herself again. 'That's my own little secret. Besides, I'm not a full initiate, admitted into the perfection of their embrace. My Christian beliefs, increasingly persuasive as I . . . age, preclude me from that.'

'Most commendable,' said Admiral Slovo, and rested his head back on the opulent pillows. Through the window he could see across the City Square to where the Cathedral of St George faced the d'Este family 'Tower of the Lions' in which he now lay. Morning was already well advanced and the distant noise of commerce wafted up to disturb the idyll. 'I hesitate to foreclose this interlude of delight,' he said, 'but shouldn't we consider the return of Duke Alfonso?'

Lucrezia snorted her contempt.

'If he visited my boudoir, I'd die of surprise rather than a cuckold's revenge,' she said. 'True, early in our marriage, he built a "secret" passage between my rooms and his, hoping to take me unawares in illicit passion, but it remains unused. Perhaps that's just as well since I've had it booby-trapped. But no, Admiral, I'd need to dress up as a cannon before he'd show any such interest as you fear!'

'Yes,' said Slovo, 'when I met the Duke he did in fact speak to me of his great love for artillery – at some length.'

'He spends his days at the cannon foundry he's created – in search of the perfect piece of ordnance. Still, it does at least further the cause of the Ferraran State which he inherited and I run. Our army is well served, even if I am not.'

'Many ladies of quality would envy your marital arrangements,' said the Admiral, 'wishing their husbands would attend more to Mars than Venus. Certainly, Duke Alfonso fought creditably when we were together last year at Ghiaradadda.'

'Yes,' said Lucrezia archly, 'he saves his performances for the battlefield.' Seeing the Admiral's attention was distracted, she added, 'Oh, I do apologize for the noise incidentally . . .'

Admiral Slovo was well aware of the cause of the sound of padding feet and the occasional sob coming from above. Duke Alfonso's two half-brothers, Giulio and Ferrante, had been imprisoned there, one above the other in windowless cells, since a bungled coup attempt five years ago. What the Admiral could not know was that they were to remain there, fed by manna descending through a hole in the ceiling, unmentioned and unlamented by their family, for fifty-three and forty-three years respectively. It had amused Duke Alfonso to house them within audible range of his intimidating wife.

A Gascon priest, similarly involved, had been less favourably treated. Since no secular prince could lawfully execute a priest, Alfonso had housed *him* in an external hanging cage and was content to let winter or hunger do the deed. In the event, there had proven to be one kind person in the Castle and he or she had dropped the priest a cloth with which to hang himself. His body still resided in the cage, a gruesome sight for the Admiral to feast his eyes upon when he'd arrived.

Aware therefore of such tokens of Ducal displeasure, Admiral Slovo still felt he had good cause to fear Alfonso's revenge. However, he was too courteous to return to the topic. Brushing her questing hand away from his privates, he said, 'Rest at ease, Duchess,' and levered himself out of bed, gathering his clothes for fear of further intimacy developing. 'At least your husband made himself most useful to us. Among other things, the Ferraran artillery proved decisive in confounding the Venetians.'

'And not just the Venetians,' said Lucrezia with a sly smile.

'Ah,' said the Admiral, climbing into his tights. 'So you've received a briefing about that then?'

'About the Te Deum and the Filing Cabinet? Of course! I insisted on full disclosure from the Vehme as a pre-condition to declaring war on so powerful a neighbour as Venice. By the by, they positively sang your praises afterwards – and rightly so. It's not everyone who gets to snuff out a religion.'

Slovo was brushing his straight, silver hair and turned to face the recumbent Duchess. 'As I constantly state,' he said, 'I fear the "snuffed" candle will one day re-light. We have retained simplicity and man-scaled civilization for a few generations more, that is all.'

'Well, as for the future,' said Lucrezia, 'the Vehme have other wonders for you to perform nearer to home.'

'Surely not Capri?'

'The Church.'

'I *wondered* when they'd dare to tackle it!' said Slovo. 'They are aware, I hope, that they cannot count on my total engagement in this project?'

'Oh yes,' Lucrezia hurried to say. 'You and I are in a similar case with our affection for Mother Church. Still, there is no harm in letting the Vehme chance their arm – and lose it.'

'You make a good case, Madame,' said the Admiral, in full agreement. 'It is written that one must not put God to the test, but I recall nothing to that effect in scripture relating to his earthly representatives. It will be an interesting experiment. What do they want of me?'

'Against so formidable an opponent, the Vehme first propose to divide before they conquer. Their aim is to split the Church.'

Slovo was helping himself to a reviving glass of wine. 'Between saints and sinners?' he asked as he poured. 'Believers and the ambitious?'

'The exact details were not vouchsafed me,' the Duchess replied. 'I am only informed that there are two separate people whom they wish you to meet. Presumably *The Book* says that your presence is required. Neither are initiates or even sympathizers, but merely those in whom the Vehme have invested hopes. The first they say you need not unduly concern yourself with. Apparently it is thought mere proximity to your company will have the desired effect. The second they wish you to "entertain", "Broaden his horizons" were their exact words.'

'And what were their names, Madame?' asked Slovo, preparing to go.

'For that information,' came the answer in a coquettish voice, 'there is a price. I first require you to "entertain" *me*. Come back to bed and "broaden my horizons". And other places . . .'

Admiral Slovo considered the prospect and reluctantly resigned himself to compliance. There was, he comforted himself, at least a certain aptness in doing to a Borgia what the Borgias had long done to the wider world.

❧ The Year 1510

*'THE FLOWERING OF THE
REFORMATION & FATHER DROZ'S
LITTLE OUTING: A symposium on faith, carnal
lust and sausage. I guiltily sow weeds in the fields of
Mother Church.'*

> *... And then the Pope made a joke about the 'Lion of Judah'
> at which I was expected to laugh. But for imagining him
> naked and painted blue I do not think I could have managed
> it. Even so, I fear I may have been less than convincing in my
> deception. Therefore please speak to him on our behalf upon
> your return. Destroy this letter.*
>
> > *Your loving brother in monotheism and melancholy,*
> > > *Rabbi Megillah.*

'So how goes it with the Roman Hebrews?' asked Numa
Droz. He was examining a crossbow quarrel, pondering ways
to improve lethality but still sufficiently bored to show an
unprecedented interest in others.

Admiral Slovo carelessly let the letter drop from his fingers,
and the night breeze bore it off the Tower, and into the
moonlit, Tuscan countryside below. 'It goes badly,' he replied
languidly, 'but that is nothing in the least novel. As head of the
community, Megillah has been skinned for the Lion money.'

'Serves him right,' smiled Droz, showing his brown peg
teeth. 'What's the Lion money then?'

'The salary and expenses of the *Custos Leonis* who looks after the symbolic, but nevertheless live, lion traditionally held on the Capitoline Hill in Rome. Surely you must have seen it?'

'No, Admiral, I haven't. I don't go to Rome to sight-see.'

But to be told who to kill, thought Slovo. 'Quite. Well, on reflection, perhaps your omission is not so surprising. The lion is tame and gentle and easily intimidated by the brutality of the Roman crowd. It therefore rarely emerges from its cage. Even so, the related cost is said to be thirty silver florins per annum and in memory of the price paid to Judas for the betrayal of the Christ-person, such a sum is yearly extracted from the Roman Hebrews. Conjoined with all the other depredations they are prey to, it presents them with no small problem.'

'Well then,' said Droz, his conversational attention span reaching its limits, 'they should kill it.'

'The lion, you mean?' queried Slovo, somewhat puzzled.

'Why not?' replied the Swiss mercenary, enviably untouched by doubt. 'The lion, the custodian, whoever . . .'

'So here we are again,' said the Admiral, idly amused. 'Your explanation and remedy for all ills: *kill it.*'

Numa Droz adopted his 'honest peasant among sophisticates' persona. 'Well, it's a maxim that always served me well,' he sad stoutly.

Admiral Slovo would have been hard put to dispute the point. Captain of the Ostia Citadel at twenty-one, roving problem-remover for three Popes by the age of thirty, possessor of a smooth and unstressed family life, Numa Droz occupied the high ground in any such argument.

Silence, save for the sounds of perpetual war between owl and vole, fell as the duo on the tower resumed their vigil, peering out into the unlit night, grading shadows and evaluating the mutation of shades.

Admiral Slovo would have been content never to speak to mankind again, but Numa Droz, for all the bloodiness of his progress from the Alps to the Apennines, retained a degree of sociability. To his mind, speech and noise were useful indicators of life – lack of them usually meaning his job was done. The corollary of this, however, was that prolonged quiet made him uneasy. He worried that he too might have crossed the great divide without realizing (another of his range of tricks).

'You're very pally with Jews, aren't you?' he said eventually.

Slovo undermined his answer by hesitation. '. . . Yes – and why not?'

Numa Droz ignored the riposte. 'We've got Jews in Canton Uri,' he said. 'Came from Heidelberg where the people gave 'em a hard time. It turned those left into a vicious bunch of daggermen: neutral, close-grained sort of folk as far as humanity goes; bad enemies. I really like them.'

'Remind me never to introduce you to my acquaintance, Rabbi Megillah,' mused Slovo.

'There's a saying about Hebrews in Uri, Admiral,' continued Droz unabashed. 'If anything's really dangerous – you know, an iffy bridge or splintery seat – "it's like a Jew with a knife", we say. Now, is that high praise or what?'

'Dangerous?' queried the young lady emerging through the Tower's trap door, catching the echo of conversation and repeating it with hot interest. 'What's so dangerous?'

'Nothing that need engage your attention,' growled Numa Droz, turning back to scan the outer darkness. Free as she was with her favours, the Lady Callypia de Marinetti would never sleep with a barbarian such as a Swiss. Knowing this, Droz was accordingly tormented with desire.

'How are you, my lady?' asked Slovo with great courtesy. 'Can you not sleep?'

The beautiful young patrician unleashed a full volley of charm at the Admiral, and then remembered that in his case her powder was damp and useless. The charm was extinguished like a light.

'I cannot sleep,' she said, reverting to tartness, 'because I am plagued by your Englishman following me: he even attempts to settle outside my door. I have come to complain.'

'She's plagued by something all right,' said the soldier who now joined them on the roof. 'Or maybe lack of something, hur hur!'

'Then you still suspect there are matters afoot, Master Cromwell?' asked Slovo gently.

'Borr ... she's up to something tonight,' said Thomas Cromwell. 'There's fires lit in there expecting quenching before cock crows, I reckon.'

To the fastidious Admiral, all speech bar his native Italian sounded like angry coughing but he recognized the control and cultivation overlying the soldier's earthy peasant tones.

'How dare ...!' exclaimed de Marinetti, for probably the fiftieth time that day. No one paid attention, for the act was wearing thin.

Cromwell dared because he was abroad and armed and fortified with the qualities expected of a Cockney Brewer's son. 'They may be all eyes and legs, these nobility,' he continued, 'but I know the spirit of the farmyard when I see it.'

'Yes ... yes, thank you,' said Admiral Slovo, only his Stoicism preventing an impermissible show of embarrassment.

'We go!' hissed Numa Droz from the parapet's edge, waving them all to silence with a compelling chop of his gauntleted hand. Cromwell permitted himself a thin-lipped smile of vindication.

For all his sympathy concerning the dictates of passion in

others, the Admiral looked sternly on de Marinetti. She had only been in his charge for a mere month: what were young people coming to?

Seeing the game was up, Callypia shrugged her tiny shoulders, expressing the Pagan innocence of her time and class.

Carried clearly on the still air, they heard the gentle rasp of gravel upon glass further along the priory wall.

'Love craves entry,' whispered Numa Droz, '(if you see what I mean). And though the bed is empty, still he must have his night to remember.'

In an impressive blur, the Swiss rose, sighted and fired his crossbow. A howl like the end of the world livened the night.

'Right in the parts!' exulted Droz, addressing de Marinetti. 'He's a fine-looking youth – but not much use to you now, I fear.'

The lady, looking wiser than her sixteen summers should permit, was already descending the stairway. Bisected by the Tower floor, she turned back to reply. 'If the ancient writers were studied,' she said, firing another full broadside of allure in order to taunt, 'in the place from which you spring, then you would know there are subtler refinements of joy than plain fornication. I go now to explore them. Sleep well, gentlemen – and you too, Swiss.'

Admiral Slovo (who knew precisely what she meant) and the soldiers who (even worse) could construct some guesses, were silenced. Prisoner though she was, de Marinetti retained the power to sow seeds that would blossom and grow, spreading their poison rest for seasons to come.

She then departed, mistress of the field.

Each wrapped in coils of unhealthy speculation, the three captors followed her down. The sobs and groans from the priory grounds continued a little longer before stopping abruptly and for ever.

What have I become, thought Admiral Slovo, remembering the child that he must once have been, *that I find cruel things funny?*

'As one professional to another,' said Thomas Cromwell, to Numa Droz the following morning, 'I would advise against your present daydreams. Would you shoot so well with your eyes removed? Would there be point in such thoughts if your manly parts were torn out?'

Droz knew the advice was both timely and well meant. He tore his eyes from Madame de Marinetti's retreating form for fear of the operation being performed literally.

'It's that bad, is it?' he asked.

'Or that good,' nodded Cromwell. 'Palatine gossip says her invention is so unique, her performance so mettlesome, that she makes monogamy a viable option. That holds obvious attractions for a Pope for, after all, he has a certain position to maintain. Alas, however, the lady's energies are ... exuberant and Pope Julius is a jealous man. He thinks a spell in this forsaken hole might cool his mistress's passions – other than for him, that is.'

Numa Droz laughed: an unnatural and unpractised sound. 'What? With all these novices and us here? Not to mention half the gentlemen of the region now wearing crossbow bolts in their codpieces.'

'Leave the "us" out of it,' said Cromwell, an edge of iron in his voice. 'I saw what was done to the Scribbiacci brothers in Rome for essaying what you have in mind. Blood waterfalled freely from the scaffold and the hangman had to be paid extra. It was most educational and accordingly, for my part, I look at her as I would my mother.'

Numa Droz acknowledged the wisdom of this. 'And, of course, the Admiral is her appointed custodian,' he said.

'Beware him, Engishman: he reads minds and is married to the stiletto.'

'He has commendable self-control,' concluded Cromwell. 'And I intend to emulate him in this respect. You should do the same. It might,' he went on, wrinkling his nose, 'enable us to transcend the present overpowering stench.'

'I know,' agreed Droz. 'Ghastly, isn't it? I hate flowers.'

Admiral Slovo, who had listened in to all this, decided there was nothing of import brewing between his two mercenaries. There was, of course, a contingency plan for the disposal of either or both but, for the present, it could lie, chill but ready, in the ice-house of his subtle calculations. He walked on.

'Must those two follow me everywhere?' snarled de Marinetti. 'Can't I even walk in a garden without—'

'Patience,' said the Prioress, 'is the open secret of happiness: lack of this quality is, I think, the seat of your troubles.'

'The seat of her troubles,' whispered Droz to Cromwell, 'is her seat.'

Callypia glowered at the blameless grass but deferred to superior spirit when she heard it. Admiral Slovo was happy merely to observe the fray, holding his own decisive forces in reserve.

'For instance.' the Prioress continued gently, 'it required patience to create this garden but, within a few decades, my restraint has borne a beautiful harvest. Look about you, child.'

For safety's sake, de Marinetti glanced briefly up at the great coloured ramparts of flowers that bordered the narrow paths. Right up to where the walls of the garden met the sky, an anarchy of starbursts and tendrils was all that met her eye. 'It is too much,' she announced. 'You have incited nature to excess.'

Admiral Slovo's judgement was not so harsh. Although

(also for safety's sake) self-trained to aesthetic indifference, he quite liked the riotous garden. The unusual degree of concealment offered rendered it an assassin's dream.

'As you may already suspect,' continued the serene old lady, 'this garden is my pride and joy. It has blossomed and flourished in direct proportion to the joy and detachment I increasingly feel and, as such, may be a divinely permitted metaphor.'

'But what if,' Master Cromwell said confidently, 'man is master of his own destiny? I heard it proposed in Antwerp that the Almighty set the universal mechanism in motion and then stepped back. Opinions vary, but perhaps he has withdrawn until the Day of Judgement – or even for ever. If so, we are alone: and these are just riotous blooms and no more. What then?'

The Prioress looked quizzically at the Admiral.

'it is a foible of mine' he said, 'to permit liberality of speech in my servitors. It amuses me because of the occasional gem of perspective that, from time to time, emerges. However, if he is being offensive . . .'

'No,' said the Prioress in a kindly voice. 'He may be English but his mind shows tolerable discernment.'

Cromwell frowned again and the observant Admiral saw the face of murder briefly surge up from its place of confinement.

'Well,' said Numa Droz, 'if we're all to be permitted to put our pike in, what I'd like to say is that this place would make a fine defensive point for the Priory. Hack them plant-things away, platform and crenellate the walls and you could hold this for days against pirates and free-companies.'

'Or lovers of the inmates,' said Cromwell, with cold anger.

The Prioress spoke up at once. 'The blooms,' she said, impelling Droz to silence, 'will not be cut. I forbid it absolutely.'

The spirit in her voice caused the little party to wake anew. De Marinetti looked at the Prioress, perhaps scenting some weak point on which to play. Admiral Slovo was obliged to suppress a flicker of surprise. The soldiers, reflexes triggered by raised voices, were instantly on duty.

'And that is my one permitted selfishness,' she continued, by way of explanation. 'Outside this garden I have surrendered my will to God but here; here is where I come to regroup. I trust you will appreciate the military metaphor there, gentlemen – and note it.'

They nodded.

'Beauty hoarded,' said de Marinetti, 'is beauty wasted.'

'Without restraint,' countered the Prioress, 'beauty is guzzled and debauched. The senses must be tamed and fed moderately – like a lion in a pleasure garden.'

The Admiral signalled his wholehearted agreement and cast his own mind cheerily back to when he himself was a mere slave of feeling: before tragedy and experience, before Marcus Aurelius and Stoicism.

Only Cromwell seemed to remain resentful of the Prioress prevailing, 'I have heard it said that the Hebrew scriptures say that before the throne of judgement, every soul must one day account for every pleasure missed.'

'Every *legitimate* pleasure,' said the Prioress. 'You really must quote accurately, mercenary.'

'Whatever,' replied Cromwell blithely. 'Legitimacy varies from sect to sect.'

A gulf of years and sadness separated the Prioress from the dangerous energies of the Englishman and she could not find it in herself to blame him for his zest. *Christ*, she recalled, *is in every man – but sometimes in heavy disguise.* 'I am pleased,' she said, 'to hear your familiarity with any scripture. Why, to think my previous impression was that the Almighty did not play an overlarge part in your life . . .'

'Whilst not, of course,' Cromwell replied, 'denying God' (and all the others nodded, observing the formalities of the age) 'it is at least arguable to consider him remote. One can regard him as the foundation of proper social order but still not require the sight of his hand at work amongst men. I suspect we are effectively orphans and alone in the world – that being so, we must surely make our own way.'

The Prioress was merely amused and this only infuriated Cromwell the more.

'If I did not know,' she replied, 'that my Redeemer liveth and will one day walk the Earth, life would be . . . insupportable. It would have no point.'

'And why should it have?' cried Cromwell, warming to his subject. 'From our puny perspective, why should we perceive any meaning? I see no need for heaven or hell or *meaning*. It is a mighty universe we inhabit, Prioress, and more than enough to get on with, in fact.'

Admiral Slovo had long ago ceased to care, and the Prioress held her peace. Meanwhile, way above (or below) all this philosophy, Callypia de Marinetti winked at Numa Droz and shifted her endless legs. Ignoring visions of red-hot pincers and the executioner's knife, and like all tiny creatures seizing at the fleeting moments life offered before the final dark, Droz winked back.

'So they are all gone?' asked Admiral Slovo calmly.

'Every one, sir,' replied the nervous novice. 'And she has not risen at her customary time. We are all most concerned.'

De Marinetti placed a (possibly) consoling arm around the young nun's shoulders and stroked her hand. 'No one is holding you responsible, my lovely,' she said. 'Our suspicions are drifting elsewhere.'

'Not I!' protested Cromwell. 'I am capable of many things—'

'Of anything, surely,' corrected Numa Droz, expressing his professional opinion.

'—but not pettiness,' Cromwell pressed on.

Admiral Slovo looked at the mercenary, pinning him with his grey eyes. A tense moment elapsed until, his mental trespass complete, Slovo was satisfied.

'I believe you,' he said. 'However, given your continual debate with the Prioress these last two weeks, and your obvious ill-will upon being worsted, our initial surmise is surely forgivable.'

'I would not harm the Prioress,' Master Cromwell maintained stoutly, just the lightest sheen adorning his brow by virtue of Slovo's scrutiny, 'or any other old lady.'

'Unless it was necessary or business,' expanded Numa Droz again.

'Naturally,' conceded Cromwell.

'Very well then,' said Slovo. 'The noose remains untenanted – for the time being. Let us go and examine the evidence first-hand.'

'There may be no case to answer,' commented Numa Droz reasonably. 'Old ladies do sleep late sometimes. My great-grandmother . . .'

'No,' said the Admiral confidently. 'This place is diminished: I can sense it. She has gone on.'

That was enough to decide things and the little party roused themselves from the breakfast table.

'You stay here,' said Slovo to the novice – and then noticed de Marinetti's flare of predatory interest. 'On second thoughts, come with us; you've had enough novelty for one day.'

The garden was bare, a green graveyard of beheaded stems.

'What hours of patient work,' marvelled Callypia, 'to sever and collect every bloom. Surely this is either a labour of love or hate . . .'

'Two closely related emotions,' commented Slovo, permitting just a modicum of contempt on the final word. 'And the Prioress's bed-chamber is . . .?' he enquired.

The novice indicated a solid-looking barrier at one end of the ravaged field.

'Brute force, if you please,' said Slovo to Numa Droz.

The great Swiss casually applied his metal-shod boot to the door, which splintered away from the violence offered it. With contrasting gentleness, he then disengaged the wounded lock. The door swung open.

Admiral Slovo walked in like Sultan Mehmed the Conqueror entering Constantinople. The others, more like the disciples at the Easter Tomb, followed nervously.

In this case the tomb was not empty. The Prioress, having left the world behind, sat peacefully composed in her bedside chair, surrounded by her transplanted earthly joys. Every surface bore bowls and vases packed with the cut flowers, even the bed and floor were thickly stewn with them so that the otherwise bare and sombre cell was today positively aglow with colour.

Whilst his charges and followers looked on in wonder, saving the image for their old age, Slovo made a search and discovered the unsealed letter propped up before a washbowl of roses.

'*I have heard my call,*' he read dispassionately to the assembled witnesses, '*and dutifully answer, being nothing loath to leave. I know my redeemer liveth.*'

Thomas Cromwell sighed.

'She always had to have the last word,' he said bitterly.

*

'She may just have felt Time's heavy hand upon her,' said Cromwell, 'and made a lucky guess.'

Admiral Slovo made his move and doomed, three turns on, Cromwell's rook to inevitable death.

'One does not bid farewell to one's oldest friends, as the Prioress did, on the basis of a guess. Imagine the embarrassment of waking the next morning!'

'Perhaps she took poison to avoid that shame,' hazarded Cromwell, grimacing at the chessboard in his unwillingness to admit defeat.

'No,' said Slovo, looking around the cleared garden. 'I have a passing familiarity with the poisoner's art. The Prioress departed at the call of Nature alone.'

'And she's been seen again!' piped the Lady de Marinetti. 'This morning! One of the novices told me.'

'I have also heard these stories,' said Admiral Slovo. 'If true, she seems to have retained a custodial interest in her former garden.'

Former was the correct word. Plagued by boredom and lust, Numa Droz had pressed the sturdier nuns into service, turning the garden into the citadel he had proposed earlier. Already, in one short week, the plants were gone, replaced by rough rubble ramparts.

'The dead,' Cromwell spat, 'are gone and spent and do not return to trouble us. That is their great merit. It has to be so for the proper ordering of things.'

'How so?' queried Admiral Slovo with polite interest at his soldier's venture into statecraft.

'Well, consider,' replied the Englishman, boldly convinced, 'if every subject disposed of by a Prince, came back to mock his Lord's decision; if every felon hung returned to flout the Law's due sentence, what then? Why, Admiral, there would be metaphysical anarchy!'

Admiral Slovo decided he rather liked the sound of that situation and was thus in favour of the two-way grave.

'Besides,' Cromwell continued, 'the one redeeming feature of the woman's death was in the proof it must have supplied her. Failing to awake to life everlasting she would – if she could – have conceded the explosion of her life-long fancies. Alas, however, she could not – for she was dead and I am right.'

Then de Marinetti gasped and pointed. Admiral Slovo smiled and Cromwell rocketed to his feet, propelling the board and chessmen into the air.

The Prioress was gliding alongside one of the walls, tending and scenting flowers that only she could see. They saw her as through a grey, gauzy film, a figure who flicked in and out of view as she passed open doorways between her world and the real one. The presence of the Admiral and his party was not acknowledged. Eventually, she entered some section of the parallel region not visible to man and disappeared from sight like an extinguished candle-flame.

Callypia de Marinetti sighed deeply and smoothed her hands down her silken gown. 'I never knew,' she purred, 'that fright could be so delicious.'

Thomas Cromwell was less sanguine. He stared after the vision, his face set with barely checked ferocity. 'I take this as an insult,' he said quietly.

'The important thing about a haunting,' said Admiral Slovo, 'is to stand still.'

'Eh?' snarled Cromwell angrily, wrenching his eyes away from the Prioress's spectre as she advanced, yet again, along the departed flowerbeds. '*Still*? What d'you mean?'

Slovo fastidiously ignored the lack of respect, putting it down to stress. Over the last two weeks, Cromwell had been positively persecuted by the ghost, both by its frequent appearances – sometimes at most inconvenient and private moments – and by the implications of its presence. He had got it into his head that everyone – even the giggly novices – was laughing at him.

'I mean,' explained the Admiral patiently, 'that we are permitted these visions through portals of communication. As you will observe from the irregularity of our view, they are random and transient. One moment she can be seen, the next she has passed from sight – only to reappear elsewhere. The correlation of dimensions between here and ... somewhere else is not precise or predictable. If one were to move about during a manifestation there would be the danger of involuntary penetration into other realms. At such moments, who knows what awful gateways gape a mere hand's breadth away from us?'

But Thomas Cromwell had been pushed too far to heed wise words. The future Chancellor of England was consulting his subconscious, travelling back down the years and communing with his roots. He was hearing the savage advice of Pagan Saxon ancestors. Even King Ambition was powerless before the winds that blew from those times and regions.

His eyes narrowed and the hands that would one day draft the dissolution of the monasteries and priories of his native land, twitched and curled with fury. 'Mebbe so,' he said, to no one in particular, the careful Court-English he was capable of replaced with a thicker, swifter dialect, 'but I reckon I'm being buggered about! And it's *like this*; I be fed up with it!'

He drew the concealed, serrated dagger that Slovo had noted on their first meeting and charged at the intermittent image of the Prioress. Admiral Slovo was intrigued to note the Englishman was still soldier enough to downgrade his anger into serviceable ferocity – and just as interested to see his theory confirmed as Cromwell was swallowed up and vanished from sight.

In her first interaction with the world since leaving it, the Prioress slowly turned to face Admiral Slovo and howled in triumph. It was not a sound that could have been emulated in life, being too octave-ranging for mortal chords. Also, somewhere in the interval of time, her eyes had been turned into fire.

Whatever the provocation, the Admiral was determined to heed his own advice. He held on to the arms of his chair and remained still; where Thomas Cromwell had gone, he did not care to follow.

Accordingly, during the long afternoon that followed, Slovo was captive witness to the hunting and harrying of Cromwell through the Prioress's new home. No one else entered the ravished garden, warned away by Slovo's terse commands. Only Numa Droz hovered alertly by the entrance, patiently awaiting the call to rescue his contract-master. Time hung heavy and horrible during the gory process but, as it turned out, there were diversions...

Before the noise of the multi-voiced howl had died away, the Prioress had sped out of sight. A few yards away, another *window* opened and Slovo saw her hurtling, most unlike an old lady, down some endless corridor. At its end stood Thomas Cromwell.

The two collided in a chaos of flapping black habit and gaudy mercenary's garb. Cromwell, bone-white but resolute, made a masterly up-and-under killing strike to the sternum region. It went up ... and up ... and through, meeting no resistance, Cromwell's whole arm following the blade. He had a moment to stand stupefied, harmlessly transfixing the Prioress. Then she laughed and blinded his right eye with a talon.

Again the vision faded.

And so it went on. A few more times, Cromwell turned to fight, his dagger passing uselessly through the spectre, while he suffered yet more grievous injuries. Thereafter, he relied exclusively on flight.

The Prioress's private heaven, hell or limbo, whatever it was, seemed full of indeterminate landscapes of white. Admiral Slovo caught glimpses of hills and plains as well as featureless interiors of the same dull hue. Sometimes, Cromwell appeared to have taken refuge within a building and would rest, heaving for breath and bright with blood, against a wall. But soon enough he would be scurrying on, driven by the sound of the Prioress's keening call.

On other occasions, a great time seemed to have elapsed and he was seen labouring over low foothills or salt-white marshes, fleeing the razor-sharp claws ever close behind. The Prioress's unearthy exultations echoed all over the drear scenes and seeped out of the portals to echo in her one-time garden. Cold winds also issued forth and streamed back the Admiral's silver hair, carrying with them the sounds of the hunt and the scent of despair.

In one of the less dramatic interludes, Admiral Slovo found himself thinking of what an Ottoman *Bashi-Bazouk* once told him (under torture, naturally). In Paradise, he had said, everything forbidden on Earth: wine, boys, a nice portrait on one's wall, all were permitted. Eternal indulgence was the reward for a life-time of restraint.

For himself, Admiral Slovo considered that total self-control should extend beyond the tomb – Stoicism being an absolute concept – but, for others, he could see the appeal of the idea. To the Prioress, for example, after three-score years and ten of peace and loving kindness, might not a spot of vengeance be most welcome? Surely, in her case, the larder of stockpiled aggression must be more than overflowing. In fact Slovo was slightly disappointed and his decision to distance himself from the world strengthened. If that was the way she acted once the leash was off, what real conviction had attended the virtuous life before? Actually it was rather shocking.

It ended – or the beginning ended – in early evening, by Admiral Slovo's time. By poor Master Cromwell's reckoning perhaps whole days or weeks had elapsed.

A series of irregular portals winked open and in a deserted town square, lit by the moon of Slovo's world, the Admiral saw Cromwell cornered – and then averted his eyes as the Prioress skinned the screaming soldier alive.

When it was done, she draped herself in the red pelt and eagerly ran off to an eternity of new wickedness. Except in dreams, Admiral Slovo never saw her again.

The obscure tides governing the display shifted and snapped the windows shut, at which point Cromwell was spewed forth on to the ground before the Admiral's feet, naked but otherwise untouched – and miraculously alive.

Less grateful than he might have been, Cromwell staggered to his feet and felt his chest and arms, half fearful that their solid attachment was illusory. 'I am whole again!' he gasped.

'Well, almost,' said Slovo gently. 'Save that she has carved the Papal Cross-keys upon your arse.'

Cromwell nearly turned to look but, higher sensibilities such as dignity now returning, he restrained himself.

'I suspect it may be permanent,' added Slovo rather gratuitously.

Cromwell nodded, 'I *will* be avenged, you know.'

Slovo smiled. 'How so? The Prioress is beyond your reach in the most profound of ways.'

It was Cromwell's turn to smile and there was a greater coldness in it than ever. Previously, his ambition had been undirected, but now it was mounted upon a mission and accordingly speeded and energized in a way that, he sensed, would last him out his days. 'She has left hostages behind, Admiral,' he said, waving his bare arm to encompass the entire priory, 'things that she cared about: bricks and mortar, institutions and a culture, a whole way of life! With these tools I'll pay her back, blow for blow, wound for wound, as she watches down, helpless to intervene. And since I'm an honest man, Slovo, after my own lights, I'll repay her with proper interest, you mark my words!'

Admiral Slovo did as he was bid and noted the simplicity and innocence of a civilization younger than his own. He firmly believed that Cromwell would be as good as his vow. Slovo also felt that though the die of history was cast, the protesting squeak of those that history would crush should be heard.

Aloud he said, 'But concerning the life to come and such; surely the Prioress *was* right, was she not?'

Cromwell looked at the Priory Tower, seeing demolition gangs and secular inheritors. 'She was right,' he agreed. 'That only makes it worse.'[14]

'He's even forbidden us the solace of sausage!' The monkish face was alight with indignation, squinting against the Roman sun. 'Can you believe that?'

Reawakened by the rebarbative images this statement conjured up, Slovo forced himself to pay attention. 'I beg your pardon?'

'Since time immemorial, eminent Admiral,' said the monk in a whiney tone, 'each brother has been granted a daily pork-and-blood sausage of the type we Germans love. By partaking so intimately in the raw components of recently living things, we draw near to the divinely created cycle of existence. Von Staupitz has now forbidden us this ration!'

231

'Give us this day our daily sausage, eh?' grinned Numa Droz, as huge and unlikely in his clerical gown as a lion in a mitre.

The monk wasn't sure whether the jest was in mockery or support but, too frightened of this monster of a 'priest' to do otherwise, accepted it as the latter. 'That's right!' he said. 'And that's not the least of his savagery. He's watering the wheat-beer as well.'

Father Droz's eyes – as evil as a goat's at the best of times – flared. 'Now *that's* not on!' he said. 'I reckon you ought to go back to Efurt and cut a blood eagle on the bastard!'

The monk was perturbed now, worried by the floodgates of 'sympathy' he'd opened. 'Oh, I see ... um, what's that?'

'A blood eagle?' answered Droz. 'The Vikings invented it – I've always admired their good old ways. First you put your man down, though it can be done on women too. Then you get 'em face to the ground and cut through the back till you see the ribs and can pull 'em up and through. It looks like they've got wings, d'you see? An eagle, get it? They can live on for hours sometimes.'

When the monk could manage no response, Droz took the open-mouthed silence for approval. 'There you are then!' he concluded. 'Simple, isn't it?'

'What I suggest,' interjected Slovo, forcing himself to try and regain control of events, 'is that you go and indulge yourself. Here is a florin. Over there is a purveyor of processed dead animals. Go and consume blood sausage therein until funds are exhausted.'

'Well, actually, Admiral,' replied the monk, 'I'm not all that hungry at the moment and—'

'I *insist*,' said Slovo, so that even Numa Droz had to fight the urge to leap forth to buy sausage. 'And do not return until you are surfeit. Otherwise I shall think your complaints of ill-usage are as empty as your monastery larder.'

The monk looked into the Admiral's eyes and saw a blasted landscape not at all to his liking. He was up and away like a greyhound.

'So, Brother Martin,' Slovo resumed to the remaining monk, 'perhaps you will have the chance to speak now. What say you about all this?'

'I think I'd best say nothing,' returned the dumpy and intimidated German.

'Sorry. That's not permitted,' replied Slovo, with great finality. 'Whilst His Holiness deliberates on your Order's complaints against their new Vicar General, we are deputed to entertain and enlighten you. We cannot entertain a silent man.'

'Yeah, that's right,' said Droz, fixing the monk with his awful gaze. 'Give us some of that tempestuous Teuton tomfoolery I've heard so much about – sausages, big women, Jew-baiting – anything that takes your fancy.'

'This is my first visit to Rome,' stumbled Brother Martin. 'I am a little overwhelmed by it all and tired, yes, very tired. Perhaps I should rest and—'

'No,' said Slovo as decisive as before. 'Tell us what you think of us Romans.'

The monk proved to have more backbone than first impressions suggested. His face directly hardened, his Latin acquired a harshness beyond that grafted on by a guttural mother-tongue. 'You are loose-livers,' he said. 'I have never seen so many people seduced by the call of the flesh.'

Admiral Slovo leaned his chin on his hand. 'Yes ... that about sums us up.'

'Present company excepted,' added the monk – but only out of politeness, not fear.

'I resent your prejudice, Brother,' said Droz, smiling horribly, in a way which told Slovo that someone, some-

233

where, would suffer before the day was out. 'But everyone's entitled to their opinions, I suppose.'

Admiral Slovo called for another flask from the wine-shop owner and its speedy arrival smoothed over the awkward lull. He sampled its contents before asking, 'So the new Augustinian General is giving your Order a hard time, is he?'

In fact Slovo knew full well that was so. Johann Von Staupitz – Thomist, Augustinian, member of the currently fashionable 'Brethren of the Common Life' and (more to the point) Vehmist – had been drafted in to do just that. Resentment boiled marginally below the violence point in the Order's German houses as a result. Two eloquent (by the standards of their type) brothers had been deputized to take their grievances to Rome for restitution and it just so happened that Brother Martin Luther was one of them. It was he that the Vehmic talent spotters had adjudged ready for the influence of Rome and Admiral Slovo's company.

'I should say so,' now replied Luther. 'A monk's life should be austere but nowhere do I find it justified that it should also be miserable. If it were not wrong to impute bad faith, I would say Von Staupitz was out to upset us for reasons of his own.'

Not knowing whether to be impressed by the monk's perspicacity or shocked at the crudity of the Vehme, Slovo pushed the flask towards the monk. 'I should have a drink,' he said, oh-so reasonably. 'You'll enjoy your time with us more. Wine dulls those parts of man which discern pain and boredom. Conversely, it awakens the inner eye for joy.'

'Life is crap, so drink and forget,' added Father Droz, nudging the container even further forward till it threatened to topple into Luther's lap.

Strangely, the monk seemed to appreciate these last words and he was thereby persuaded. Downing the wine in one mighty convulsion of the throat, he smacked his lips and drew a pudgy hand across them to mop up the residue.

Admiral Slovo was both encouraged and repelled. Not even the pirates he used to know consumed brain-stunning liquor with such indecent relish. Wine was, he realized, a powerful weapon against a man used to drinking in beer-quantities. The monk's defences were now breached and open to the attack of new ideas and sensations.

'Right then,' Slovo said, gathering together his gloves and scrip, 'since your colleague is off enjoying himself with death-by-a-thousand-sausages, we shall be away. What would you like to do?'

Luther looked about, symbolically taking in the mighty City, one-time home of Empire and now the hub of Faith. The first assault of alcohol was making it all seem full of infinite possibility. 'I should like,' he said, 'to ... go to church.'

Admiral Slovo saw propriety win a momentary victory during the monk's hesitation. It didn't matter. They'd planned for just such eventualities ...

It had taken an inordinate amount of money and the calling-in of several favours to get Numa Droz to dress as a priest. Not only did he have a low opinion of the cloth, he was also much attached to his rainbow silks and flamboyant hats.

Admiral Slovo had won him over eventually but it'd been an uphill struggle. The Admiral did not number any six foot eight inch clerics among his acquaintance and so had to commission the necessary disguise as a special – and expensive – secret. But this had proved to be simplicity itself compared with coaching the mercenary to behave in a manner even distantly approaching that expected.

However, Droz was warming to the role and beginning to

enjoy the pantomime. After Mass at the Church of the Repentant St Mary the Egyptian, he sat with Luther and the Admiral outside a nearby Neapolitan baker's-cum-resthouse, enjoying a lunch of pizza[15] and watching the lively life of the adjacent *Bordelletto*.

'I *enjoyed* that sermon,' said Numa Droz. 'It certainly stuck the knife in the Pelagian heresy!'

'Is that why you kept shouting "Orthodox"?' asked Luther.

'Well, you can't clap in church, can you?' answered the Swiss, giving Slovo a *who-is-this-yokel?* look. 'It reminded me of a talk I once gave to a load of captured Janissaries. My oath! Nigh on half of 'em renounced Islam on the spot!'

'And the other half?' asked Luther.

'We stuck 'em on stakes, matey!' Suddenly Droz recalled who and what he was currently meant to be. 'I mean, that's what they do to us – and anyway, they were all apostates!'

'The Janissaries,' explained Slovo to the monk, thinking a little interlude wouldn't go amiss, 'are recruited from a levy of Christian children imposed on the territories conquered by the Ottomans. They are raised as fanatical moslems and serve as the Sultan's elite troops.'

'I have heard of them,' said Luther, 'but would question whether the term "apostate" is appropriate. Full consent to salvation can only be given in adulthood.'

'Can it?' said Droz innocently. 'If you say so.'

The monk looked a little shocked but let it pass. He was plainly more exercised by the proximity of the church in which they'd just worshipped to Rome's throbbing red-light district. Admiral Slovo noted the direction of his burning gaze.

'Is something troubling you?' he asked.

'I'm not sure,' said the monk, creasing his brow. 'Do you see what I see?'

Admiral Slovo and Numa Droz obligingly looked but saw nothing untoward.

Luther turned to them in some agitation, not all, Slovo suspected, of innocent origin.

'I've just seen men openly consorting with women of easy virtue,' gasped the monk. 'Look! He's negotiating with her! They should be whipped!'

'Well,' observed Droz amiably, 'maybe they will be, though it costs a little extra, I understand.'

'No, no, no!' said the monk. 'I refer to this open ... traffic – and beside a church as well. To think that next door to a House of God wherein the sanctuary light shines before the Body of Christ, they are performing such enormities!'

'It's how you got here,' said Slovo, disarmingly.

'Are you saying my mother—' roared Luther, rising to his feet.

'My reference was to the mechanics of the procreative act, not your personal antecedents' came the calm reply. 'In a city where men of quality tend to marry late, you are somewhat intolerant of the demands of human nature.'

'I am mortified to hear you speak like this,' said Luther, shaking so much with indignation that he had to sit down again.

'It so happens that I am singularly well qualified to do so,' claimed Slovo.

'Are you *admitting* that you—' interrupted the monk, 'with the taste of communion still in your mouth?'

'No,' said Slovo, annoyingly failing to join in with the mounting wave of emotion. 'I am not admitting what you might think, though there would be little shame in it if I did. It just so happens that my tastes are more restrained.'

'And specialized,' added Numa Droz candidly.

'What I was referring to,' the Admiral continued, 'was that one of my early occupations in His Holiness's service

237

was the supervising of the great *Social Register*. This involved enumerating all the whores plying their trade in Rome, but, being lazy, I gave up counting after nigh on seven thousand freely answered to that calling. All that, mark you, in a city of fifty to sixty thousand souls. Ultimately, for fear of scandalizing both His Holiness and posterity, my finished return included only the true professionals of fourteen hundred or so. Of that number,' he went on, 'nigh on five hundred were foreigners, especially imported. And since it was obvious that none of these "unfortunates" starved from lack of trade, it must be accepted that they were well patronized. That being so, if a sin is so universally practised, is it any longer sin?'

Before Luther could make the predictable point that murder and theft were pretty widespread too, but that didn't make them all right, Admiral Slovo waved Numa Droz on to say his piece. The polished double-act caught the monk on the hop.

'Anyway,' said Droz in his priestly role, 'I've got this theory. The purpose of the sexual act is breeding, right?'

'Yes,' Luther agreed cautiously. 'Such is the Church's teaching, based on natural law.'

'So, a sexual act is a procreative act and, conversely, a procreative act is a sexual one. Well then,' said Droz triumphantly, pleased at having remembered his lines all the way through, 'by that formula, any act which excludes procreation isn't sexual, is it? If you take precautions or venture some of the more daring stuff the ladies over there offer, there's no chance of a baby, and thus no sexual business and thus no sin, geddit?'

'Um . . .' replied Luther, frowning monstrously. Slovo saw that he oh-so *wanted* to embrace this radical revision of developed natural law but stubborn honesty was bringing him back, time and again, to the flaws within it. Pretty soon, worrying away at the edges, he'd be able to drive a coach-and-four through one of the resulting gaps. The Admiral therefore prepared some propositions to meet the monk if and when he emerged. Slovo was determined that the weary hours spent coaching Droz to carry out his very first abstract argument should not go to waste.

Fortunately, at that exact moment, when all was in the balance, the powdered mushrooms that had been covertly introduced to Luther's wine took effect. Slovo merely wished to make him more liberal and welcoming than hitherto, and it had been simplicity itself, for someone who'd spent two decades in the company of the Borgias, to doctor Luther's drink. The monk's attention had been seized by a passing *Puttane* with endless legs in gold hose; in a trice the deed was done – and the world thereby changed.

Luther looked at Slovo and Droz anew, a fresh vivacious light in his slit eyes. 'I see what you mean,' he said slowly. 'Hadn't ever thought of it that way before. So you *could* say it's the intention that counts, not the deed, couldn't you?'

'Absolutely,' replied the Admiral, not really listening any more, confident his job was done.

'I mean,' Luther sprinted on, 'if ever a monk got to Heaven by monkery, it ought to be me. I've done my bit, ruined my knees in prayer and gone without beer and sausage for days on end to save my soul.'

'And a lifetime without the flushed-pink diversions over there,' smirked Droz. 'No wonder you're so worked up!'

'You're right,' agreed the monk. 'I reckon God should be more forgiving than man is, and men forgive almost *anything*. So, as long as you believe—'

'The Just shall live by faith,' mused Admiral Slovo, and – catching the monk's chemically affected mind at *just* the right moment – inadvertently supplied the cornerstone of a whole new theology. Unknown to Slovo, the idea that would split Europe in two and put the Grim Reaper on to overtime had just been born.

'Right!' shouted Luther, standing up in his excitement. 'Justification by faith alone – Ooo-wee!' He punched the air and gyrated his bovine hips in a masterful, four centuries premature, impersonation of James Brown, 'godfather of Soul'.

'I feeeeeeeeeel gooooooooooooooooood!' he sang, and the nearby ladies stared at him.

'Over to you, I think,' said Slovo to Droz. Things had gone terribly well – now for phase two of the plan.

'I have some business to conduct elsewhere,' Slovo explained to the dancing German. 'However, Father Droz here will be with you for the rest of this little outing. He will take good care of you.'

'S'right,' rumbled the Swiss, pleased that things were now moving into his specialist sphere. 'Don't worry, I've brought a spare sword . . .'

Unwilling to actually witness the spiritual squalor of what Numa Droz called a good night out, Admiral Slovo went home and occupied himself with the sort of things he did when people weren't watching. He was awaiting the inevitable.

It came at dawn in the form of a Burgundian Officer of the Watch. 'Would the honoured Admiral be so good,' he'd asked, puzzled but pleased to find Slovo dressed and waiting, 'to attend the Castel Sant'Angelo and vouch for two malefactors who dare to claim acquaintance?'

Admiral Slovo followed on at his leisure, having advanced in the world beyond blind obedience to the summons of some mercenary. In the *Palazzo del Senatore*, he waited until the coast was clear and then gave the contents of his money-scrip to an old beggar-lady who was crouching in a doorway. Then he hurried off before anyone spotted the shameful deed. It would not do for his painfully acquired image to be compromised by public knowledge of pointless kindness. One of his many enemies might conclude he was getting soft and make a move against him.

Even so, he'd felt impelled to make the gesture. Doubtless he would be richly rewarded, as usual, by the Vehme; land and money, and access to people and pleasure seemed to be theirs in infinite supply. There remained, though, some guilt about his compliance with their demands. Only a little, however ...

Then, mentally braced against the tedium of active life, he entered the Sant' Angelo – and found Numa Droz and Martin Luther holding court.

The Watchmen, who were only hireling shephereds after all, were wary of Droz and had not attempted to disarm him. He was, Slovo straightaway realized, in that most unpredictable of phases where the waves of euphoria are set to crash against the cliffs of hangover. The Admiral accordingly kept communication to the minimum. The Swiss looked back red-eyed and noted the acknowledgement of a job well done. He felt pleased, but these things were tricky to judge.

Luther, by contrast, was making noise enough for three, reliving the night's exploits under the amused eyes of the Watch. He plainly had no idea how to hang or handle a sword, was boastful drunk and didn't know or care that he'd split his monk's habit from neck to arse.

'Hello, Admiral,' he shouted, weaving about unsteadily. '*What* a time we've had!'

'We finally caught up with them making a fighting retreat from the *Bordelletto*,' said the Burgundian, smiling wryly. 'There's probably two dead and a lot more who'll need patching, no one of any importance though. You obviously know them and your word's good with me. What's it to be, sir, the informal garrotte, a proper hanging or shall I let them go?'

Admiral Slovo paused for a few seconds before replying – just out of sadism really. Martin Luther sobered considerably in the interval.

'The last option, I think,' the Admiral said eventually.

'If you're sure,' replied the Burgundian, signalling to his men to clear the way. 'But if they're either priest or monk, then I'm a Frenchman!'

'No,' admitted Slovo, to the man's evident relief. 'You're not a Frenchman.'

Outside in the comparative cool of the morning, Luther started to come off the boil. Slovo had chosen the 'Thousand Star' mushroom because of the reportedly gentle and benign return to earth it gave. Never again would the monk feel as good or live so fully as he had done these last few hours, but the warm memory would linger on, like the fading perfume in a lost loved-one's clothes. It would keep him going for a while – long enough for it to be too late to turn back.

'Ah – Admiral,' Luther rhapsodized as they walked along. 'I don't know what to say . . .'

'Good,' said Slovo, but to no avail.

'I've had the best night of my miserable life, I have. Mind you, I'm scandalized that a priest of Rome should know what Father Droz knows!'

'Please,' said Admiral Slovo, raising his black-gloved hand, 'no details, I beg of you.'

'We had opportunity for thought as well, you know, amidst all the . . . doing,' said Luther, pouting and offended. 'It was strange, my perception of time seemed to go funny; the hours stretched on and on.'

'They did when you started talking!' complained Numa Droz, raising his eyes to Heaven.

'Father Droz is like a soldier in many respects,' the monk went on regardless. 'He has their fatalistic attitudes, most unlike a normal priest.'

'All I said,' protested Droz, 'was that if a pike-head's got your name on it, it's got your name on it and there's nothing you can do.'

'It's just *so* in accord with my new insight,' said Luther, ignoring him. '*We live by faith alone.* If you're justified by faith you're saved, if you're not, you're not – and there's nothing you can do about it! See?'

When Luther added to himself, 'I must think about this some more; it has such profound implications . . .' then Slovo knew that the deed was done.

The monk would be given all the opportunity to think that he wanted. Johann Von Staupitz was under orders to cherish Luther upon his return and allow him free rein. The German Augustinian Order would have switched dramatically from over-severity to discreditable laxity when Brother Martin got back to Efurt. In order to disorientate, he who had been his sausage-stealing enemy would become his patron, friend and teacher.

'The thing is,' said Admiral to monk, transfixing Luther with cold eyes, 'to think your own thoughts, become sure of them and then don't budge. Nail your colours to the mast.'

'Nail . . . to the mast!' echoed Luther, fixing the advice in his befuddled brain.

Admiral Slovo was no prophet or seer, but perhaps long association with the Vehme had granted him gifts of insight. Whatever the cause, he saw ahead and felt impelled to add: 'Well, nail them to something anyway.'[16]

'What could we say, Admiral?' asked the Welsh Vehmist. 'Your name was cropping up at nigh on every Council meeting and the praise was getting wilder.'

Admiral Slovo was looking at the distant activity in and around his villa and thinking how marvellous it was at last to be free of care. 'Was it actually all that much?' he queried, albeit without great interest. 'Didn't you have myriad other agents burrowing away through the woodwork?'

'None so gloriously favoured by success and omen,' replied the Vehmist. 'You were featuring in *The Book* with monotonous regularity, once we could see it, slipping with perfect fit into the predicted roles; those man-shaped spaces in history we'd allocated to be filled by one of our own. A Council member told me there'd not been such fulfilments of scripture since Attilla appeared on the scene.'

'I'm not sure,' said Slovo, 'that the comparison is altogether flattering.'

'Everyone has different parts to play,' explained the Welshman. 'We don't necessarily approve of everything that's predicted, but what is written is written and some of it you just can't get round. You, however, we could applaud. You were worth all the tolerance and patience expended on you.'

'You think so?' said the Admiral, tracking the movements of a tiny fishing smack on the glittering waters below. He was jealous of the fisherman's short and ignorant life.

'Undoubtedly,' answered the Vehmist, wondering what was so absorbing about a stupid plank-and-rope boat when they were discussing the turning of the world. 'After the event, we saw how needful it was for you to be there for the inspiration of Thomas Cromwell. It was awesome to see the fulfilment of Pletho's words in so *small* a way – I mean – flowers and a branded bum! Fancy those insignificant things wreaking, by the gears and pulleys of position and power, such mighty violence on history!'

'You would soon tire of it if you'd been as close to the machinery as I have,' warned Slovo. 'The cogs slip and grind and they spit blood. People are the grist under the mill-wheels. What emerges, that cake you call history, is bound together with gore.'

'It was always so,' replied the Vehmist blithely. 'But please do not think us so crude or superficial as to aim for mere visible events. True, we wish for Cromwell-the-catalyst to purge the Church and religious-houses from his native land but that is not the entirety of it. All the foretellings, the anti-Papal legislation, the dictated divorce, the martyrs and creation of another Protestant super-power are incidentals. Do you think we'd really stretch forth our hand to create the ... "Church of England"?'

'Possibly not,' said Slovo to humour him. 'There's small pleasure in seeing an abortion get up and walk away.'

'Just so, Admiral. As it happens, Cromwell, our little joint creation, will succeed beyond our wildest expectations. But even so, we have others in place to serve our desires. No, the crux of the matter is to destroy a way of life, a vital social support system for the poor and needy, as well as ideological centres of resistance to us. We want to knock a prop away, bring the edifice down, and let someone else build anew in its place. It's in our mind to provide a mighty leg-up for the land-seizing classes, the secular and nationalist proto-bourgeoisie, you understand. In selling them the expansive monastery lands – as he shall – King Fatso VIII of England will sign the death warrant of his kind and there is also a certain beauty in seeing that social algebra start to work through.'

'And with Luther it is just the same only writ large,' said Admiral Slovo, assisting him.

'Exactly,' smiled the Vehmist. 'And, as a by-product, all

245

the chopping and changing and cynicism will discredit religion for the masses. The whole thing is so elegant.'

'It was bound to come,' said Slovo indifferently. 'The rumblings of reformation were heard throughout even my life.'

'Debatable, Admiral,' countered the the Vehmist. 'It takes individuals, men acting under free-will to turn those "rumblings" into proper thunder and lightning. The Reformation needs its gardeners before it can flower. What you, and we, have caused to live will grow and change Europe – and thus the world. The playing out of that particular game occupies two full pages of *The Book*. Seeing it through is to be our major preoccupation for the next half-millennium!'

'I did well out of it, I suppose,' said Slovo wistfully. 'Bracciolini's[17] personal, annotated copies of Lucretius's *On the Nature of Things* and Epictetus's *Encheiridion*. Quite some finds!'

'We had to send his heir floating under the Bridge of Sighs to acquire them,' agreed the Vehmist. 'He wouldn't sell, you see.'

'They certainly kept me diverted for upward of a month,' said Slovo, indicating he thought the arrangement well worth it. 'The outpourings of Lucretius were quite scandalizing however. Epicurianism is the antithesis of Stoicism!'

'There will be room for both persuasions in our world, Admiral,' said the Vehmist, in liberal mode. 'And in so saying I'm reminded that it's you we have to thank for there being such a world to look forward to ... The prophecies focused and converged, all matters appeared to come to a point – and at its centre was you.'

'Mere chance,' said Slovo.

'All predicted,' the Vehmist objected. 'Because of you, there was a Grand General Council meeting, one of only two

246

ever convened – and that previous one was to note the conversion of the Emperor Constantine.[18]

'This Council,' asked Slovo, 'it wouldn't have been six summers ago, would it?'

'That's right,' answered the Vehmist. 'In the Damascus Casbah, away from prying monotheistic eyes.'

'I *thought* I discerned a certain thinning in the ranks of high society,' said the Admiral, pleased even at this stage in his life to have a wild supposition confirmed. 'I had Vatican security look into it.'

'I know – you scamp, you.'

'But nothing came back to me.'

'I should hope not, Admiral. It was the most vital of ventures, and far from lightly undertaken. Our wisest and best people, those who'd spent their life in analysis of *The Book*, couldn't see beyond the crisis that was developing. We sensed either the ending or success of our plans. There were even suggestions that the day of the gods' release was at hand.'

'No,' smiled Slovo. 'Nothing so minor. They're still tucked safely away. I looked in on them not so long ago.'

Piqued by such blasphemous levity, the Vehmist spoke more coldly. 'It turned out to be an even greater issue, if such there could be. It was the day, the one day, that you were born for. We – and the rest of creation – had to hold our breath and await your kind decision.'

Admiral Slovo looked at the continuing, living world around him; his home and children, the birds and the sea, and he pondered the attractions of Apocalypse *now*. 'I wonder,' he thought aloud, 'if I decided right?'

❧ The Year 1520

*'A LIGHT TO (AND FROM) THE
GENTILES: In which I decide the fate of the
Universe and become Lord of the Isle of Capri.'*

'The clockwork is being wound,' said the flamboyant young dandy, smiling as he spoke. 'Your presence is required.'

'I beg your pardon?' replied Admiral Slovo, shocked, even here in this wayside wineshop, at the invasion of his privacy. But the dandy had already gone – vanished most unnaturally into nothing.

'Fires are being stoked high,' added a dark, lascivious merchant from another nearby table. 'Matters are near to the boil. Your presence is required.'

'If you do not desist, I will stab you,' answered the Admiral gently but firmly. After all, what point was there in his present vertiginous position if he could not socialize unaccosted? Slovo, sad to say, no longer had any leeway of patience for humans. In this case, none was needed, however, for the merchant was also . . . gone.

'Desist from what?' queried the Admiral's companion, the Rabbi Megillah. He was unsettled by the intrusion of knife-talk – Rome's ubiquitous, third-favourite topic. 'To whom are you speaking?'

The Admiral turned back to his flask and goblet, the

merest ripple on his ocean of composure now smoothed. 'To no one, I suspect,' he replied. 'Kindly overlook the matter.'

His long years as ghetto-leader had trained Megillah not to distinguish between gentile request and gentile command.

'. . . though, of course, we aspire to reunion with the Land in Messianic times,' he continued, faultlessly from the break in the conversation, 'where an even greater number of mitzvah – relating to the Temple and farming and so on – will be available for performance. This will further enhance the degree of sanctification and holiness amongst the children of Israel, which is the pre-requirement for the Messianic presence.'

Admiral Slovo nodded his understanding. 'Whereupon,' he prompted, 'you will presumably be the foretold "light to the gentile nations" and history (being merely the record of the deeds of the wicked) will equally presumably cease . . .'

'Er . . . perhaps,' answered Megillah, a trifle nervously and brisker than his normal style. 'The issue impinges upon the eschatological beliefs of your own faith and could be construed as, er . . . contradictory at certain points. One likes to leave the subject unexpounded and rely on divinely ordained goodwill to permit co-existence in God's good time.'

Admiral Slovo was born half a millennium before such declarations could be taken at their face value and so construed it (only partly correctly, as it happened) to be a reference to the Inquisition.

'Just so,' he said, waving a calming, gauntleted hand over the theological difficulties of his friend. 'Time will tell, I always say. Our dust will answer to one call or another, I'm sure.'

'Indeed,' agreed Megillah diffidently, obliged by the age to fear traps even from the friends of his comparative youth.

'I do so . . . enjoy our talks,' said the Admiral slowly, surprised at his own use of such an emotional term. 'They quite counter an equal number of hours spent attending to His Holiness's Babylonian travails. One naturally suspects the survival of pockets of good faith and idealism, but it is refreshing nevertheless to actually encounter them. I recall that . . .'

'Your presence is required.'

'Can you see him? Is he real?' Slovo asked Megillah calmly.

When the Rabbi cautiously nodded his white-topped head, the Admiral turned to face the voice. 'Yes, you're real, enough,' he said, prodding a Swiss guardsman in the chest. 'So I will listen – but no more than that.'

The guard had seen a great deal in a short life and certainly too much to worry about honour or insults. On duty, he could not be offended. 'Your presence is required,' he repeated evenly.

'By His Holiness and now?' Slovo helpfully expanded.

The guardsman's eyes glittered slightly in assent. 'My message is delivered,' he said. 'Make or mar as you will.' Three steps backward and he was gone as suddenly as he'd arrived.

'You should go,' advised Rabbi Megillah, as gently as he could. 'We are doing nothing here—'

'Precisely!' said the Admiral, smiling tightly. 'I am increasingly attached to *nothing*, whilst the calls to *something* grow dimmer by the day. And when that something is the murky labyrinth of His Apostolic Holiness's world, the sentiment is infinitely multiplied.'

Megillah recognized the mental state all too well, but naive friendship still caused him to shake his head and tut-tut.

'I know, I know,' said Admiral Slovo, levering himself up and dropping some coins on their table, 'but what can he do to me? What can he take that I value? My disposition makes me a free man in a world of slaves. Disappearing messengers and Swiss escorts, both be damned; come and walk with me awhile. Tell me some more about your end of the Universe.'

The two old men pottered off.

At the end of the *Via Sacra*, on the point of leaving the old Roman Forum, they paused before the ancient Arch of Titus.

'Everything is there,' observed the Rabbi, 'recorded in stone by Emperor Titus's craftsmen. The spirit of rebellion, human strife, the loss of all that we held dear manifested in the structure of our Temple.'

'But the triumph shown,' interjected the Admiral, 'is that of a dead Emperor of a dead Empire. Whereas you, the vanquished tribe, are still extant. Who then is the actual victor? There is that comfort to be drawn here.'

Rabbit Megillah nodded. 'I concede,' he smiled, 'there might, on reflection, be a multiplicity of lessons contained within this monument.'

'They may have your Menorah,' said Slovo, ponting to the scene of the sacred Temple candelabrum being borne aloft by exulting Romans, 'but what good did it do them, eh?'

The Rabbi was never given the opportunity to answer.

The carved images and decorations of the Arch began to boil and writhe, rising in and out of the depth of the stone like tiny figures in a snake-pit.

Slovo heard Rabbi Megillah gasp and thus knew that he was not alone in this between-world. However, since his companion was by profession and birth a natural victim, there was precious little comfort in that.

Suddenly, from deep inside the Arch's interior, a life-size head and torso burst forwards with enormous force. As the stone strained and bulged, a man's face broke through into the open. He screamed and his eyes were full of horror.

A second and third figure joined the first in similar

manner, as if they'd been hurled against a permeable membrane. They struggled fiercely, striving to be fully free, howling horribly all the while, but could get no further.

Then, in answer to a higher, inaudible command, the trio fell instantly silent and fixed their gaze upon Slovo and Megillah. A great quiet prevailed until even Admiral Slovo felt it oppressive. Eventually the first figure spoke.

'I, Titus,' it said, and then drew slightly back into the Arch.

'I, Vespasian,' said the second and likewise retreated.

'I, Josephus,' said the third; and the other two returned.

'We burn!' they shouted in unison. 'We suffer! We suffer in Hell!'

'For what I did!' soloed the Emperor Titus.

'For what I took!' added his predecessor, Vespasian.

'For what I wrote!' said Josephus, the renegade and historian.

'Help us! Save us! We burn!' the chorus was renewed and with desperate gestures they indicated one particular part of the now mobile frieze surrounding them.

Admiral Slovo tracked along the line of sight.

'They are stretching for the Menorah,' he observed to the awe-struck Megillah.

'It is time!' howled Titus, clearly in great pain.

'Put it back!' gasped Vespasian.

'It is tiiiiiiiiiime!' agreed Josephus and the others joined in his screech.

The three, suddenly seized with renewed panic, struggled all the more vigorously but to no avail. Try as they might, they could not free more than head or hands, nor reach a finger's width nearer the tiny engraved symbol of their desires. As before, they seemed to have heard some secret signal and it was not long in being enforced.

From the Arch's unguessable depths came claws and

grapples which fastened on to the unfortunate three, tearing their flesh and drawing blood. Slowly but inexorably, though fighting with the strength of fear, they were drawn back until lost from sight. A final pitiful sob issued from one as the stone surface closed over his mouth and then all was quiet once more. The Arch was no longer alive.

'*Blah blah blah, blah-blah*,' said a nearby voice in due course, allowing Slovo to revive from his reverie and thus notice that he had returned to the world he knew.

'Your presence is required,' repeated the voice. 'I'll say that just once more and then: violence.'

The Admiral recognized the tone, and the tracing of its owner gradually grew as a priority in his mind, thus compelling him to re-set his thoughts.

'Master Droz?' he said, turning to face the giant Swiss Captain. 'How are you?'

'Exasperated,' replied the Swiss, 'but implacable. Why will you not listen to me, honoured Admiral?'

'I was deep in thought, Droz; pondering the course of the wise man in response to curious messages.'

'Ah, well, I can settle that for you, Admiral. He responds to them promptly; particularly when I am the bearer. What's up with that Jew?'

'He is pondering likewise, I suspect.'

'He could at least say hello. No good comes of all this thinking, you see. That is why God granted us instincts: to save us from slavery to fallible reason.'

Admiral Slovo, who, if he cared for anything, cared for his Stoic beliefs, suppressed a shudder. 'I propose a deal, Master Swiss,' he said swiftly. 'I will comply with your wishes in every single particular and, in return, you spare me your natural philosophy. How's that?'

'Done, Admiral – though you deprive me of my rebuke

regarding your treatment of my sergeant-at-arms in the wineshop. This from you, Admiral – a man I call my friend!'

They both laughed, the Swiss with a bellow, the Admiral with a dried-up bark of amusement, at the absurdity of the notion of friendship between such as they. Then Slovo allowed Numa Droz to lead the way, leaving Rabbi Megillah still rapt with shock before the silent Arch.

'Don't fret, Master Droz,' said the Admiral, consolingly, 'life is full of disappointments. However, on this day of portents, you may escort me to yet another.'

'Admiral,' said Leo X, Christ's senior (recognized) representative on Earth, 'you have kept us waiting!'

Admiral Slovo parried this demand for an explanation by treating it as a statement of fact – thereby letting down the massed courtiers, priests and guards, who had been anticipating his discomfiture. They should have known of old that the Papal Investigator was poor sport in the tormenting stakes.

'Everything comes to him who waits,' said the Admiral politely, lazily selecting one of the more shop-worn phrases out of his vast collection of clichés.

'Not poxing well fast enough, it doesn't!' roared the Pope. 'Ach! Sit on this, you Caprisi . . . Admiral!'

Slovo affected not to notice the Pope's insulting thumb gesture, whilst registering that there was sadly little left of Giovanni Medici, 'the Golden Florentine', son of Lorenzo the Magnificent and youthful companion of Michelangelo. Life had turned him into Leo X, in whom appetite had prevailed over reason in Admiral Slovo's stern judgement, and there was now a permanent sheen of grease on his chin to prove it.

Leo looked ill and his short temper bubbled forth from

deeper springs than the revenge of over-indulgence. The effect was so profound that the Admiral drew modestly from his drying well of human sympathy and actually felt sorry for his master.

'If I had someone else with a brain whom I could call on,' said the Pope, petulantly flinging a fig at his advisors, who shied from it as they would a cannonball, 'someone with better hearing and more obedient legs, then rest assured I'd do so. However, I'm stuck with you, aren't I, Ad-mir-al?'

Slovo sensed that, even for him, this might not be the best time for a witty remark. There was more ill will than sunshine in the room as far as he was concerned. Any one of the career or just plain personal enemies gathered there would have been both swift and happy to implement any Papal decision to deal with him. Moreover, something so novel as to be interesting was afoot and he preferred not to miss it. So Admiral Slovo smiled and said nothing, and the Pope's acid twinge passed like a cloud.

Leo was uncharacteristically deep in thought and was obviously troubled. 'I have a dream . . .' he started – it was a standard opening recommended by the rhetorical schools of the day, a perennial favourite. 'In fact, I get it all the time now,' he continued in a less elevated rush. 'At first I put it down to the cucumber brandy, but the same thing kept coming back, again and again. It's burning me up, Slovo. I tell you, somehow, I don't know how, but it's been revealed to me I'm going to die, that I'm hellbound, if this thing isn't solved!'

'All this in the month since we last met?' Slovo asked, unable to accept the change in the once robust Pope.

'I've kept things from you,' answered Leo weakly. 'But I can't hide or ignore the matter any more: I want you to stop these Menorah dreams.'

'And the thrust of these nocturnal visitations is that you should replace the said Menorah, I assume,' Slovo said coolly.

'Yes . . .'

'And you wish me to do so on your behalf,' Slovo went on, enjoying the stance of omnipotence.

'Yes,' answered Leo coldly. 'And if you persevere in such prophecy, I may conceive that you are, in fact, there in my dreams and possibly even conducting them. If I were to come to such a conclusion, Admiral, it would not be a happy day for you.'

Slovo gave way with a good-natured bow, and Leo pressed on.

'I do indeed wish you to locate and replace this relic. For better or for worse, I have no one else to whom I can entrust such madness. Pirate you may be—'

'Ex-pirate,' protested Slovo mildly, 'and mostly under Papal licence.'

'A Stoic . . .'

The Admiral stoically accepted the charge.

'And a sodomite, so one hears.'

Once again, Slovo thought it perhaps best to say nothing.

'But useful,' Leo concluded. 'Besides,' he went on, mustering a hollow laugh at some unshared knowledge, 'you come highly recommended from a source you'd doubtless admire.'

'A reference to the Pagan Emperors appearing in your dreams, I take it?' ventured the Admiral.

Leo X, vague amusement instantly forgotten, gripped the arms of his throne and tried to catch Slovo's eye, looking for he knew not what.

'A lucky guess,' said the Admiral innocently. 'And yes, I will do this thing, Your Holiness. By all appearances, it would seem I have been chosen.'

At this Leo waved on a loitering attendant and Admiral Slovo discovered that he knew him well.

'Hello, Leto,' he said brightly. 'So you haven't been burnt yet, you old bugger!'

Giulio Pomponio Leto, foremost classical scholar in Italy, frowned at the Admiral from under his sword-straight Roman fringe. As so often with kindred spirits, he and the Admiral cordially hated each other.

'Hello, Admiral,' replied Leto, his face forcing a smile but his voice full of stiletto-messages. 'How gratifying to see you once more.'

'The Menorah! The Menorah!' roared Leo impatiently, catching Leto on the back of the head with a well-aimed fig. 'Less of this chit-chat! Tell him about the Menorah and let me get back to normal. Don't you know there are forests full of deer and boar out there waiting for me? My cellarman is dying of boredom and my mistresses are getting out of practice (or so they tell me).'

Thus prodded, Leto began. 'The Menorah,' he recited, looking through and beyond Admiral Slovo, 'the sacred candelabrum of the Hebrew people, removed from the Temple in Jerusalem by the Emperor Titus after the fall of that City in the seventieth year of our era. Subsequently stored in the Temple of Jupiter on the Palatine Hill and in all probability sacrilegiously looted from there during the sack of Rome by Alaric the Goth. Thus departing from the clear light of history, it enters into legend and subsequent reports of its fate are various. These are—' and Leto fastidiously began to count off the options in what he thought to be suitably gruff Roman terms. 'One: loss in North Africa during...'

But by then, Admiral Slovo had tuned out all except the salient points (distinguished by the speaker's sudden loss of interest).

Leo X, to whom history was merely tragedy best decently forgotten, listened in wonder, amazed that Leto's students could bring themselves to attend to him, let alone (allegedly) sleep with him. He picked up another fig, intending to spur matters on again, but then charitably thought better of it. He might not be able to repeat his last direct hit.

'So there you are, Admiral,' Leo interrupted a supposedly elegant anecdote about Visigothic government, 'an impossible task to be accomplished without delay. My advisors tell me it's one of the great mysteries of the age – though people seem to have been happy enough to leave it unsolved up to now. Hard master that I am, I give you one year, calculating that I'll last just about that long. If you've not resolved things by then, don't bother coming back. Dead or alive, I will have arranged a welcome you'd not enjoy. So stay in Mauritania or Syria or wherever you end up. My shade will come there to torment you and tell you what a bad servant you are and then, in due course, you'll die and go to Hell.'

'That all seems fair enough,' said Admiral Slovo concisely.

'You think so?' replied Leo, raising one eyebrow. 'What an easy-going man you are! There is, of course, a plus side to all this for you. I will provide every form and type of document, making all Christendom your playground. You are not to want for any material assistance, I assure you. And if things *do* get sorted out through your good offices, then . . .' The Pope reflected deeply but soon lost patience. '. . . Oh, anything you like: money, pardons – whatever,' he said irritably. 'So long as it doesn't outrage posterity or let in the Turks.'

'Done!' said Admiral Slovo and turned smartly on his heels so that Leo might not see the wide smile on his face. Within seconds, he had taken a score of long-legged strides to the great double door and put his hand upon its latch. 'This commission will see me out!' he exulted. 'With all the books – and all the sex – and all the opportunities for selfless good' (Stoicism finally making its stern voice heard) 'that I have ever wanted! I can tell the Vehme to go and—'

And then, quite inexplicably, in leaving the Papal throne room, Admiral Slovo re-entered it.

He never knew if it actually was the room he had just left or a perfect copy. He felt inexplicably old and tired as he tried to work it all out and took a few steps forward.

'Hello, Slovo,' said the vast demon-creature squatting on and all over the throne, its voice like a juicy chime. 'I don't suppose you planned on meeting me so soon!'

Far away, an inner version of Admiral Slovo was petrified and screaming, but it was ignored in favour of the victorious Stoic whole. 'That depends,' he managed coolly. 'Who are you?'

The demonic servitors, swarming about their master, howled and crashed their wings. The sense of outrage at Slovo's non-recognition was palpable, but overshadowed by the dripping steam and sulphur. Already the priceless wall murals were beginning to peel.

'My name,' screamed the demon, 'is ... changing!' Giant tears of bronze seeped from its hooded eyes and fell to the floor, crushing those beneath. 'Your friend, the Rabbi, would call me ... *The Dybbuk*, and that will suffice. As to whom I am: look about!'

Admiral Slovo accepted the invitation. For the first time he noticed that there was more of death than life – however loosely defined – in the room. Vast tumuli of ill-treated bodies, some of them almost human, lined the walls in undignified fashion. A few component parts of them still moved feebly, thus catching the attention of the roving demonic soldiery who then rushed in to finish the job.

The Admiral had seen battlefields before and was quite

comfortable with them. In this case however, he would have been a lot happier had the blood pools been a nice, normal red.

'There is war in Hell,' smiled the Dybbuk. 'And now a New Order prevails!'

A flying thing flew down close to Slovo's face and lisped, 'New Order! New Order!' to make the point. It had the head of a beautiful girl on a body of indescribable leathery horror.

The Dybbuk daintily adjusted the Papal Tiara hat adorning its warty head and fixed most of its eyes on the Admiral as though awaiting some response.

'Congratulations,' said Slovo eventually.

'Thank you, Admiral,' the Dybbuk replied. 'You'll soon notice the difference, I'm sure.'

Slovo languidly waved his arm to indicate the throne room in general. 'Have I not already done so?' he queried, swiftly withdrawing his hand from the rapt attentions of a multi-jawed orange nightmare.

'Exactly,' agreed the Dybbuk. 'Your puny presence here confirms it. We are not the lazy old-guard, waiting for the *Book of Revelation* to get rolling in its own sweet time. No, we are the Young Turks!'

'Turks?' said Slovo, somewhat puzzled. True, the Dybbuk looked as unsympathetic as some of the Ottomans he'd met and/or killed, but he couldn't quite see the connection.

'The phrase comes from after your time, man-creature,' explained the Dybbuk loftily, 'but you get the general drift. We are the ones who get things moving!' The Dybbuk gestured with his titanic head, causing the mock Papal Crown to fall. Another instantly appeared in its place.

'And is there anything I can do for you?' replied Slovo politely.

Just for sport, the Dybbuk yawned monstrously and turned its head inside out. The Admiral couldn't help but gag.

'Yes, there is,' it said when normality was resumed and its mouth pointed outward again. 'I want you to visit old friends, that's all.'

'Given my history and temperament, my friends are few in number,' countered Slovo. 'There's Rabbi Megillah, I suppose.'

'No,' said the Dybbuk, briskly, 'not the foreskin-less one: *not* him.'

'Well, there isn't anyone else really,' protested Admiral Slovo.

'Think on, Admiral,' grinned the Dybbuk. 'I know the hearts of men better than anyone and there are still a few who think warmly of you.'

'This is all to do with the Menorah business, isn't it?' said Slovo, resignedly. 'Not only have I got to find it but you want me to exhume my best-forgotten past, searching amongst the debris for . . . friends.'

'That's about the shape of it, old boy,' laughed the Dybbuk. 'You don't think I'd be wasting time talking to such a limited life-form as you if there wasn't some bigger issue at stake? I can't explain too much, of course; one has to stick to the script and human free-will is required – you being the selected representative. All I can do is direct you on your way and speed things up. Visit your old friends, Slovo!'

'Script?' asked the Admiral, slapping off the attentions of a hermaphrodite incubus (or succubus?). 'What script?'

'Oh, you know all the old Doomsday stories, Slovo,' said the Dybbuk. 'Don't you ever read your Bible?'

'Frequently,' said Slovo truthfully.

'Well then, you should be intimately familiar with all the end-of-Time scenarios. Most of them involve the rebuilding of the Jerusalem Temple, and for that you require the Menorah.'

'Hence Pope Leo's torments and the pleas of the Emperors...'

'... and your presence here, yes, yes,' interrupted the Dybbuk impatiently. 'All my own work. As I've said, I want to get the ball rolling early and catch the enemy unawares. The old boss wouldn't have that so he had to go. Now I'm in charge and I'm going to help you to help things along. Go and see your old friends, Slovo!'

'So you keep saying,' pointed out the Admiral reasonably, 'but if you *are* the new Prince of Darkness, why all this worry about scripts and rules? Surely it would be more in keeping for you to play the game entirely as you wish, regardless of any regulations.'

'I don't know why I'm bothering to bandy words with you,' said the Dybbuk slowly, opening and closing all his eyes in a formation dance. 'The rules just *are*; they predate the whole struggle and can't be overturned. I mean, just look what merely trying to subvert them does to me!'

Admiral Slovo looked carefully as he had been bidden, and had he not been born too early to know of the phenomenon, he would have recognized the play of enormous G-force on the Dybbuk's pulpy skin.

'That is the price of resisting the regulations in the slightest respect,' it said. 'My flesh ripples and my eyes strain as though in the path of a monstrous wind. I suffer every bit as much as your precious Pope and Emperors, I'll have you know. Why, even ageing you three years was a major drain on my energies.'

'*I beg your pardon?*' enquired Slovo evenly.

'I told you before,' said the Dybbuk in terse tones, 'I can't direct your feet, only speed them along. We can't be bothered to wait three whole years whilst you gallivant round the

Orient, fruitlessly questioning the natives and digging holes. No, I've fast-forwarded those years so as to cut out your useless search and get you to *go and see your friends!*'

Slovo now recalled the added burden of age he had felt on first entering the room. Three years nearer the cold and peace of the grave, but not a memory to show for it. He didn't know whether to feel pleased or outraged. Either way, there was no point protesting; what was gone was gone. But he did ask to be updated.

'Pope Leo only gave me a year, and promised dire consequences should I fail. Since you appear to be the sole source for this section of my biography, perhaps you'd be good enough to explain what happened?'

'He died,' replied the Dybbuk bluntly. 'In hideous agony, poor chap. The surgeons found that his brain was all dried up like an old prune. It was likewise with his successor, Adrian VI; he only lasted two years under my relentless pressure. Right now I'm giving ... what's his name?'

An ethereal, translucent creature, half dragonfly, half fair maiden, flew up to the Dybbuk's ear. 'Clement VII!' it sang sweetly. 'Clement VII!'

'That's right, thank you,' agreed the Dybbuk, reaching out and juicily crunching the creature in one huge hand. Red-green blood and ichor spilled over his fingers. 'Clement VII, that's the one I'm giving a torrid time of it right now. So I tell you, you needn't worry about your welcome back in Rome; you're needed as much as ever!'

'Well, thank you for that at least,' said Slovo dryly.

'Don't mention it,' replied the Dybbuk affably. 'You've provided me with a degree of amusement these last few years and of course, I have high hopes for you in the future. You really are a nasty piece of work on the quiet, aren't you?'

Admiral Slovo answered with one of his 'I do what I have

to' gestures. 'I am a victim of my times,' he said in his own defence.

'Hmmm,' said the Dybbuk dubiously. Well, you're wasting your time with all this "natural virtue" business, you know, all you Stoic chaps end up down here with me in the end.'

Slovo smiled. 'But there again,' he said, 'you are the Prince of Lies, are you not?'

The Dybbuk decently conceded the point with a shrug. 'There's no pleasing you, is there!' He huffily flicked one enormous finger at Slovo, causing the throne room to spit him out.

As he was ejected, Slovo caught the Dybbuk's final words, 'GO AND SEE YOUR FRIENDS!'

There were some advantages to a proxy tour of the dangerous sixteenth-century world: awaking in his lodgings, Admiral Slovo found himself lighter, healthily tanned and adorned with several new scars he was glad not to recall receiving.

In his sea-chest there was a framed pair of golden, winged socks, labelled as the former possession of the last Roman Emperor, Constantine XI Palaiologos;[19] an indecent statuette of a pathic from Baalbek; gold coin in plenty (Slovo's piratic impulses had never really been purged); and a stone from the Wailing Wall for Megillah. It looked in fact as if it had been a fun trip – aside from the glaring lack of menorahs.

Like the good and frightened Caprisi woman she was, the Admiral's housekeeper had kept the place well stocked in his absence, anticipating a sudden return as per the wise bridesmaids of Christ's parable. To be flung home by the gesture of a demon was about as sudden a return as could be imagined, but Slovo still found the makings of a passable pre-dawn breakfast awaiting him.

Seated with a flask of sack, some bread and onions, he watched the faithful sun rise over the dome of Santa Croce and thought about times past. Later, in his library, he browsed through the great bound volume of Marcus Aurelius's *Meditations* upon its brass eagle lectern, until he could postpone decision no more.

There was nothing else that could be done, he concluded. Since the Menorah continued to be lost he would have to visit his friends. Fetching his favourite whetstone, he began to ply his best stiletto upon it.

'I'm very sorry to intrude, Harold,' said Admiral Slovo, 'but tell me, would you consider me a friend?'

'Oh yes,' replied the stocky, red-faced man sitting opposite, 'I should think so.'

Slovo heaved a silent sigh of relief. In his brief trudge around Rome he'd feared that the short list of those who'd make such a confession was already exhausted.

'After all,' the man continued, 'it was you that secured me permission to reside in Rome. You've been to good old England; we've shared a few flasks together and outfaced that ... unnecessary duelling charge. If that's not friendship, what is?'

'What indeed?' smiled the Admiral in return, thankful for the simpler standards of the Northern races. 'You know, you're an interesting case, Harold Godwine: your Italian grows less barbarous each time we meet. Not many English could have settled in so fully.

'Ah well,' said Godwine, acknowledging what he took to be a compliment, 'I have a pressing reason for doing so. As you well know, I did not come to Rome to enjoy myself but to save my soul!'

Admiral Slovo was mildly troubled. 'Whilst not a priest or

theologian,' he said gently, 'I would still advise caution on your *proximate sanctity* theory, Harold.'

'It makes sense to me, Admiral. Being so close to so many people striving for holiness, bang next door to God's chosen representative, some benefit's bound to rub off. Besides, it's got to be easier for me here – no Scots or Welsh!'

'Ah, yes . . .' said Slovo, fearful that he'd unwittingly lit a fuse. It turned out he had.

'I've had a good life,' said Godwine, rehearsed-reflectively. 'I make no apologies for it (except when I'm in church). I've killed lots of Scots and Welsh: almost as many as one could wish for.'

Slovo tried half-heartedly to stem the tide.

'I have encountered these remnant Celtic peoples . . .'

'The Scots are not Celts, Admiral,' interrupted Godwine, on, over and through Slovo's comment. 'They're blood of my blood, which just makes it all the more interesting. I mean to say, I've nothing against them personally (well, maybe the Welsh . . .). Individually, I rather like them. It's just that when they're gathered in convenient clumps I can't resist the desire to chuck the whole quiver amongst them. That's just the way it is, I'm afraid. Scotsmen are what the longbow was invented for, that's what I say.'

'Absolutely, Harold . . .' said the Admiral, swept along.

'I mean, I'd rather kill Welshies instead. But they mostly threw the towel in long before my time so there's not much chance of a decent ruck there. See what I mean? If the Scots weren't neighbouring my country, I could probably leave them alone – but they do – so I can't . . .'

'Indeed,' agreed the Admiral politely, wondering what was for dinner.

'Mind you, it was Flodden Field[20] that finished me. I overindulged myself so much there, there was no place left for me to go, no professional mountain left to scale. Might as well spend the rest of my life in the Borgo[21], praying for forgiveness I said – so here I am. Borr! Flodden! Now, *there* was a battle, never mind a flukish Bannockburn ... Did I ever tell you about Flodden, Admiral?'

'I believe you may have, Harold; perhaps once ...'

'Save us! What a sight that was. They lost – now listen to this – their King, James IV: twelve Earls; nineteen Barons; three hundred-odd Knights and lairds; the Archbishop of St Andrews; two assorted bishops; two abbots and the Provost of Edinburgh. Oh – and most the army as well. We just stood off their *schiltrons*[22] and poured in the old clothyard till they were collapsing in waves and there weren't no room for the dead to fall. Talk about "Flowers of the Forest", ho ho! What do you think about bagpipes, Admiral?'

'Well, I try not to let the subject rule my life but ...'

'I *hate* them. The Scots play them constantly, you know – and some North English too – which makes 'em honorary Scots in my book. Anyway, when we eventually got stuck in – at Flodden, this is – I made a point of seeking out the pipers – just to let them know what I thought of the noise they make. *And* I got me two clan chiefs as well; their claymores are up in my trophy room along with all the other family treasures. I took their ears as well but they went all nasty and I couldn't keep 'em.'

Admiral Slovo thought he had spotted the glint of a possible escape from the present carnival of carnage.

'You mentioned your family, Harold; were they also soldiers and travellers such as yourself?'

'Oh yes,' said Godwine, 'wanderers, soldiers and crusaders all – very sound on the Scots, too. There was Tostig Godwine, for instance. Now, he was a Varangian[23] and only got out of Constantinople by the skin of his axe when the 1204 Crusaders came rampaging in. Then there was Gash "Death from Wessex" Godwine who ... But look, why just talk, when I've got this huge family tree I can show you in the trophy room. Come upstairs and see it; the light's better up there anyway.'

'Billed and bowed' into submission, Slovo mechanically followed Godwine up the cramped stairway. Despite all the inducements to doze, he could not be at peace: something was troubling his mind, something preventing a merciful switching-off.

Then, as he trod on the top step it occurred to him. 'Why,' he asked, 'is the light better in the trophy room?'

'Because,' answered Godwine brightly, 'of what Tostig the Varangian got out of Constantinople *with*. The Family's held on to it ever since and I'm quite attached to the thing. I mean, it's not only valuable but practical too. Look, it holds seven bloody great big candles ...'

'I am sorry to hear of your friend Godwine,' said Pope Clement VII. 'A tragic accident.'

'Thank you, Your Holiness,' said Admiral Slovo. 'Stilettos are dangerous things to set about cleaning by mere candle-light; people are always accidentally falling on them.'

'Perhaps he didn't know it was loaded,' tittered a Cardinal whom relative career failure had made bold. The Pope silenced him with a glance.

'And you have the Menorah secure, Admiral?'

'It was, of course, Godwine's dying wish that I take custody of the object. It is now with my savings, Your Holiness – and there are few places more secret and secure than that. All that remains is to restore it to its proper siting.'

'Which is where?' asked Clement with genuine curiosity.

'I'm seeking advice on that, Your Holiness,' said Slovo.

'Give it to ussssss ...' lisped an oily black Eel/Man

crossover, leaning casually on the back of the Papal throne. 'Give it to ussssss!'

With difficulty, Admiral Slovo averted his gaze from the Dybbuk's emissary who was, it became obvious, invisible and inaudible to all bar him.

'I beg your pardon, Holiness?'

'I *said*, Admiral, that my nocturnal sufferings are much abated now that the Menorah is at least in our custody. All that remains is to make them cease altogether.'

'I shall not rest until that is so,' said Slovo, affecting just the right amount of weariness-acquired-in-the-course-of-service.

'No!' said the Eel-thing, advancing menacingly down the Hall. 'You will give it to ussssss.' Slovo noticed that its mouth was improbably packed with teeth.

'Then go about your business, faithful servant,' said Clement. 'Relieve me of my dreams and you shall have all that was promised you.'

Admiral Slovo sprang the trap. 'The Lordship of Capri?' he asked. 'Public absolution for all my sins?' The latter raised a gasp from the assembled clergy and advisors. It was a lot to ask for.

'Capri certainly', replied the Pope hesitantly. 'I shall have to see about the other thing – there may be scandal.'

Slovo was content. Possession of the sybaritic island was in any case merely an open invitation to a fresh universe of sin.

The Eel creature, now perilously close, leaned forward to whisper noisomely in the Admiral's ear. 'Give it, through free-will, to us,' it said, 'and you shall have every book and bottom you have ever desired.'

Admiral Slovo was thus given cause to think anew all the way to the door – which once again opened on the unexpected: this time there was a walled expanse of lawn, decorated in the fashionable precision of the age with generous quantities of flowers and fruit trees, and presided over by none other than Rabbi Megillah.

'Hello Rabbi,' said Slovo, like the veteran he was, 'what is beyond these high walls I wonder?'

'Nothing,' said a wizened old man, emerging from his place of concealment in a bush. 'I have looked, and a blue void extends infinitely in all directions. We are quite adrift.'

'I *know* you,' said Slovo, gesturing dismissively with the stiletto he had instantly drawn. 'I heard that you were dying.'

The old man smiled thinly. 'So I am,' he said. 'In fact I am presently on my death-bed – but also granted one last great chance to be here.'

'That's nice,' said Slovo, 'for your life was not attended by any real success. I am, you see, quite familiar with your career, Master Machiavelli. We even met on one occasion; whilst jointly making diplomatic supplications to the King of France.'

'I do not recall you,' said Niccolo Machiavelli, his smile the merest bit thinner than before.

'That's unsurprising, sir, given the ignominious end to your mission and my part in securing same. Now; what was it the Florentine Seigniory's enquiry said of you? *He has advanced the frontiers of blithering ineptitude to hitherto inconceivable limits.* Or something like that.'

'I have been constantly attended by ill-fortune,' snapped Machiavelli. 'But I am a man of affairs and action. I have been called here today for that very reason.'

'To do what?' enquired Rabbi Megillah.

'I've no idea,' admitted Machiavelli.

'Nor me,' echoed Megillah.

'And I am too indifferent to explain,' said Admiral Slovo. 'So shall we merely stroll and admire the flowers?'

A noise like a demon's sigh filled whatever universe or

thought-construct they were within and sudden illumination fell upon Slovo's companions.

'I will take the Menorah,' offered Megillah quietly, 'and arrange safe custody. It will be held ready until called for in the proper course of things. I now know why I am here, the very reason for my creation, and I offer my fate and the lives of my descendants to this noble end. Give it to me, Admiral, and to him whom I represent.'

'Whereas I,' said Machiavelli, looking on Megillah with disdain, 'am deputed to argue the contrary. I have been granted wisdom about you, Admiral Slovo, and what I am told points implacably to you making a different and bolder decision. Seeing what you have seen, Admiral, are you *really* willing to have events played out in God's good time? Are you *really* going to act to preserve the status quo? I think not.'

Megillah and Machiavelli's eyes were fixed upon Slovo's impassive face. He was looking out into the blue yonder, considering his alternatives.

'I have reviewed your lifetime, Admiral,' continued Machiavelli, plainly enthused by his task, 'your battles and sacked cities, your murders and acts of betrayal. I sense a certain ... ambivalence in you concerning them. There is disgust, yes – but at what? You have acted in the World that the enemy has made. He now calls on you to extend it for ever – the gall of the creature! However, dull reason has not totally subdued you, has it? There is a certain beauty to a burning town that you have noted – is that not so? You have appreciated the *uncomplicated* pleasure of placing someone in the Tiber on a permanent basis. In short, Admiral, you have heard my Master's call in the groans of the World, and you long to respond.'

'The Admiral is a Stoic,' interrupted Rabbi Megillah, 'and therefore immune to—'

'Men justify surrender to failure and call it philosophy,'

laughed Machiavelli. 'I am talking of a wilder, older way here, Hebrew; something that satisfies all that goes to make a man, not merely the skin called civilization. Give the Menorah to us, Admiral Slovo; give it of your own free-will and we will have such times, such clarity.'

Slovo was seen to lick his lips.

'On the one hand,' Machiavelli sped on, scenting victory, 'is offered more of the same tedious mess that passes for normality. But where is the passion? Where is the drama that quickens the pulse on waking? On the other hand, however—'

Machiavelli stopped speaking because Rabbi Megillah had felled him with a kick and a vicious chop to the throat. Incongruous as a whale with a musket, the Rabbi produced a blade and watered the Dybbuk's lawn with Machiavelli's life-blood.

'The Lord strengthens my arm,' Megillah said by way of explanation, straightening up most unlike a Renaissance man in his seventies, and levelling the knife at Admiral Slovo's Adam's apple. His cold eyes were a summation of all the Admiral's worst enemies combined. It was very impressive. 'Give me the damn thing,' he said, 'and now!'

Admiral Slovo smiled. 'The one great fault I've perceived in life,' he said, 'is that, up to now, the good have always lacked conviction. It's yours.'

'We shan't meet again,' said Megillah. 'Not in this World.'

'No,' agreed Admiral Slovo in a neutral tone, looking around him at the bustle of Ostia Port.

'I am sorry about the knife business,' continued the Rabbi. 'It must have seemed very unpleasant.'

'But necessary,' replied Slovo easily. 'Think no more about it, Rabbi: all my friendships seem to end in knife-play sooner or later. But turning aside to more practical considerations, are you sure you don't require an escort? I can arrange a galley within hours.'

'Thank you, but no, Admiral. We are well fortified already – and it is best you do not know where we sail.'

Slovo saw the truth in this and suppressed his curiosity. In the week since their sudden return from the Dybbuk's garden, matters had been more than fully discussed, and now there was little left to say. The Papal afflictions had ceased, and it was therefore assumed that the arrangements made were approved of. The burden of the Apocalypse had passed from the Admiral's hands and all that remained was to forget and to work hard upon his temporary weakness as revealed by Machiavelli's blandishments. He thought there would just be time for that before he, in turn, was called from life. As Lord of Capri, meanwhile, there would be consoling sights and sensations enough.

'There are sanctuaries available to us,' continued Rabbi Megillah, seeking to apologize for his need for secrecy, 'citadels of holiness and powerhouses of prayer, against which the Evil One (save in the final days) strives in vain. The Menorah has only to reach such – be it in Zion or Muscovy or Ukrainia – to be safe until called upon.'

'But getting there?' countered Slovo, who, more than most men, knew the Sea as the mother of Chaos and confounder of all plans.

'We have Yehuda,' said Megillah, stretching to tap the shoulder of the smiling gentle-giant of a simpleton beside him. 'The Evil One (may his name be blotted out) has no power against the innocent. Thus, till we reach our destination, the Menorah will not leave the pack secured to Yehuda's back. And, I have the guns Pope Clement provided, so, we have done what we can and all else is left to God.'

Admiral Slovo conceded that there might, after all, be

grounds for mild confidence. The score of dark-eyed ghetto-youths selected as crew had been ill-treated enough by life to be a match for any passing pirates. A few of the toughest might once even have found a place on his own ships.

'I'll tell you one thing for certain,' Megillah suddenly blurted out, 'I shall have to answer for the death of Machiavelli.'

'I will stand in the queue before you,' said Slovo, 'and beside the recounting of my misdeeds, yours shall appear as nothing.'

'We will stand together.'

Admiral Slovo felt an unwelcome corpse-twitch of emotion.

'And that day,' the Rabbi went on, 'there will be no more differences between us, nor ever again. We *shall* meet once more, this time never to part.'

Megillah and the Admiral embraced briefly by way of Earthly farewell. There were tears in the Rabbi's eyes and, if Admiral Slovo had not had all feeling excised in youth, his own eyes would have watered.

The Hebrew party set off for their sailing within the hour and Slovo wandered away to cast a professional glance over a visiting Venetian *Galeass* and its revolutionary firepower. As he walked along, he was accosted by a flower girl.

'No, thank you,' he said. 'I have unhappy memories of flowers and gardens.'

The little girl nodded, looking wiser than her years and wickeder than her occupation. 'You shall *not* meet again,' she said slyly. 'Your destinations are not the same.'

'I beg your pardon?' said Slovo, covertly retrieving his stiletto.

'The one and only sin,' she went on, 'that is never forgiven, that is a certain passport to Hell, is that called *anomie* or despair.'

Slovo swiftly backed away. Three paces behind however,

his retreat was blocked by the harbour wall. Like most of the sailors of the age, he had chosen not to learn to swim.

From her basket of blooms the girl drew out a translucent parchment package. Within it some dark powder shifted and swirled.

'This is all the Dybbuk could brew at such notice,' she gloated, 'but it is the finest, blackest despair, and more than enough for an old-man's lifetime. Here, he presents it to you with his compliments!'

The flower girl had vanished into nothing before the missile burst in his face, coating him with its dusty contents.

When he had cleared his eyes, the Admiral looked out on a world freshly drained of all colour and meaning, realizing that justice was just a word and that some farewells really are for ever.

❧The Year ?

'ENVOI: The Devil's gift-box contains only unsweet sorrow. A comfortable life, another wife and additions to the tribe of Slovo. A bath seems increasingly attractive however.'

In 1525, King Francis I of France was still weeping bitter tears about losing his freedom and a good section of his army at the battle of Pavia. On Capri, Admiral Slovo and the Vehmist were still arguing the toss.

'The Dybbuk didn't last long after what you did to him,' the Vehmist was saying. 'He fell to someone marginally more ruthless than he, and since then there's been coup and counter-coup. First the "Gradualists" and then the "Impatients" and so on. What else can you expect from conviction-individualists? I'm told that at one point there was even a "Peace" faction!'

Admiral Slovo appeared uninterested by the news of his cosmic handiwork and a change of tack seemed called for to hold his attention.

'So, Admiral,' said the visitor, maintaining the conversational flow admirably on his own, 'what's it like living in despair?'

'A daily Stoic exercise,' replied Slovo crisply. 'And also something of an ordeal – hence my decision to have a bath. I find myself unable to continue.'

'So remarriage, breeding, the adoption of waifs, none of them could distract you?' the Vehmist enquired, though plainly not out of any great concern.

'For the briefest of moments only – sexual congress early on in the union, before novelty faded – and at the birth of children; only then. But my curse overpowers their charm.' Slovo hesitated and added, 'I do trust my family, blood and otherwise, will be left in peace?'

'No,' said the Welshman. 'We won't recruit your offspring or adoptees. There's no hint of them in *The Book* and times are changing. We're looking for different types nowadays.'

'I'm reassured. They have had little enough from me without inheriting your attentions.'

The Vehmist looked reproachfully at the Admiral. 'But they'll live in our world,' he said. 'And now can't you find it in your heart to forgive us for your parents?'

'And entire family,' added Slovo.

'. . . and entire family,' the Vehmist conceded.

'No,' said Admiral Slovo.

The Welshman shrugged and looked away.

'Cold, cold heart,' he said, but left it at that. In producing a piece of theatre it was not essential for the actors to love the management. It was only an exhausted husk the Vehme were losing anyway. He helped himself to another glass of wine, before unwisely voicing some additional thoughts.

'We gave you a more interesting life than they would have done,' he said. 'But for us, you and your Stoicism would have been a mere shaking of a tiny fist against the greater dark. Like it or not, we gifted you with something to believe in. Your family offered only the half-hearted hand-me-downs of tradition.'

Admiral Slovo regarded him for a short while. 'And what,' he finally snapped, 'gives you the wild confidence to think you ever knew what I believed?'

'I must confess,' said the Vehmist, in jocular tone, 'that was the subject of some speculation. We didn't think it really mattered but—'

'I was never a theologian,' interrupted Slovo, shocked at his desire to make secret things clear, 'I have no patience with demands to float clear of the material world. These are not reasonable requests to make in a harsh universe. Men do what they must and then, and only then, what they can. I claim no difference from that.'

'But, on occasion,' said the Welshman, expanding the theme in mockery, 'when circumstances permitted and the coast was clear, you raised your eyes to the stars.' He waved dramatically towards the cloudless sky.

Admiral Slovo nodded.

'I had my own faith, my own ideas before ever you explained your system to me, or Michelangelo listed the captive gods.'

'I still think our ignorance is excusable,' said the Vehimist. 'There was precious little evidence to go on. Whatever you may or may not have believed does not seem to have informed your actions.'

The Admiral permitted himself the indulgence of explanation. 'It's simply put,' he began. 'I *believed* life was a vale of tears and hard on failure – you saw to that. I *hoped* that what the Church taught was true, but I *feared* that nothing was true and everything was permissible.'

'Nothing of what you say detracts from the achievement of your years on earth.'

'From where I sit,' said Admiral Slovo, 'I see only a lifetime of petty concessions and compromises.'

The Vehmist laughed with a peculiarly liquid chuckle. 'Nonsense, Admiral. That's just the Dybbuk speaking. None of your sins or virtues were little ones. At certain times, and in your own quiet way, you bestrode the globe like a titan.'

'If you say so.'

'We do. You swayed the course of history a degree or two. Who else set a Reformation in motion, commissioned the Sistine Chapel ceiling and defeated two gods – Dybbuk and Te Deum – *and* glued the Tudors to a shaky throne? But for you the World would be a very different place and much less to our liking.'

'It somehow fails to comfort,' said Slovo.

'Do not shrink away from your creations; *they* are your children, Admiral,' said the Vehmist. 'Admit paternity with pride! Would you perhaps be convinced of your value by the knowledge that a statue of you is commissioned for the Hall of the Vehmic Citadel where you experienced your initiation all those long years ago? There you will stand, in marble depiction of classical dress, beside Mars and Horus-Hadrian and oversee the new generations of our people. We will tell them of you and you will see the light of admiration in their eyes.'

'Just as long,' replied Slovo, not so impressed or grateful as he ought to be, 'as they do not detect any similar light of life in mine.'

'Well, it is possible,' admitted the Vehmist. 'After your demise it's our intention to draw down your *ka*, your residual essence, to inhabit the image of stone. The book of Hermes Trismegistus has provided us with the means and it has worked before. We do not like to lose our most illustrious servants. Your imprisoned semi-divinity will be able to discern potential greatness in those who pass before it – as occurred with yourself. Better that than the Hades or oblivion awaiting the rest of your soul, surely?'

'Not at all,' said Admiral Slovo. 'I absolutely forbid it!'

'Sorry. It's non-negotiable. Do you want to see *The Book* now, before you go?'

Slovo saw no point in further protest, but found that

curiosity lingered on even in a mind that hadn't long to live. 'Since you've brought it,' he said.

The Vehmist made a conjuration with his hands and from nowhere a vast tome appeared, resting firmly upon nothing. Around and about, the air was agitated with half-glanced swirls of red and purple: signs of *The Book*'s demonic-guardians.

'Read and learn,' Slovo was told. 'You've deserved it.'

After token hesitation, Admiral Slovo arose and walked to where this great honour was waiting. The filaments of colour, sensing permission, made grudging way for him, leaving an odour of carrion.

To touch, it was like any other book in Slovo's library, though bound so as to last for whole civilizations of use. He lifted the heavy front board and, caring all too little for the past, made straightaway for the volume's hinder parts.

The Vehmist came round to join him. 'Ah – now this,' he said, pointing to a particular verse, 'concerns what is yet to come.'

'*St Peter*,' read Slovo, albeit with difficulty, for he had neglected his study of the earlier forms of Greek, '*shall be . . . shown the Sun, Sol Invictus, and taken on a . . . tour of Rome. The churches?*'

'Places of worship,' nodded the Vehmist, like a tutor pleased with his pupil. 'But yes, essentially churches.'

'*The churches shall be filled with light and then be silent.*'

'Very good,' said the Vehmist, betraying some surprise at the lack of assistance required. 'The Great Analytic Council of the Vehme interpret it all thus: that the body of St Peter will be discovered beneath the great construct bearing his name, and it will be exhumed in disgrace and dragged through the streets of Rome by the mob. All the churches, chapels and cathedrals will be set ablaze and then left, burnt-out and abandoned. We will find other, less defiled, sites for our neo-temples.'

'I see . . .' said Slovo.

'Before this you will find predicted three great universal conflicts, each more savage than the last, bringing half the world to ruin. None *appear* to be of our making but all serve our ultimate advantage.'

'But of course,' replied Admiral Slovo.

The Vehmist seemed a little disappointed by Slovo's reaction and was anxious that he be properly impressed.

'The concluding pages are sealed even to me,' he confessed, 'but looking ahead as far as permitted, we find reference to a time when man lives elsewhere than Mother Earth, though where or how that can be we cannot presently conceive.'

Slovo prevented the Vehmist's hand from speeding forward through the pages. 'Just at the moment,' he said, politely apologetic, 'I am more intrigued to see those pages which refer to me.'

'Oh?' said the Vehmist, surprised and discountenanced by such unexpected, self-regarding myopia. 'Very well then.'

He turned back in *The Book* to a section with which he was plainly familiar, and left Slovo to peruse as he wished, whilst he reinvestigated the pleasures of the view over the Gulf. After all, the Admiral had a tongue in his head should he encounter difficulties in translation.

Admiral Slovo read for a long time and saw, in neat array, his entire life foretold. Long before he was even born, the writer had travelled in Slovo's most private thoughts and foreseen all his days from birth to death, today. Slovo couldn't help feeling that he needn't have bothered to have actually *lived* his life.

He wished with all his ice-coated heart that he could find some fault, some fall from perfection, in the Vehme's consummate cycle of prediction and fulfilment – and for the first and last time his prayers were promptly and properly answered.

'This line here,' he asked, succeeding in concealing the rising excitement from his voice, 'what does it mean?'

The Vehmist leant over to read. '*And he will hold the key*,' he pronounced, with ease born of prior acquaintance, '*and the usurper will thus not prevail*. That's a reference to your crucial role in the matter of the Dybbuk and its attempt to bring on the end of everything. The key, that's you; the usurper, that's the Dybbuk – and due to you, it didn't prevail, did it?'

'I see,' said Slovo and savoured a moment of quiet triumph. 'However,' he then went on, as though musing aloud, 'might there not be an alternative reading of the text?'

'No,' said the Vehmist, returning to his vigil over the water to Naples.

'Oh, I don't know,' Slovo persevered. 'Might not "the usurper" be the Vehme – you do seek to usurp, don't you? Might not "the key" be this?'

The Vehmist whirled about to see Admiral Slovo holding up an elaborate key, secured on a stout chain about his neck. The Welshman made to speak ... thought on, and then sought to speak again – but could not, as his universe crashed in ruins about him.

'To the prison of the gods?' he quavered, when he could at last muster sufficient voice to talk. His wide eyes never left the elevated key. 'To the chamber below Rome?'

Admiral Slovo nodded but was kind enough not to smile.

'But ... but you said the door was sealed – secured with a seal.'

'I did and it is,' agreed Slovo. 'But that's just wax – a ruse. Didn't you ever wonder about the Cross-Keys symbol of the Papal emblem? One key to the Gates of Heaven for sure, but the second to some other place. What an unobservant lot you turned out to be! Yes, sirrah, the objects of your ambition and worship are held by lock and key, hapless captives of a Church that's wiser than it looks. What a shame I never paid it the attention it deserves! Still, that's life. No, you'll never liberate your masters without permission – or without this key.'

'So . . .' said the Vehmist, advancing a step.

The Admiral held the key higher. 'A dying Pope told me,' he said. 'Poor old Julius, he never had much luck. It was I who found him expiring alone in some dive, and he was worried that the key each Pope inherits might fall into improper hands. And so it did, of course: that is to say, *mine*. Being me, I bagged the thing before handing the dead Julius on – just a reflex action really, and a quite shameful betrayal of trust. Right at the end, you see, Julius had my word – I promised to act in good faith. But now I'm glad I lied; it turns out to have been worth all the interrogations and falsehoods. At the time I didn't even know what I proposed to do with the thing – sell or bequeath it to the Vehme, one presumes . . .'

'Just so, Admiral, just so,' said the Welshman, hungrily extending his cupped hands.

'But now I realize that can't be. *The Book* must be fulfilled, mustn't it? After all, everything else it said of me came true.'

'NO,' said the Vehmist, taking another step. 'We—'

'Sorry, no, *you* must not prevail,' Slovo corrected, swiftly impaling the Vehmist with a lightning stiletto-thrust to the eye.

Lax in passing on the message of death, the Vehmist's brain caused his body to stagger two paces on, the blade still protruding from his face, before he fell like a supplicant at Slovo's feet.

Meanwhile, *The Book* roared into flame, scorching the Admiral's back and arm as it did so. Within seconds it was consumed into nothing. The red and purple demon-trails plummeted to join the conflagration and then were gone.

Slovo toed the dead Vehmist off to roll away down towards Naples, boorishly scattering a host of feeding birds as he went. Unexpectedly, the Admiral found it within himself to construct a laugh and his distant house-servants turned to stare at the unprecedented sound. As far as the Dybbuk's parting gift allowed, Admiral Slovo's final moments on earth were happy ones.

He took the key from its chain and pushed it, end on, deep into the soft lawn. Centuries later, the Archaeologist would find it and, in due course and for want of any better use, present it to the Victoria and Albert Museum.

His life's work thus complete, Slovo was free to stroll home through the beautiful garden and back to the chore the Vehmist had interrupted.

'Oh man,' he recited as he went, more than ever glad of the *Meditations* now he was on his final journey, '*citizenship of this great World-City has been yours. Whether for five or five-score years, what is that to you? You are not ejected from the City by any unjust judge or tyrant, but by the self-same Nature which brought you into it. Pass on your way then with a smiling face, under the smile of him who bids you go.*'

Admiral Slovo duly looked to the sky and smiled. There was the hope of peace, of escape from being Admiral Slovo – and paradise in knowing nothing. The bath would be cold by now, but that needn't deter him. If his worst fears were confirmed, it would be plenty hot enough where he was going.

NOTES

1 Ancient philosophy placing an emphasis on life lived in accordance
with the awesome order perceived in Nature, on restraint and self-
containment, and virtue as a duty and its own reward. In the
Roman context, and indeed to the present day, it is associated with
a certain stern-mindedness and what might be termed the 'repub-
lican virtues'. Its appeal seems to rest upon the opportunity for a
rational ordering of life, and an escape from the pointless storms of
human nature. '... whenever the virtues begin to lose their central
place, Stoic patterns of thought and action at once reappear.
Stoicism remains one of the permanent moral possibilities within
the cultures of the West.' (Alasdair MacIntyre, *After Virtue*, 1981)

On the other hand, the great classicist Professor E. Griffiths
brutally dismisses it as 'the shield of the despairing; mere gift-
wrapping round the death-wish.'

2 George Gemistus Pletho (or Plethon) (c. 1335–1450?). A Byzantine
philosopher and scholar. Best known for the introduction of
Strabo's *Geography* to the West (thus indirectly permitting Colum-
bus's discovery of America), for founding a philosophical academy
at Mistra in Greece, for social engineering in the doomed Byzantine
Empire and aiming to replace orthodox Christianity with a revised
form of Neo-Platonism. Visiting Italy, he reawoke the European
interest in Plato, after the Aristotle-obsessed Middle Ages, and
inspired Cosimo de'Medici to found the famous Platonic Academy
in Florence. His school of thought was revised and popularized by
the infamous Sigismondo Malatesta of Rimini, and was in mild
vogue in Admiral Slovo's time thanks to Malatesta's recovery of
Pietho's bones from Greece (whilst in mercenary service for Venice,
fighting the Turks), and his subsequent display and veneration of
them in the Church of San Francisco in Rimini. For this and worse
sins, Sigismondo was uniquely 'canonized to Hell' by the Pope in
1462.

3 The great Roman House of Orsini, as well as many Italian cities,

made the understandable (but not forgivable) error of supporting Charles VIII's seemingly invincible but ultimately unsuccessful invasion of Italy in 1494.

4 Fra Bartolommeo della Porta's portrayal of Admiral Slovo, in his *Last Judgement* of 1499, may still be seen, albeit in sad ruined form, in the Museo di San Marco in Florence. Look for the savagely afflicted hawk-faced man.

5 Actually, a tribute to the preservative qualities of alcohol and the resilience of the human frame, Prince Alamshah lasted out until 1503, the despair of his doting family.

6 Curiously, history does relate that, whilst copying before the masterful frescoes of Masaccio at the Church of the Carmine, Michelangelo Buonarroti's nose was broken by a fellow pupil whose efforts he had been deriding. The pupil was indeed expelled and exiled for this temporary lapse. The nose did not heal correctly and the consequent disfigurement forever after distressed and depressed its owner.

7 *Cruel Man before the Castle of Pandemonium*, the strangest of Torrigiano's surviving works, has long puzzled the select few who have viewed it at Windsor. 'What can have inspired this one vision of sick distortion in a lifetime of otherwise conventional artistic toil?' (from *Notes towards a catalogue of the pictures in the Royal keeping at Windsor Castle*, 1964, by Sir Anthony Blunt, Keeper of the Queen's Pictures (to 1979)).

8 Prince Arthur died three years later, 2/4/1502, aged 16, of something called 'the sweating sickness'. Henry survived a further seven years before he was laid to rest in the glorious and imposing memorial constructed under his painstaking specifications by Pietro Torrigiani in Westminster Abbey.

9 Admiral Slovo was being suspiciously percipient. His words serve as a cruel summary of Machiavelli's public life. The casual dispersing of his pride and joy, the Florentine citizen militia, by invading Spanish troops, was only six years away.

10 If Michelangelo is to be believed, then they arrived prematurely, since Cortes did not set sail until 1519, 13 years in the future. Perhaps Quetzalcoatl and Huitzilopochtli, given their supernatural talents, knew when the game was over and gave themselves up.

11 Michelangelo's great work in the Sistine, completed in October 1512, after 4½ years of super-human toil and savage arguments

with Pope Julius, survives – and acording to Admiral Slovo permitted its creator to do the same. The Colossus, a three times life-size bronze, was less fortunate, being torn down by an unappreciate Bolognan mob after a mere four years. It passed into the possession of Alfonso d'Este, Duke of Ferrara, who reforged its bronze into a giant cannon, ironically dubbed 'La Julia'. Alfonso did however retain intact the 600-pound head – for unknown purposes.

12 Pope Julius refers to Cambrai in North-East France, near the Burgundian Netherlands. Hence the association known to history as the League of Cambrai, contracted on 10/12/1508.

13 In fact he was – cut into nine pieces in a petty skirmish in Navarre in 1507. Clearly, the good news took time to travel.

14 It was always known that Thomas Cromwell had, as a young man, served as a mercenary in Italy. However, the period's true formative power was not, until now, suspected.

15 An earlier invention than you might think.

16 Which he duly did, seven years later, appropriately enough on All Saints Day, to the door of All Saints Church at Wittenberg.

17 Poggio Bracciolini. Famous Florentine Latinist and 'discoverer' of lost classical texts. 1380–1459.

18 Presumably Emperor Constantine the Great (274?–337) who proclaimed Christianity the state religion of the Roman Empire.

19 Constantine XI was last seen alive on 29/5/1453, advancing alone and sword in hand, towards the Turkish army storming into his City after an eight-week siege. Allegedly, his socks were the sole means by which his body was eventually recognized and recovered.

20 Flodden Field. 9/9/1513. Battle between the English and invading Scots near Branxton, Northumberland. Possibly the most crushing of all the Scottish defeats.

21 The English quarter of Rome since the first Anglo-Saxon pilgrims. The name derives from the English for Borough.

22 Traditional Scottish fighting formation. A tight clump of spear- or pikemen.

23 The Byzantine Emperor's axe-wielding 'foreign legion' and bodyguard unit, largely composed of North Europeans and, after 1066, Englishmen.

CRITICAL WAVE

THE EUROPEAN SCIENCE FICTION & FANTASY REVIEW

"CRITICAL WAVE is the most consistently interesting and intelligent review on the sf scene."
- Michael Moorcock.

"One of the best of the business journals... I never miss a copy..." - Bruce Sterling.

"Intelligent and informative, one of my key sources of news, reviews and comments." - Stephen Baxter.

"I don't feel informed until I've read it."
- Ramsey Campbell.

"Don't waver - get WAVE!" - Brian W Aldiss.

CRITICAL WAVE is published six times per year and has established a reputation for hard-hitting news coverage, perceptive essays on the state of the genre and incisive reviews of the latest books, comics and movies. Regular features include publishing news, portfolios by Europe's leading sf and fantasy artists, extensive club, comic mart and convention listings, interviews with prominent authors and editors, fiction market reports, fanzine and magazine reviews and convention reports.

Previous contributors have included: MICHAEL MOORCOCK, IAIN BANKS, CLIVE BARKER, LISA TUTTLE, BOB SHAW, COLIN GREENLAND, DAVID LANGFORD, ROBERT HOLDSTOCK, GARRY KILWORTH, SHAUN HUTSON, DAVID WINGROVE, TERRY PRATCHETT, RAMSEY CAMPBELL, LARRY NIVEN, BRIAN W ALDISS, ANNE GAY, STEPHEN BAXTER, RAYMOND FEIST, CHRIS CLAREMONT and STORM CONSTANTINE.

A six issue subscription costs only eight pounds and fifty pence or a sample copy one pound and ninety-five pence; these rates only apply to the UK, overseas readers should contact the address below for further details. Cheques or postal orders should be made payable to "Critical Wave Publications" and sent to: M Tudor, 845 Alum Rock Road, Birmingham, B8 2AG. Please allow 30 days for delivery.